DEAD IN
DUBAI

Marilynn Larew

THE
ARTEMIS
HUNTER
PRESS

Artemis Hunter Press
20 New Park Road
New Park, Pennsylvania 17352
www.marilynnlarew.com

Publisher's Note: This is a work of fiction. Names, characters, places, and incidents are a product of the author's imagination. Locales and public names are sometimes used for atmospheric purposes. Any resemblance to actual people, living or dead, or to businesses, companies, events, institutions, or locales is completely coincidental.

DEAD IN DUBAI
Marilynn Larew -- 1st ed.
ISBN 978-0-9910912-3-2

Praise for *The Spider Catchers*

"Larew portrays Lee as an effective analyst who's looking for a way out of the CIA, and readers will likely enjoy the frenzied action she gets into, as when she's close to a suicide bomber's blast or dodging a guard in an office late at night. A solid introduction to a new thriller series."
—*Kirkus Reviews*

"A white-knuckled spy thriller about human trafficking, dirty money, and the funding of terrorism. Readers who love a clandestine novel will be pleased with the way Larew weaves her mystery . . . This book was a riveting read, and the onset of a sequel is cause for excitement."
—*Chanticleer Reviews*

"There is plenty of action and suspense offered, and the reader will be on the edge of their seat more than once."
—*The Book Junkie*

". . . a mystery that is gritty dealing with spies, terrorists, sex trade that keeps you guessing about who are the good guys and bad guys . . . I like Lee's character she is tough, does what is necessary and falls apart after the fact. She thinks on her feet."
—*readalot*

"A strong female protagonist, plenty of physical action, and lively dialogue kept me turning the pages to discover what would happen next."
—*Queen of All She Reads*

"[R]eally fine entertainment and launch of a new series . . . Authentic and action-packed."
—Leslie Gardner, *e-thriller.com*

The Lee Carruthers Series

The Spider Catchers (Lee Carruthers #1)
Dead in Dubai (Lee Carruthers #2)

For Autumn Terry
the newest family member
and
Karl
always

Chapter 1

IS THERE LIFE after the CIA? I wondered as I stamped my foot into the bindings of first one ski and then the other. I was among the few early birds on the slopes. The view was spectacular! Snowy hills covered with pine trees stretched away and away. I lowered my goggles and pushed off. As I gathered speed I laughed aloud at the awesome feel of the wind in my face, the best antidote to my time in the Algerian desert I could think of. Halfway down the *piste*, something buzzed past my face. Then I heard a crack. Somebody was shooting at me? I bent as far down as I could and snowplowed to the side of the run, stopping just before I got to the trees. Great! Nothing. Not even a knife. I ripped off my goggles and kicked out of the bindings. Stepping carefully into the woods bent almost double, I advanced with a ski pole in each hand. I wish my gear wasn't burgundy, I thought. On the other hand, I hadn't expected to have to channel the Fourth Mountain Brigade that morning. I heard steps crunching toward me in the snow and ducked behind a tree. A man in black wearing a black face mask, his rifle held lightly in his right hand, slipped carefully forward, scanning to the left and to the right. He was looking too high to see me. When he was half a meter away, I yelled and launched myself at him with the ski poles thrust forward, but he deflected them with the rifle. He raised the rifle for another shot. I threw myself at him again, and he dropped the rifle. I grabbed it, and swung it hard, hitting him in the left shoulder. I reversed the rifle, backed up and fired. Off-balance. Tried again. He turned and ran. Should I follow him? What would I do with him if I caught him? I considered the rifle. I could hardly take it back to the ski lodge with me. I dropped the clip and whacked it up against the side of the tree, sending a jolt all the way down to my toes, and buried it in the snow by the side of the trail, throwing the clip as far as I could into the woods. I retrieved my ski poles and stood panting, heart pounding. I started to tremble and told my body it would have to wait until I got to the bottom of the slope, but it paid no attention, so I trembled.

"Who?" I asked myself. "Who?" I sat down with my back against a tree for a count of five hundred before I stopped shaking. Blowback from Morocco?

I stomped the snow off my boots and slipped them into the ski bindings. I couldn't find my goggles, but I wanted to be in cover as soon as possible, so I didn't spend much time looking for them. With a shooter in play, I felt terribly exposed. Maybe the shooter had a friend. Unarmed. I was unarmed. Not even a nail file. I wanted a gun and badly. Where could I get a gun in the peaceful countryside of Switzerland? Breaking into a gun shop was always an option.

At the bottom of the slope, I kicked my way out of my skis and carried them back in to the rack. I felt cold deep down inside, and gin seemed advisable. A drink in the lounge? Too public. Back in the room I made one of my very dry martinis—gin and a cube of ice. Maybe that would help me unscramble my brain. I looked at my watch. Ten thirty. Drinking in the morning was a sure sign of something or other. I finished the drink, but I was still cold. I took a long, hot shower and lay curled up under the duvet, remembering.

I had been sent to Morocco to find a missing colleague and wound up fighting my way out of a terrorist camp. They killed Kemal. I touched the bloodstained pearl hanging around my neck. I killed his killer, but Kemal was still dead.

Would the Pure Warriors of Islam send an assassin all the way to Switzerland to get me? Possible, but it seemed unlikely. Whoever he was, he knew me, and I didn't know him. I went to sleep listing the people who might want to kill me.

When I woke, I ordered lunch from room service. The waiter who delivered it looked like an Arab. Arab guest workers in Switzerland? The shooter could disappear into the crowd of Arab workers. He might even be one of them. If I couldn't find and neutralize him, I was going to have to cut and run. I hate to do that, but I disapprove of assassination, particularly my own.

Chapter 2

WHEN I WOKE up, it was dinnertime. I put on a long black velvet skirt and a creamy silk shirt and settled a bunch of golden chains around my neck. There were a few wrinkles at my green eyes and the corners of my mouth. Laugh marks, I called them. My long brown hair had a few strands of silver. I left them. As the Queen Mother once said, I earned every one of them.

The lounge was full of Beautiful People standing by a huge stone fireplace, working hard to impress each other. Oh, how I wanted a gun. I felt naked without one. A gorgeous man handed me a mug of hot buttered rum with enough rum in it to flatten a British sailor.

"You're new," he said. He had melting eyes and a touch of a French accent.

I took a sip of my drink and put it down on a nearby table. I once got sick on hot buttered rum and the smell of it made me faintly nauseous. "I'm an Aquarius? You?"

For a moment he looked puzzled, but then it clicked, and he threw his head back and laughed a central casting kind of laugh. Could teeth that regular be real? People turned to look and then returned to their celebrity minuet.

"Do you come here often?" he asked, his eyes alight with fun. "I'm Ricky."

Ricky began to identify the celebrities. "The woman with the pink dress and red face is Calliope Weathers, the frozen food heiress. That handsome hunk she's talking to is Hector Sampson, the Olympic ski star."

He looked faintly jealous.

"Who's the blonde?" I asked. "The one with the cleavage."

He smiled. "Brandi. That's B-r-a-n-d-i. She's a model working on her fourth husband, the man with the glasses standing next to her. He's Jason Rector, the German armaments heir. The short woman with the curly hair he's talking to is Samantha, a 'Got Talent' finalist."

Celebrities make me faintly nauseous too, so I cut his patter short before he had identified even half the people clustered around the fireplace. "I think I'm suitably impressed. And hungry."

He ushered me into the dining room, his hand held lightly at my elbow. The cuisine was "international," which satisfied the celebrities, but I had just come from Paris. Still, they could probably fix a simple steak-frites without doing much damage. I tensed. The waiter looked like an Arab. I relaxed, but paranoids sometimes have enemies. After our main courses, he flamed our crèmes brûlées dramatically. It wasn't bad, but I've had better.

Afterward, we sat on a large interior decorator sofa, sipping brandy, and he looked at me with his soft chocolate eyes. I put my glass down. Enough, I thought. He escorted me up in the elevator. At the door to my room, I turned to bid him good night. He kissed my hand and started to put his arms around me. I stepped aside.

"I have a twenty-four-hour rule," I said.

He looked confused. "*Pardon?*"

"I never sleep with a guy until I've known him for twenty-four hours."

He looked startled but kissed my hands longingly. "Until tomorrow, then."

I shut the door on him. Ski instructor or gigolo? Probably both. Why was he hitting on me when there were any number of celebrity chicks downstairs? I'm not that hot.

I did going-to-bed things and put myself in bed. It was only by chance that I was looking at the door when I turned out the light. I saw a pair of shoes against the light under the door. I got up. All I could see through the peephole was a large ear and then the back of a person in a hoodie walking away.

I sat on the bed for a while thinking. I'm as brave as the next girl, but being shot at and having some creep lurking outside my door were a bit much for one day. I had to go to Dubai anyway. Did I really need to ski anymore? If I did, I could go to the Mall of the Emirates, and hit Ski Dubai. While the laptop was booting, I went to the safe and removed my alternate identity. No girl should leave home without one. The first flight out was a pain, a milk run that stopped at every landing field until it got to Vienna. I booked a flight on it with a connecting flight to Paris. Then, with my alternate identity, I booked a flight from Vienna to Abu Dhabi. I finished packing and was going to bed again when there was a knock on the door. Looking through the peephole, I saw Ricky holding a bottle of champagne and a bunch of flowers. As if. I ignored him and went to bed.

The next morning I was at the desk checking out when my handsome friend arrived.

"Not leaving us already?" he asked, a look of desolation on his face.

"'Fraid so," I replied. "A crisis at the office. I will get them for this. This is the first holiday I've had in two years. Since you're here, would you mind taking my skis back?" I handed him the claim check.

"I will take you to the airport," he said.

"Thank you, but I've sent for a taxi."

"No. No. I will take you. Cancel the taxi," he ordered the desk clerk and took the handle of my roll-on. "It's not far to my car."

I had hoped to get away without anybody noticing, but short of slugging him I could think of no way to escape, so I let him hand me into the car and fasten my seatbelt for me. Tenderly. He was giving me the creeps.

He drove at speed down the curving mountain road, all the while shooting languishing glances at me, a combination not designed to contribute to my feeling of security. Parking illegally outside the terminal, he escorted me to the check-in desk and then through security, the languishing looks never diminishing. He saw me through the gate and down the ramp. I waved. He certainly was determined to see me board that plane. Why?

Just as the steward was about to close the door, a tall man rushed into the cabin and strode, bent forward, down the aisle past me, looking like a stork in a hurry. Forty, with a receding hairline and metal-framed glasses, his pinched lips made him resemble a Calvinist accountant. I kicked back, fastened my seatbelt over a blanket, and tried to sleep. I gave up and thought about Dubai.

As I was leaving the Agency, I had refused to go to Dubai to find out about George Branson. George's wife, Cynthia, turned up at my apartment in Paris to hire me to find him, doubtless sent by my former boss, Sidney Worthington. According to her, George hadn't been home in over two years, and she wanted me to find him so she could serve divorce papers on him. She wanted to marry somebody who came home at the end of the day. They had given her the brush-off at Langley, but she kept at them. Eventually, they sent her to Sidney. I don't know why. Sidney's a money man, but they sent her to him. Maybe they thought he had a nicer way of telling her to get lost? It looked like he had sicced Cynthia on me. I decided I might as well take the job while I figured out what to do with the rest of my life. After all, I had a head start. I knew where he was.

Why didn't the Agency just tell her he was dead? They knew he was dead. They just didn't know why, striking when you consider that the CIA had tons of people in and around Dubai, and it was their business to know why their operatives were dead. It looked like straight detective work—finding out what George had been up to and why he was dead. The only really interesting thing was the little brass key she gave me. She said George had sent it to her from Istanbul the previous January.

Chapter 3

I WAS PULLING my roll-on down the concourse when my nostrils were assaulted by the scent of Viennese coffee. The restaurant had tables on the concourse, so I stopped and ordered *kaffee mit schlag*, fighting off the attempt by a dirndl-clad lassie with flaxen braids to sell me a sweet roll. I figured the coffee was enough to put me in a sugar coma. Instead, I virtuously ordered a plain baguette with butter. My principles did not require me to refuse the cherry jam that came with it, however. I was sipping the hot, sweet brew when my accountant friend dropped into a chair at a table as far away from me as he could get and ordered plain coffee, no sugar. Calvin has a lot to answer for.

I studied him as I worked on the baguette. He watched the people as they came and went along the concourse, refusing to glance in my direction. Was he following me? Why would he follow me? I paid my bill and strolled along, looking in shop windows. At a newsstand, I bought a copy of *Le Monde* and a paperback with a bare-chested hunk embracing a blonde in a dress that showed her entire spinal column, and let the guy get ahead of me. That made him nervous, so he turned into a shop full of tacky statuettes of yodeling couples to let me get in front again. It looked like he really was following me. The window across the concourse had as fine a collection of Coach handbags as I have ever seen, so I went inside and lingered, looking at the bags and discussing their merits with the salesclerk. He really was following me, because he had to loiter conspicuously to make sure he didn't lose me. He began shifting from foot to foot and looking at his watch, as if waiting for someone. I shook my head regretfully and strolled out past him without a glance. The devil made me do it.

I ambled toward the gate for the Paris flight, stopping to window shop along the way, but eventually I got there. I sat with my back to the wall in one of those orange chairs shaped to some alien's rear and began to read the paper. He sat down gratefully and stared at me until the flight was called. I was ahead of him in line. I waited until I was almost at the gate, when I stepped out of the line and started scrambling frantically in my backpack as if looking for my boarding pass. He was trapped. I faded back in the line, and when I saw him go down the ramp, I faded out of the line entirely.

The flight to Abu Dhabi was uneventful.

Abu Dhabi is the capital of the United Arab Emirates, a string of small Arabic states with their fronts to the Persian Gulf across from Iran and their backs to the Rub' al Khali, the "empty place," in the Saudi Arabian desert. A strip of inhabited greenery six hundred kilometers long and, in some places, as much as thirty kilometers wide that has been painfully constructed using desalinated water from the gulf. If you know Dubai, Abu Dhabi is on a separate planet. Because it has the largest oil reserves of any of the Emirates, the emir didn't start to think about other kinds of development until just recently, but now the Emirate has high-rise buildings and expressways, too, and is spreading toward Dubai at a fast rate. Soon the two will meet and have no discernible boundary, like Dubai and Sharjah, which is the next Emirate along in the string.

All the way from Vienna, I'd been worrying about how the Pure Warriors of Islam knew I was in Switzerland. Followed my trail from Paris? I was sure they would like payback for that shoot-out in Morocco, but they must have better things to do than chase me. Kidnapping tourists to raise money, for instance. I shifted in the seat. Airplane seats are almost as uncomfortable as airport seats. Did I really know the shooter was one of the terrorists? Did I even know he was an Arab? Neither my gigolo friend, who was so interested in making sure I got on the plane, nor the Calvinist accountant was an Arab. Al Qaeda certainly had Western supporters, men willing to do a little light money collecting and assassination for them, but the Pure Warriors were too new to have a European infrastructure, weren't they? Had I really slipped them in Vienna? Only time would tell. I felt a cold draft on my right hip where the Glock ought to be.

Coming into Dubai is like visiting Disneyland. It's full of Technicolor sights and disco sounds. The creation of Emir Mohammed bin Rashid Al Maktoum, Dubai is an international economic node of free trade and no taxes that has attracted the headquarters of some of the most important corporations in the world. Big in the world's gold and diamond trade, it is also the world's money-laundering capital. The new port and airport at Jebel Ali were in operation, and an enormous US Navy aircraft carrier was docked there, making all the container ships beside it look like toys. New high-rise towers with offices and apartments had sprung up to meet the port since I'd been here last, each with its own string of yachts docked nearby, floating up and down like ducks waiting to be fed. Dozens of new towers lined the roads into town, a tribute to business' need to invest their ill-gotten gains. The traffic into the center had grown exponentially, too, since my last visit.

It made me question the wisdom of staying at my favorite hotel overlooking the dhow docks on the creek. If I was going to have to beat my way through traffic like that every time I wanted to go anywhere, I might have to stay at one of the new international celebrity hutches on the other side of the creek. I wished I could stay at the Bur Dubai in sinful luxury just once. The Emirate's logo caravanserai was built in the shape of a dhow in full sail, and it dripped decadence from every pore. Somehow I didn't think Cynthia Branson would spring for that, so I had to settle for my usual hotel with its usual Businessman's Special room, all chrome and black leather, with a bed the size of that aircraft carrier and a view of Deira on one side and across the creek to Bur Dubai on the other. I would hardly make a dent in that bed. It was built to accommodate a sultan and his whole harem.

I got the little bottles of gin from the minibar, mixed a drink, and, choosing the Deira view, sat looking at Dubai Creek, the original water source that had made the old pearl fishing village possible. It divided Dubai into two unequal parts. Deira, to the northeast, was the first section developed after the Oil Rush made the Emirate rich. It had the airport, the Gold Souk, some banks and hotels, including my own, and the earliest and least glitzy of the shopping malls. But Dubai had the least oil deposits of all the Emirates, and it had to learn other ways to make a living. Thus the emir's Dream of Dubai as an international economic powerhouse and tourist destination. Thus phantasmagorical Dubai.

The old pearl fishing village across the creek in Bur Dubai can hardly be found now that developers have created huge skyscrapers and gigantic malls, like the Mall of the Emirates, with its high-end shops, its ATMs dispensing gold bars, and Ski Dubai, the indoor ski resort supported year-round by a massive air-conditioning plant. It is in that direction, southwest toward Abu Dubai, that golf courses, gated communities of bungalows transported from Hollywood, the tallest skyscrapers, and the new free port of Jebel Ali have sprung up like flowers in the desert after a rain. Dubai is a dream, all right, I thought. A hashish dream. After a while, it made my teeth hurt.

I finished my drink and called my former boss, at Langley. Sidney runs a money-laundering unit at Langley that deals with the profits from organized crime, drug smuggling, gunrunning, human trafficking, and terrorism funding. I used to work for him in Paris. I used to do a little more than hack into Geneva banks, though—little assignments that were outside my job description as an analyst, until the last time when I got a good friend killed. And nearly got me killed too, but that comes with the territory.

"Why did you send Cynthia Branson to me, Sidney?" I asked.

He coughed. "She has a right to know whether her husband is dead or alive," he said.

"You know he's dead. You told me so. You could've told her that. Why didn't you?"

He was silent.

"Sidney, if I'm going to do this, I need to know what you know. What was George doing? Why was he in Dubai? He came ashore carrying a false passport, you said. You did mean he's dead?"

"Yes. That's what I meant."

"How do you know?"

"Roger Findley from the consulate identified him."

I thought about that. "He identified the body as George Branson?"

"No. He didn't identify him to the Dubai people at all. He identified the fingerprints and told us. He told them he couldn't identify the man."

"They were using fingerprints? Why?"

He coughed again. "Because the face was unidentifiable. He'd been shot in the back of the head."

"Executed?"

"Yes."

"How did they know he was American?"

"He was carrying an American passport in the name of Gil Brady. They asked the consulate if anybody by that name was known to be missing and attached the fingerprints. Findley told them he'd check the fingerprints across IAFIS. After a couple of days, he told them the man wasn't in the database."

"Okay, that takes care of that. What was George doing in Dubai in the first place? Let me rephrase that. What was George doing in Dubai that got him executed?"

"We don't know," Sidney replied.

"I don't believe that," I said flatly.

"Neither do I, but that's what they tell me. Nor do I know why they wanted me to get you to go to Dubai and find out."

"They asked for me specifically?" I asked.

"They did."

That rocked me. What particular skills did I have that made me more suited to find out why George Branson was dead than, say, any of the operatives they had in Dubai?

"And you don't know what he was doing in Dubai right then? What he had been doing? Surely they know what he was supposed to have been doing."

"You'd think. All they say they know, or all they'll tell me, is that he was supposed to be working on weapons smuggling from the former Soviet arsenal."

"Well, that narrows it down," I said sarcastically. "Had he ever been in Istanbul?"

"He was in Istanbul when they lost contact with him."

"And when was this?"

He sounded apologetic. "Two years ago."

"The mystery here, Sidney, is not that they want to know why George is dead carrying a false passport," I said, "but why they hadn't missed him earlier. Sidney, I don't believe them. This is one of their hustles. I can't see any reason why they couldn't just give Mrs. Branson a death certificate and cough up his pension."

"Neither can I," he said and ended the call.

I couldn't decide whether this was unusual or not, given the Agency's habit of double-dealing. Maybe it wasn't a Pure Warrior who shot at me in Switzerland. The guys who had been interested in me weren't Arabs. Maybe it was because I was coming to Dubai to look into the death of George Branson. That worried me. If they, whoever they were, had followed me to Switzerland from Paris, they probably knew I was going to look into George Branson's death in Dubai. But who were they? And how did they know? Whoever they were, it meant that I probably hadn't slipped them in Vienna.

The consulate used to be in a high-rise office building in Bur Dubai with a bunch of other consulates, but we decided that it was tacky to share space with Nicaragua, so we built a sprawling single-story complex just across the creek from my hotel. It wasn't as ugly as the federal prison clone they built in Istanbul—probably the building permit people wouldn't allow that, but it must have displaced several hundred families.

Decompressing from the Agency was going to take me some time. It felt really strange to show my passport at the gate rather than my CIA creds, and I had to be escorted along the hall to Roger Findley's office just like any other stranger. Roger Findley had never been my favorite guy, and I wasn't very high on his hit parade, either. Stooped and pale from years spent sitting behind a desk, he had gray hair, gimlet eyes, and a smoker's cough. He was wearing the formal Dubai costume—short-sleeved white shirt open at the neck and khakis. Informal was a T-shirt and khakis. He didn't bother to rise when I was ushered into his office.

"Not Sidney's little pet anymore, eh, Carruthers?" he said sourly.

"No. I have at last achieved emancipation," I replied and took his visitor's chair without invitation. The furniture in the office and the assortment of pictures and plaques on the walls put him at a mid-rank. I would've thought that he had served enough time to be higher up on the totem pole than that.

"What do you want?" he demanded. He's never going to make deputy director with manners like that, I thought, although he was probably more polite to higher-ranking people. I was not only low ranking, I didn't work for the Agency anymore. I didn't exist.

"You identified George Branson."

"Yes."

"How did he die?"

"Shot in the back of the head."

"Then how did you identify him?" I knew the answer, but I wanted to see what he would tell me.

"His passport." Chatty so-and-so.

"Sidney said he was flying a false flag," I said.

He winced at my slang. "False in the sense that the US passport was issued to Gil Brady. The picture was George Branson's. So were the fingerprints."

"Fingerprints?"

He shifted in his chair. "The police gave me his fingerprints."

Just what Sidney had told me. I looked at him thoughtfully. "I'll need to see his things, wallet, certainly, and whatever else he had on him."

He straightened a few things on his desk. "I don't have them." A sly look of triumph flashed across his face before he could suppress it. "I sent them with the passport to Langley."

"And what did you do with George?" I inquired curiously.

"Had him cremated."

He was enjoying himself just a bit too much.

"Identified as?"

"Oh, Gil Brady. That was the name on the passport." He passed his hand across his head. "Of course."

I continued to look thoughtfully at him. The silence lengthened, and I let it. He broke first.

"Now if that's all . . ."

I stood up. "It is by no means all, Roger," I said briskly. "I'll need to see his file." I thought for a minute that he was going to have a stroke.

"You can't see his file," he blustered. "It's an internal Agency file. You are no longer an employee of the CIA and therefore are not entitled to see it."

I smiled sweetly. "I may no longer work for the Agency, Roger, but I am doing Sidney Worthington's bidding. I think you'd better let me see the file."

He was torn between the satisfaction of refusing me access and the possibility of Sidney's displeasure. Sidney's displeasure is well known in the Agency. He slapped his hand on his desk, making a pencil can jump, and led me to a workstation. In a few minutes the monitor began displaying George Branson's file. George had been working for Felix Gringikov, a Belarusian merchant of death, in all the hellholes of Africa. Why was Sidney interested in a Belarusian arms dealer? But it wasn't Sidney, was it? Somebody else wanted to know about George Branson's death and thought I could find out.

George had done good work. There were long reports about his comings and goings from Belarus to Congo and other hellholes. He recorded what he sold and to whom. The occasional short analytic bits about the players were all interesting to me. Belarus supply sergeants vied for space with African warlords and Middle Eastern rebels. I used to chase some of that money, but I'd never seen any of George's reports. Why not? They might have helped me. Roger wouldn't let me take notes, the obstructive bastard, but he eventually left the workstation, and I entered a basic chronology into my iPhone and as much of the rest as I could, but it was slow. I think the thumbs of the current generation of kids have evolved. Mine are not designed for that kind of work. I scrolled on down to the end of the file and found no financial data. I decided I needed to get the file from Sidney; there was too much detail that I needed to study, so I told Roger I was finished, and he guided me rapidly out the door into the arms of a Marine escort. I was as glad to see the last of him as he was to see me go.

I looked at my watch. I had just enough time before the bank closed to visit my safety deposit box and take care of the draft on my hip. I lifted a Glock 26 out of the box, loaded it, and racked a round into the chamber before I seated the gun in its holster. The knife went into a scabbard on my left ankle. I felt normal for the first time since I left Paris. Normal and grateful. I dropped the box of hollow points in my pack and removed half of the stack of hundred-dollar bills. There was another identity there, but I left it. I already had two in play.

The question was who to see first. Was it too early to go to Ralph Prince's hookah bar in Bur Dubai? Ralph was a retired gunrunner, and he would know what was happening in the gun trade. Willy Soo? He was a stockbroker and would know where the money was coming from and going to. Akbar Khan in the gold souk? He would know where a different kind of money was moving. I decided on Ralph's. I know something about money but very little about the details of gunrunning.

I lay on the bed and stared out the window at the setting sun, trying to put the pieces I had into some coherent pattern, but I had too few pieces and no clue as to what the finished pattern might look like. I dozed for a while, and then it was time to go to Ralph's.

A nice long soak in a tub full of pine-scented bubbles left me tingling and more relaxed than I had been since the ski mask shot at me in Switzerland. I concluded that Ralph's place required something higher up the clothing scale than the blue jeans I had been wearing. Only Emirati women were required to wrap themselves in black in Dubai, so I chose a rose-colored cotton pants suit. The top had vines and flowers embroidered around the neck and sleeves with little mirrors and pearls in among the leaves. With the top alone I would be wearing more clothing than ninety-five percent of the other women at Ralph's. I looked at myself in the mirror. I always felt elated when I wore something brightly colored in a Muslim country, because I had spent far too much of my working life in a black suit. I added a touch of blush to my cheeks and was about to twist my hair into the usual chignon when I stopped. In Dubai I didn't have to cover my hair! Three cheers! I brushed it down and looked in the mirror again.

"God," I thought, "I'm disguised as a girl."

What to do with the Glock? I got out what looked like a black clutch purse and was really a holster. I inserted the Glock into it. The sides of the purse were Velcro and one end was open so that I could slip my hand in to grip the gun butt. When I jerked the catch of the bag down, the Glock was in my hand, and all I had to do was raise the other hand and fire. Maybe I should get somebody to make me one in gold lamé. Black looked so dull.

It was just after ten when I went downstairs and asked the doorman to get me a taxi. Dubai was not as difficult to drive in as many Arab cities, because they had oodles of space and divided roads everywhere, but they did have the problem of Arab drivers, who regarded lane markers as mere suggestions and had powerful feelings of entitlement. At least half of the population seemed to be on the road at any given time. Even at that late hour, the traffic showed no signs of diminishing. Maybe they run two shifts? Even Paris winds down by four in the morning, but not Dubai.

Ralph's place, the South Seas, occupied a utilitarian single-story concrete block building which been painted ocher within living memory. It probably looked a bit chipped in the daylight, but at night it was fine.

Inside, I found bamboo tables with thatched umbrellas and high-backed wicker chairs with cushions covered in bright prints. The ground floor, which could be air-conditioned all year around, had a bar, bamboo and thatched, and a DJ who played mixes for those who want-ed to use the small dance floor or just dream over their bubble pipes. Ralph himself was working the door.

"Lee, baby! How are you? Where you been?" He start-ed to hug me and stopped.

"Don't want to get arrested?" I asked. A British couple had been sentenced to jail recently for kissing in public. Or had they been having sex on the beach?

He hugged me. "Oh, funny. I never want to see the in-side of a jail again," he said fervently. He stood back to look at me and saw a tall woman with green eyes and long brown hair. I saw a retired buccaneer, running to fat a bit but still as handsome as ever. He had crinkly wrinkles around his eyes and a rakish smile, although the purity of his profile, which had once made maidens swoon, was blurred with time and good living. He wore jeans and a sport shirt.

"I'm good, Ralph, and how are you?"

"Never better, kiddo, never better." He patted me, waved at the bartender, and led me upstairs away from the noise the DJ was making. In the winter the Dubai nights were cool enough to enjoy the rooftop bar, and the breez-es were balmy that night. The decoration up there was bamboo and bright prints too, but without the umbrellas. Smooth space music played instead of the DJ, and the view over the creek to the glass towers of Deira was spec-tacular. With a clear idea of what would sell in Dubai, Ralph had put his waitresses in bikini tops and grass skirts.

Looking around, I said, "Can we talk?"

He ushered me to a table in the corner. "I'll be right back," he said.

I had stopped smoking some time ago and only really wanted a cigarette after making love satisfactorily or after somebody made a serious attempt to kill me, but the scent of the fruit-flavored smoke coming from the bubble pipes was seductive, so I sat back, inhaled happily, and looked around.

Ralph had opened the place shortly after he was expelled from Djibouti for gunrunning. He'd been operating from there for a long time, and the authorities seemed quite happy to take his money for their discretion, until one day his financial arrangements for a shipment collapsed, and his supplier shot him as an inducement not to let it happen again. The authorities threw him in jail until he could come up with some money to get out. As he told the story later, it was summer, and they let him bleed on the filthy floor of a fetid cell for a while to make their point before they got him medical attention. As a result, he couldn't raise his left arm above his shoulder any longer. When they let him out, which they did as soon as the weather cooled and they decided he really didn't have any more money, he flew to Dubai, lifted his stash, and bought into a hamburger joint. He rapidly decided that he didn't like the way hamburger grease clung to his body even after he showered, so he sold the hamburger joint and opened the hookah bar instead. It looked like he was doing more than all right. He came back with two martinis, and we sat telling each other lies for a while, enjoying the coolness and watching life on the creek.

"You're twitchy, girl," he said.

"What do you mean?"

"You're sitting in the corner with your back to the railing, and you keep scanning the room."

I rolled my shoulders. "I have a very strong feeling that I'm being watched."

He looked at me seriously. "Working again?"

"Just a little job, Ralph. I'm out of the Agency now."

"Congratulations," he said. "I always thought you could do better than that."

I smiled. "A woman wants me to find her husband so she can divorce him."

"Nothing in that to make you twitchy, so come on. Don't hold out on me."

I looked out over the creek and made up my mind. Well, why not? "A couple of days ago when I was skiing in Switzerland, a guy took a shot at me. Got away. All I saw was a guy in black wearing a black mask. Could've been anybody." I looked out over the creek again.

"So who's on the short list?" he asked.

I took a sip of my drink. "I don't know. The obvious is a bunch of Moroccan terrorists I had a dustup with, but would they follow me all the way to Switzerland? The two guys who have showed unusual interest in my movements were Caucasian, not Arab. I have no idea what it could be about, and that makes me nervous."

Ralph looked me seriously. "Excuse me," he said and went across to the bar, where I saw him make a phone call.

"You hungry, girl?" he asked when he came back.

"Yeah, I'm hungry, but I'm too lazy to move."

"Say no more! How about a nice thick T-bone steak, rare, and fries?"

"I wouldn't say no," I said and laughed.

Ralph's kitchen served an elementary menu of burgers and steaks, the kind of thing he liked to eat himself. From the looks of the crowd, a substantial number of locals and tourists agreed with him.

"I haven't eaten yet, myself. We will have steaks. Meanwhile," he said and wiggled his eyebrows like Groucho Marx, "we will have another drink."

"One's enough, Ralph. I'm working."

"And you want more than my pale white body."

"As you say."

He waved to a waitress and ordered a bottle of good Bordeaux, which he knew I could not resist. While we waited for it and our steaks, I told him about George and showed him the photo in my cell.

"That's Gil Brady. I think he used to work for Gringikov."

"Used to?"

"Haven't seen him a while. He may have been collateral damage."

"What do you mean?" I asked.

"Gringikov disappeared. Maybe Brady did too. There has been a turf war recently in the local gunrunning community. The gun trade brought you to me?"

"That and your animal magnetism."

He snorted and thought a bit.

"Business is good, you know."

"Always is."

"The airport and the port at Jebel Ali are free trade zones, and nobody pays much attention to what's coming in or going out or what kind of money is being used to pay for it. And there are a lot of customers."

"Nothing new in that," I said.

"Half the freight forwarders in the Emirate deal from time to time, just two-bit stuff, but now since other business has been so bad, more people are dealing. More in guns than in drugs, maybe. Hard to tell. Women seem to be the specialty of the South Asians right now. There's been some jostling, some pushing and shoving recently. Felix Gringikov used to be number one, but he disappeared in mysterious circumstances about two years ago."

I remembered that George Branson worked for him, and he hadn't been seen in two years. "People think the Agency got him?"

"Yeah, they do, but I'm not so sure about that. Not that I don't think they'd do it, you understand. It's just that there was a lot of turbulence in the business just before he disappeared."

"What kind of turbulence?"

"The police in Sharjah seized a couple of Gringikov's shipments, a thing that has never happened before."

"Didn't pay the usual bribes? No. He wouldn't have neglected something like that. It's a fundamental cost of doing business. A tipoff?"

"I think so," Ralph said. "And then there was some rough stuff at the airport. Damage to Gringikov's planes, his handlers roughed up, one pilot beat up so badly he had to be taken to the hospital."

"Dubai?"

"No. Sharjah. That's where they all hang out."

"What are they thinking of? The emir of Sharjah is very conservative."

"They do some free work for him occasionally. Sharjah's a nice place to do business, but the emir doesn't like publicity. Gringikov was actually warned by the authorities."

"No, really? What's the chronology?"

"What?"

"How close was this rough stuff to the time Gringikov disappeared?"

"He disappeared about a month later."

"So, we have intercepted shipments escalating to violence at the airport, followed by Gringikov disappearing. What's the time span?"

He sat back as our steaks came. After the wine ceremony, he replied, "A couple of months altogether, I'd guess."

"And who has taken his place?"

"Nobody yet. Gringikov's outfit is still in business, but it's not moving much through here. Sergei Malyakov is the leading contender, but he's not alone."

We turned to our meals. The steak was as good as I expected from any kitchen of Ralph's and the fries were thin and crisp. The Bordeaux was exceptional. I said so.

Ralph stopped cutting his steak and grinned. "A lot of places in Dubai are not just overrated, they're overpriced too. I think a moderate markup is better business than a gouge."

"A good philosophy. Looks like you're making money."

"That's the reason. Good food, good drinks, reasonable prices, and good *sheesha*."

I returned to the gun trade. "Has the 'turbulence' in the competition to replace Gringikov been violent?"

"Not here, except for the pilot who had to be taken to the hospital. The things that happened to Gringikov in Sharjah were extremely unusual. That's usually neutral territory for everybody, but there have been violence and snitching elsewhere. You know the former Soviet Union is leaking weapons?"

I raised my eyebrow. "Do tell."

He went on. "Yeah. Okay. Ukraine, Belarus, Georgia, the Stans."

"I know we've been worried about their nuclear arsenal."

"So far as I know, nothing nuclear has moved. It's the small stuff, AKs, RPGs, and ammunition. These people burn off a hell of a lot of ammo. No fire discipline at all, although there's not much discipline of any kind among twelve-year-olds hopped up on amphetamines. A shipment belonging to Gringikov's outfit went bad in Bangkok last year. Based on a tip, the Thai police seized a cargo of the usual small stuff plus a dismantled Soviet attack helicopter. That flight originated in the Emirates. The plane was an Ilyushin owned by a woman who lives in Sharjah. She said she knew nothing about any arms, she just leased the plane to some guy. Money came through Deutsche Bank. How could she think the deal wasn't straight? Yada, yada, yada, and if she had known they were moving guns she would have never leased the plane to them."

"Or she would have charged more. What's her name?"

"Wait for it." He paused, grinning. "Malyakov."

"The missus, is she? I hope she got her money up front. Was the tip part of Malyakov's attempt to take over?"

"Could be."

"They've seized the plane too, haven't they? And they'll keep it."

"It's a rickety old heap, not long for this world anyway, and it was insured."

We paused to sip our wine and admire Malyakov's footwork.

"Other players?" I asked.

"A few. A Brit name of Willoughby, in a minor way. Walter W. Willoughby. Ex-SAS, cashiered."

"He sounds familiar."

"He should. He and a few friends tried to pull off a coup in the Comoros not long ago."

"Ah, yes. And he's loose? I thought they convicted him and threw him in jail."

"They did. He served until the media went away and then 'escaped.'"

"I wonder how much that cost."

"A pretty penny, I imagine. And then there's an Australian called Two-Time Thompson, so-called because he sells his stuff more than once."

"Sounds dangerous."

"Oh, it is. He just got out of the hospital."

"I'm surprised they didn't kill him."

"So was he, but they just beat the crap out of him and left him crippled as a lesson to the others. I think he's out of business for good."

"I should think so. Ralph, I think you got out at the right time. Gunrunning is no longer the sport of gentlemen," I said.

"It's not just the sport of men these days. Did I tell you about Phuong Nguyen? A tiny, little Vietnamese doll who may be tougher than all the men put together."

"You're making that up!"

He put his hand on his heart. "Swear to God. She's about five feet tall, long black hair, looks as sweet as a kumquat. The daughter, they say, of a prominent Vietnamese pirate family that works the Gulf of Thailand from Ca Mau to Singapore. It's just a little organization, but mean. Deals mostly with the Muslims in the Philippines, I think. Come to think of it, you might want to talk to her. I've heard she had a thing going with Gil Brady." He stopped and waved to a nearby guy in khaki safari clothes. "There's Willoughby now."

Chapter 4

THE GUY CAME over. He was chunky by nature as well as good living. Blonde hair mixed with gray. Bushy eyebrows, bushy mustache, a red complexion. From the sun? Probably from the booze. He looked like a British army sergeant major gone to seed. Ralph introduced us. Willoughby finished his beer and waved for another before he shook my hand.

"She's looking for Gil Brady," Ralph said.

He looked at me out of watery blue eyes. "Why?" he asked, draining about a third of the beer from the new bottle.

"His wife needs to find him. She wants to divorce him," I replied.

"Not surprised. Haven't seen him lately. He works for Gringikov or did. He may have disappeared when Gringikov did."

"When was the last time you saw him?" I asked.

He thought, an activity that appeared unusual to him. He burped. "Dunno—been a while." With that he wandered away toward a pair of tourist girls wearing slip dresses. Or slips.

Ralph apologized. "I said he might know something. I never said he was couth."

I stood up. "Time to go, guy. It's been a long day."

"I invested a steak and a bottle of good wine and a martini and that doesn't get me anything?"

"In your dreams, boy," I said. "If that's the way it is, I'll buy my own steak."

He laughed. "You driving?" he asked.

I shook my head. "Took a taxi."

"I'll drive you back then."

I waited at the door while he gave some instructions to his floor man. I felt eyes on me and turned back toward the room. A guy in a blue T-shirt was staring at me appraisingly. His hair and eyebrows were brown, and his eyes were chips of sapphire to match his shirt. I looked at him, and he turned away.

Ralph's car was a low-slung red sports job. "My midlife-crisis-mobile." He grinned as he helped me in. I hoped he wasn't going to have to use a crowbar to get me out.

The roads were still moderately crowded, and Ralph was tooling along in the center lane when a black SUV cut in front of us, close enough that if we had had another layer of paint it would have hit us.

"What the hell?" Ralph downshifted, almost causing the car in the back to rear-end us. The SUV cut into the inside lane, causing grief there too, and turned off onto the road to the palace.

"The emir's teenage son?" I asked jokingly.

"No. He drives a red Maserati. And more politely."

"Is there a lot of that here now? I remember a lot of lane straddling and driving fast in the slow lanes and slow in the fast lanes, but nobody ever cut me off."

"It is unusual," he said. "Never had it happen before."

Back at the hotel we stopped at the door of my room, and he gave me a long, sweet, remembering kiss. I really did like the old buccaneer, but I shook my head, and my eyes filled with tears. I touched Kemal's pearl. Ralph put his finger under the chain and drew it out.

"That blood?" he asked.

I nodded.

"You'll forget faster if you stop wearing it."

"I don't want to forget."

I really do like the old pirate, I thought as I undressed and got in bed, putting the Glock and the iPhone on the floor beside me. I was looking at the door when I turned out the light, or I would have missed it—a pair of feet against the light. Again. I scooped up the Glock and ran to the door. I looked through the peephole just in time to see the back of a man going away. He had black hair.

I hadn't slipped them in Vienna.

Chapter 5

I LOVE THE breakfast in international hotels. They cater to every taste and religion in the world. Where else could I snag bacon, sausage, liverwurst, flatbread with cheese and olives, plus Chinese dumplings? I sat in the corner and looked over the room as I ate. A man in khaki facing the windows had his back to me so I couldn't see his face; everybody else looked innocuous.

I was exceedingly surprised to look up and see Ralph awake at that hour and standing by my table. Beside him stood a lanky guy with a buzz cut, wearing a blue work shirt with the sleeves rolled up and faded jeans held up by a wide belt with USMC stamped on the buckle. The ensemble was finished off by a pair of scuffed combat boots. All he needed was a cigarette hanging out of the side of his mouth for him to be the Marlboro Man.

He looked familiar. The guy in the blue T-shirt? I gestured to the men to sit down. "Okay, Ralph, what are you up to?"

"This is Fred Atkins. He needs a job. You need a partner."

"I work alone, Ralph. You know that."

"Yeah, I know you do. I've seen the scars." He stopped to smile reminiscently, shook himself, and went on. "You got a bunch of Arab terrorists looking for you and maybe another bunch shooting at you. They're coming at you from all sides, and you've only got one pair of eyes. You need another pair."

"My last partner is dead," I said flatly.

"So be more careful with this one," he said.

I looked at Atkins. "Ralph, I don't need the Marlboro Man."

"You need somebody with the right moves," Ralph said. "He's got them."

"Marine," I said to Atkins.

He nodded.

"So why are you on the beach in Dubai?" I asked.

"The Corps and I had a disagreement."

"You going to tell me about it?"

"No."

"Fair enough," I said.

I closed my eyes and heard Kemal say, "They won't take your manhood away if you have backup." Backing me up had cost him his life. We had walked carelessly into a situation we couldn't handle, and one of us had died. If both of us had been armed and walking consciously it might not have happened. I turned back to Atkins. "No."

He smiled a lazy smile. "Can't we just be friends?"

I looked steadily at him. "No."

He shrugged. "Everybody needs somebody."

"No. Go back to bed, Ralph. I work alone."

After Ralph and the Marlboro Man had left, I went back to the room and began trying to find Willy Soo, money man extraordinaire. There are few Chinese families that have gone from the slums of Canton to the east end of London and sent a son to the London School of Economics. Willy landed in Dubai after a stop-off in Singapore. He knew the score in at least four languages. The last number I had for him was at HSBC. He was no longer there. They suggested I try Citibank. He wasn't there either. And they had no suggestions. Cursing all banks and bankers, I applied to the Internet and found Willy Soo, investment counselor, with an address in one of the elegant new towers in Jumeirah. Trust Willy to light where the money was. I called the office number and got a young man who spoke down his nose in Oxbridge. He attempted to stonewall me, but Willy picked up and tanked right over him.

"Lee, baby! Long time no see!"

Willy doted on 1950s film noir, but his accent was pure Whitechapel. The Arabs loved him.

"Willy, love, how about dinner?" I asked.

"You want something," he hooted.

"Only the charm of your company and your Singapore cunning," I laughed.

"It'll cost you."

"But it will be worth it, won't it, love?" I asked and made arrangements for us to meet at a restaurant the concierge said would have white tablecloths but would only cost me an arm and a leg. He would be worth every mouthful of the dinner I was going to buy for him. That nailed down, I phoned down for a pot of coffee, and set out in search of merchants of death.

There are two bad things about leaving the Agency. The first was the lack of a regular paycheck, and the second, and worse, was the loss of Mike Donovan, Sidney Worthington's premier researcher. I live with my head in computers, so I can do my own research if I have to, but it's just another thing I have to do. When I worked for the Agency, I could press a button and reams of information would flow from Mike's computer to mine. Now I have to do the heavy lifting myself.

I wasn't going to suffer for lack of data. There were over half a million entries for Felix Gringikov and Sergei Malyakov. At that point I stopped. Unless I wanted to spend all my time on the computer, I needed to find a replacement for Mike. The coffeepot was empty when I remembered Jerry, to give him his full name, Gerald Cabot Winslow III, mercifully called Jerry. He was at MIT when I was at Yale, my roommate's lover for a while. We ran into each other at a hacker's convention in '09, and before it was over, he had invited me to invest a little money and become a partner in his IT security startup in Boston, hacking the hackers. At that time I was not mortally sick of the Agency, so I declined, but we kept in touch. His company prospered, and he continued to suggest that I come to Boston, although he said I should have taken him up on it in '09, because the value of the company's stock had taken off, and it would cost me a lot more to buy in.

Jerry must have somebody who could run Gringikov and Malyakov through the Internet and provide me with coherent bios, chase their money, maybe look for George Branson/Gil Brady. I looked at my watch. It was still too early to call Boston, so I fought my way determinedly across six lanes of traffic to the dhow docks, and bought a sandwich, which I ate as I walked along, dodging cargo pallets and guys heaving boxes onto dhows. It was easy to deduce the character of the ship's captain by the way the cargo was loaded. The dependable men had their cargo stowed in an orderly fashion, all stacked up and squared away. The more insouciant types had the cargo thrown in in any old way, or piled up and looking as if it would shift in the mildest kind of a breeze. I wiped my hands on my jeans and continued along the dock, looking for the sagging and beat-up old dhow that belonged to my friend Sinbad. He would know what was going across the Persian Gulf to Iran, but he was also likely to know other things about the world of illegal commerce.

I first met Sinbad when he pulled me, wrinkled and sunburned, from the Persian Gulf, where a bunch of bad guys had thrown me when they caught me draining the hard drive of their computer into a flash drive. He dried me off with a towel that was not terribly clean and sent me back to my hotel from the dhow dock on Dubai Creek.

Sinbad boat's wasn't there, not even among the old wrecks pulled up in the mud beyond the dock. As I went back, I stopped here and there to ask about Sinbad. Nobody seemed to know where he was, but then nobody would tell me if he was running machine tools to Iran, would they? I'd just have to wait until he got back. After dodging a crate that would have split my skull if it had hit me, I quit while I was winning and went back to the hotel. It was likely to be a late night again. I thought longingly of a nice quiet night reading some brain candy on my Kindle. In my dreams.

It was still early in Boston, so early that Jerry answered his own phone.

"Have you decided to become an honest woman and come to work with me?" he asked when I identified myself.

"Not this week, Jerry. I need a favor. Have you got somebody who can do some basic Internet research and a little light financial hacking for me?"

"That's the kind of thing you make your living doing," he observed.

"Used to make a living doing," I said. "I'm out of the Agency now, and I need some research done."

"Came to your senses, did you? What kind of research and why don't you come to Boston?" he asked.

"I'm in Dubai . . ."

"Dubai!"

"In Dubai looking into the death of a CIA operative," I continued. "He was working for Felix Gringikov, a Belarusian arms dealer. I need to know about Gringikov and a rival dealer, Sergei Malyakov—their backgrounds, their dealings, their money—all of it."

"Tell me about it." I heard his chair squeak as he settled back into it.

So I told him about it—or at least what I knew about it then.

"I don't like the sound of this, Lee," he said.

"I don't like it much myself, Jerry. That's why I need the research done. I need to know what I'm up against."

"I can tell you what you're up against," he said. "Two arms dealers and a dead CIA agent . . ."

"And I'm going to get myself killed," I finished. "Don't go there, Jerry. I don't have time to do this stuff."

"What are you going to do after you finish this case?" he asked.

"I don't know, Jerry. One thing at a time. I need this research done."

"And what if I refuse?"

"Jerry, I'll go somewhere else if I have to."

"And find somebody you can trust? Okay, I'll do it or get it done. The price will be a visit to Boston to look over the operation."

"Pure blackmail, Jerry."

"Got it in one. What do you want from us?"

"Bios of Felix Gringikov and Sergei Malyakov. There are over half a million entries for the two of them. I need coherent bios. What financial information you can find."

"Okay. I'll call you this time tomorrow."

"Jerry . . ." I protested, but all I got was a dial tone.

I checked my watch and called Con Owen. He was an ink-stained wretch of the first water, an English expat who had worked for every English-language sheet in the Emirates in his time, as well as a couple of Arabic ones. When the Arabs found out that his Arabic reading ability was practically nil, they fired him, although they still admired his legendary ability to curse.

"I'm on deadline," he barked.

"How can you be on deadline?" I asked. "You publish online."

"Online is always on deadline. When did you get into town? What do you want?"

"Yesterday. The charm of your company for a libation or two."

He grunted. "Seven, at Tipples."
"Done," I said.

Tipples was like a lot of other bars around the world, made
for guys who dreamed of wearing foreign correspondent
trench coats and were willing to pay for the privilege of
drinking in the company of working hacks, a few of whom
sat hunched over beers watching soccer games on the TVs.
Tipples' smoke-stained walls had the usual decorations—
pictures of the owner with football players and starlets,
out-of-date girlie calendars, and yellowing news stories
stuck up with browning cellophane tape. The bar was an
old and scarred slab of wood, and the tables and booths
were equally ancient and scarred. Beer mats with the
names of defunct breweries were stacked next to paper
napkin holders, right beside the crusted ketchup bottles. It
could have been imported from 1920s Berlin. They say the
owners got it at a bomb sale in Beirut in the early seven-
ties. The whole place was a violation of everything Dubai
stood for, and most of the clientele didn't match the ambi-
ence, except in their dreams. Besides the media hacks,
there were a couple of soaks out of central casting sup-
porting the bar, but the rest of the customers were wearing
natty suiting of a Savile Row persuasion or sporty T-shirts
with the names of football teams on the front and prefad-
ed jeans tucked into desert boots.

Owen waved from a booth in the rear. He had already
started, probably early in the day. He stood up to shake my
hand, and I kissed him on his wrinkled cheek. He was a bit
stooped from all the years bent over a keyboard, and his
hair, what there was left of it on his bony skull, was a yellowing white, as was his drooping mustache. He claimed
he arrived on the plane that took the last Brit troops out in
1971, and I had no reason to doubt it. His age was impos-
sible to estimate. He hadn't changed since the first time I
saw him, probably because he was pickled in alcohol. I
ordered a beer. I don't like beer. That might help me stay

sober. We chatted about this and that: the Emirates part in the air war against the Islamic State, the continuing recovery of the construction industry, the tallest building in the world. Con finished his drink and ordered another.

"So what do you want?" he asked.

"Information," I replied and shelled some peanuts.

He took a healthy swig of the new drink. "Don't we all? Any particular information?"

I poured some beer and took a sip. I still didn't like beer.

"The recent turmoil in the arms trade," I replied.

"I don't know what you're talking about," he said. He looked into his drink and screwed it around on the beer mat.

"Come on, Con. It doesn't happen in Dubai without your permission."

He didn't look up. "This isn't the States. I don't work for *The Washington Post*," he muttered defensively.

I never thought Owen had much of a backbone, or he wouldn't have spent his life in Lotus Land, but this looked less like laziness and more like pure funk.

"I know you don't, but you know what's going on."

He looked up, his eyes red and his shoulders sagging. "I can't print anything about the arms dealers."

"I'm not asking you to print it, Con," I countered. "I'm just asking you to tell me about it."

Owen looked toward the bar and stiffened. I looked around. A pair of hefty guys in jeans and sunglasses who had just come in leaned up against the bar, staring in our direction. I looked back at Owen. He began to slide out of the booth. I put my hand on his arm to detain him.

"You must know what's going on. You've been here forever."

He shook my hand off and threw a fistful of dirhams on the table. He looked over his shoulder again.

"I don't think even the police know what's going on. Maybe especially the police."

The guys followed him outside. I stood in the doorway and watched. They shoved him up against the wall. He put his hands up pleadingly and shook his head. They let him go, and he walked away, his shoulders sagging even more. One of the men got into a BMW and drove off. The other leaned up against the wall and stared at me. I leaned in the doorway and stared back at him.

"Hi," I heard and turned around. The Marlboro Man was leaning against the wall by the door. I moved out of the doorway.

"Lots of wall propping going on," he remarked.

"What are you doing here? How did you find me?"

"Just taking in the sights. It's not hard to find a Western woman in Dubai, a thing you might remember if you want to stay healthy."

I flagged a passing taxi. Just what I needed. Fred Atkins telling me what to do.

Chapter 6

WILLY SOO HAD put on a little weight since the last time I saw him, but he still looked sharp, about five foot seven, with a round face of pale ivory, jet black hair, and dark brown eyes that verged on black. He didn't precisely glitter when he walked, but he radiated money, from his hand-made silk suit to his equally handmade black loafers. He might occasionally sound like Whitechapel, but he was Dubai all the way.

"Lee!" He kissed me on both cheeks. "You're looking glam!"

And so I was, in a slinky black crêpe dress cut on the bias with a V neck that was interesting but not actionable. The pushed-up sleeves served to hide the scars on my left shoulder. Kemal's pearl hung in its place, and the Glock was in its place too, inside the little clutch bag.

Willy turned around. "Have a dekko at the whistle and flute," he said, the street urchin emerging from the silk suit. His Whitechapel came and went. It was currently in the ascendant.

"Your suit?"

"Yair."

"You're mixing vernaculars, Willy. That's Australian," I said as the maître d' ushered us to our table. The concierge had bagged me a table by the window, which would earn him a nice tip tomorrow. Nighttime Dubai sparkled as if unaware of any financial crisis. We were fluttered over until we had ordered drinks and were perusing the menu. This took us through the first martinis. The only solution I could see was to stay until I tried everything. I finally surrendered to the duck confit, and Willy had the pork.

"I always like to eat pork in Muslim countries." He grinned.

He went into conference with the wine waiter, and I put in a bid for the Haute-Medoc Bordeaux. I had visited the Château Belle-Vue on a case the previous year and found that particular vintage worthy of revisiting. The waiter turned my way, suddenly aware of my existence. I was Ordering Wine While Being a Woman. He agreed, and Willy capitulated after making a spirited pitch for one from the Château Reynard Mondesir.

"How can you resist a château with a name like that?" he asked.

"Because pretty views are better than desirable foxes," I replied.

The three of us had no trouble in choosing a Muscadet to go with our lobster and salmon ravioli starters.

The food was delectable, and the service a perfect ballet. We made desultory conversation with our starters.

"So what brings you to Dubai, lovely lady?"

"I'm looking for a missing person who is connected to the arms trade," I replied. I looked around. The tables were nicely spaced, but anybody who was interested could hear our conversation. "We'll talk about it later. You have had an eventful career since we last met, I must say."

He raised an eyebrow. "You want to talk about bundling subprime mortgages?" he asked incredulously.

I shook my head. He tasted the ravioli and rolled his eyes in pretended ecstasy. They were good but maybe not that good. "My last billet was at Citibank," he said. "I could tell the bus was going off the cliff. The Abu Dhabi deal was an act of desperation." He looked to see if I was following him.

I was way ahead of him. "So it was. And Abu Dhabi got stung."

Abu Dhabi had agreed to buy $7.5 billion worth of Citi stock to be converted into shares with an eleven percent annual return. Abu Dhabi was obligated to purchase the stock in 2010 and 2011. At the time of the contract, Citi stock was trading at around thirty-five dollars a share, but it was now trading at a tenth of that.

"Can they get out of the deal?" I asked curiously. "Doing business in Abu Dhabi will become problematic for Citi if they stick it to the emir."

"They'll either get out of it or be awarded enormous damages. Abu Dhabi is charging fraudulent misrepresentation."

"And did they? Misrepresent, I mean."

"Don't ask, eh?" He took a bite of asparagus. "About that time, my father died, so I decided to get out."

I fished a piece of lobster out of its little pasta coat and dipped it into the sauce. "Taking your clients with you?"

"You bet. I took them with me and got them into safe waters before the balloon went bust. Anyway, my father left the family holdings in Singapore to my sister and me." He popped a piece of salmon into his mouth and chewed.

After we'd finished the ravioli, Willy sat back, twirling his wine glass in his fingers.

"I've never liked her husband, and he would certainly have made my life a misery if I'd gone back there, so I let them buy me out at their price." He smiled thinly. "They thought they got a good deal. They did. I lost a little, but I had dollars when the bust came, and they had a freight forwarding company at a time when there was very little freight to forward." His Whitechapel accent had disappeared entirely in favor of Oxbridge as spoken in the City.

"How are they doing?"

"They've had to sell the condo in Bali, poor dears," he said, "but they're hanging in. Anyway, I'm out on my own, and my clients are burning incense to my photo every day. Nobody lost a penny."

"Take my portfolio. Please," I said, making way for the waiter to place my duck and risotto in front of me.

"I will." He looked happily at his pork.

I waited for the waiter to complete the wine ritual. Willy tasted the Bordeaux and nodded. I did the same. It was every bit as good as I remembered.

"Now, my dear, is it your portfolio we're talking about?"

"Not right now, but I'm open to suggestion. I've quit the Agency and need to rearrange my investments."

"You stayed longer than I expected. Then what do you want of me?"

I forked in some duck and paused to savor it. "A little local gossip for starters," I said. "I talked to Con Owen this afternoon, and he was very antsy, didn't want to talk to me. What's the matter with him?"

Willy chuckled, spreading some mustard on his pork. "He found out that he's mortal. Security picked him up couple of weeks ago and held him for three days before releasing him. He hasn't been the same since. Of course, he wasn't exactly Victoria Cross material before he went in."

"But what for?"

"Covering the corruption cases a little too enthusiastically."

"What?"

"We've got a bunch of high-level corruption cases working, eleven of them involving thirty-four well-connected punters and almost a billion dollars. A billion here, a billion there, and pretty soon you're talking real money."

"And he was investigating them? That doesn't sound like Con."

"Oh, no. He made the mistake of writing clear prose. He can do that when he's moderately sober. Made the Emirate look bad. That's a no-no for our emir. I imagine they threatened his residence visa. He's too old and lazy to start over again somewhere else, the silly sod."

"I don't get it. The news agencies ran stories on the corruption cases at the time, although I don't think I knew there were so many of them." I finished my wine, and the waiter filled my glass before Willy could reach the bottle.

"Lee, the local media have always treated the government and the royals with kid gloves. It was easy to run positive stories about Sheikh Mohammed and his Dream when things were good. When the economy tanked, ugly things started crawling out from under rocks. The establishment would rather take care of those unsightly things quietly, but they attracted outside attention."

"I remember. It was a dump-on-Dubai time, as I recall. Anybody who ever thought the Palm Jumeirah project was ridiculous said so in a loud and raucous voice. Built on sand was a favorite headline."

"And the underwater hotel?"

"That too. Sounded pretty spiteful."

"Too right."

"You've fallen into Australiese, again, mate," I said, grinning.

"Too right," he said unrepentantly. "Spent a couple of years in Sydney, didn't I? Great people, the Aussies. Anyway, economic reporters are pretty puritanical folks. If you're making money, it's bound to be sinful. It was that spiteful tone, that glee, that hurt most, I think. It tarnished The Dream. Most of the local media walked very carefully. The government likes to pretend there is no censorship here, but there is a pretty high level of surveillance. Everybody knows the penalty for stepping out of line. Most people think the phones are tapped, and a lot of people believe they monitor e-mail and web use."

"They follow people?" I asked.

He raised an eyebrow.

I nodded. "Somebody was on Con. They may be on me now."

"That may not be good, Lee, although they can always find a foreigner if they want to. These one-person states are all alike. At least nobody follows you into the loo to see if you flush the toilet, like they do in Singapore," he said. "They have the local boys pretty well in hand. Now they're trying to muzzle the wire services too."

"Good luck with that," I said cynically.

"They've had a fair amount of luck so far. The resident correspondents have their visas to consider, and the guys coming in from the outside are vulnerable in other ways. For instance, in April, Security picked up a guy from Bloomberg News when he arrived at the airport. They let him go after a couple of hours, but they warned him to be 'sensible.' He was tailed everywhere he went, you know, muscular guys wearing sunglasses. So very few people would talk to him. Word around the bars is that his hotel room was bugged too. Of course, those journos do exaggerate a bit. The cops busted into his room and took photographs of him with a prostitute, which was maybe a put-up job."

"And maybe not," I said.

"Too right. The poor guy was grabbed on his way out too. They tossed his luggage, deleted his photos, confiscated some tapes."

"And they think that will muzzle Bloomberg?" I laughed. "That kind of behavior will just invite the sort of coverage they're trying to prevent."

"It has. It has also alienated that part of the world financial press not already on their case. They may be wired in some very modern ways, but they don't really understand the Western media. They've been insulated from the real world for a long time."

"Forever," I said.

We contemplated the dessert menu. I chose the cheese plate, and Willy selected the peanut butter brulée. While we ate, we talked about the strange ways of money and the stranger ways of the people who have it. I thought it was funny that the Rothschilds would be helping to liquidate Dubai World's more salable assets.

He sighed in content. "That was wonderful! Thank you, lovely lady."

"You're welcome," I said. "Let's go somewhere for coffee." I summoned a waiter.

The cheeky street urchin emerged again. "My place or yours?"

"A sheesha bar was more what I had in mind," I said as I added up the check, added the tip, and signed it. For Dubai, I'd gotten away easily, although for the amount I'd spent you could feed an African family of five for half a year. I still hadn't asked questions I wanted answered. Con Owen was afraid for his posh lifestyle. That satisfied my curiosity about him, but in the larger scheme of things it would not butter any parsnips.

Chapter 7

"WHAT DO YOU want to know about the arms trade?" he asked.

"Felix Gringikov and Sergei Malyakov," I replied.

He thought for a moment. "The Berlin, I think," he said.

I shook my head. "Not a place I remember."

"They come and go. Probably opened since you were here last. It's at the Arab Towers Hotel, and it's hot right now. They should be there."

"They?"

"Wait for it," he said.

He drove back toward the airport and crossed the creek on the new Al Maktoum Bridge into the Bur Dubai district, the oldest section of town, where, sometimes, for a moment, you could believe that you were in the old pearl fishing town. We turned onto Jumeirah Road and drove toward Jebel Ali. As we passed I could see the lacy domes and minarets of the Fatimid-style Jumeirah Mosque, lighted against the night sky. The Arab Towers Hotel was at least six stars, possibly seven. A sheikh opened the door for me, and his son and heir took the keys from Willy and screeched away to the parking lot. Willy winced.

It was the witching hour when we arrived. Willy was greeted with enthusiasm, and we were seated side by side on a black banquette against the wall where we had a good view of the whole room. A bottle of champagne appeared at once. The club was decorated in a chic Art Deco style, all black and white, with glass tables and black upholstered chrome side chairs. Epicene Victor and Victorias lounged sensuously over period cars or waved tennis racquets or danced cheek to cheek in black sketches on white walls. A four-piece band was belting out some loud jazz.

I eyed the champagne hesitantly. We had consumed, after all, the best part of two bottles of wine with dinner, not to mention the martini starters.

"It's the only way I could get a table without standing in line. I want to show you some people," Willy said and sipped the wine. I took a small sip. It was good champagne, but I visualized what my head would look like in the morning and put the glass down.

"I need to switch to ginger ale if I want to be able to focus my eyes tomorrow." I looked at my watch. "Today."

Willy waved our waiter down and ordered ginger ale. The waiter brought another wine glass and poured me some ginger ale. He tucked the bottle into the wine cooler, right next to the champagne. Either he was understanding of people who didn't drink alcohol or no behavior was regarded as bizarre in Dubai. Willy looked around the room. The music was beginning to affect my sinuses.

"See that man over there?" He nodded toward a man leaving the dance floor. "The one with the large gold medal? You need to know about him."

I saw him. He was good-looking, almost six feet tall, with dark, expensively styled hair, broad shoulders, and a practiced smile which revealed white teeth which seemed too good to be true. He was wearing skintight Levis, a white silk poet's shirt with flowing sleeves, and the aforementioned big gold medallion nestled in curling chest hair. He looked like a male model or a TV anchorman.

"Who is he?" I asked.

"Sergei Malyakov," he replied.

"The arms dealer?" I asked.

"The very same," he replied. "Isn't he handsome?" he asked in a sweet voice.

"The Russian diet has improved remarkably since the fall of the Soviet Union."

"It has for some. He looks as if he never ate a potato in his life, doesn't he? In fact, he looks quite like the current Russian president."

"He doesn't have that ferret look that Putin has, does he?"

Malyakov was leading a busty, hippy woman by the hand. Her prominent cheekbones said Slav; her heavily made-up face was framed in swirling blonde Farrah Fawcett hair. She was poured into a magenta dress that barely covered her breasts and fluttered down to flirt with her knees. The spaghetti straps that held the top up looked severely strained. The couple took their places at a table in the far corner, where an obsequious waiter took a bottle from the ice bucket and filled their tiny glasses to the brim. Vodka, probably Imperial Vodka. Seated, the woman looked naked except for a necklace of large stones. Chandelier earrings with equally large stones escaped from her hair and cascaded almost to her shoulders, threatening to distend her earlobes. I did not make the mistake of thinking the stones were zircons.

Two large men with short hair and bulges under the arms of their too-tight suit coats stood behind the pair, feet braced and arms folded in front of them. Neither would ever dance *Swan Lake*. A young man approached the Malyakov table, a look of petition on his face. The two guards unfolded their arms, and one shook his head. The other had such a thick neck he probably couldn't. The young man flinched and turned away. The Malyakovs appeared not to notice.

"Who's the Natasha?" I asked.

"That's no Natasha, that's his wife Natalie. The man is, as I said, Sergei Alexievitch Malyakov, He intends to become the most important arms dealer in the region now that Gringikov has disappeared."

"You're sure she's not a Natasha?" I asked.

"Let's say a retired Natasha. She runs an escort service now."

I raised an eyebrow.

"And they have a large villa in Sharjah."

"Sharjah is quiet," I commented.

"She owns more than escorts."

"Like what?" I asked.

"Like a couple of Ilyushins and an Antonov."

"An Antonov! The biplane?"

"Yes. Cute little thing. Short takeoff and landing. Not much cargo space, but you don't need much if you're only inserting a couple of guys."

I nodded in agreement.

"And an executive jet, a Gulfstream G150."

"That seems to cover the field," I said.

"Oh, they've got the field covered, all right."

Singly or in pairs, a procession of men, some South Asian, some Arabs, some were probably Russian, Slavic, anyway, approached the table where the couple held court. Each appeared to report briefly and listen to instructions from Malyakov. Occasionally, Malyakov summoned a waiter who poured a drink for a favored one from the bottle of Remy Martin in the middle of the table. Two of the favored men looked Levantine, maybe Lebanese, possibly Syrian. They chatted amiably with the Malyakovs for a while, and then Natalie summoned a pair of slender South Asian girls from a nearby table of women, and they joined the men as they left.

"Who are the men?"

"I don't know. I'll see what I can find out and let you know," he said.

"Discreetly."

He looked at me seriously. "Of course. Ever met a financial counselor who was indiscreet?"

"I didn't mean to hurt your feelings," I said.

Then two men joined the group, and Malyakov himself poured them a drink. One was tall with a face fit for Roman coin, and the other was shorter with a dark complexion and pockmarks on his face. They looked supremely uncomfortable in expensive leisure outfits.

"And they are?" I asked.

Willy smiled. "The one on the left is Abdel Fawaz, an Iranian who worked for Citi when I was there. He left last year to become CEO of the newly formed Dubai–Persian Bank. The other is Rajiv Kumar, a Pakistani who heads Dubai-Persian's online operations."

"Iranian. That's interesting."

"You always did have a talent for understatement."

"More accustomed to wearing suits, I would guess," I commented.

"You're right. The Dubai–Persian bank was founded immediately after Gringikov disappeared. They're hoping he doesn't return. They have a lot of Malyakov's business."

Conversation at the table became animated for a while. When they finished their drinks, the bankers shook hands with Malyakov and retired to a table some distance away, where they were promptly joined by two luscious ladies, their generous attributes stressing the diamante spaghetti straps holding up their bright satin dresses.

"And the ladies?"

"Oh they *are* Natashas, part of Madame Malyakov's stable."

"A reward for services rendered?"

"And for services yet to come."

"And do they provide prohibited financial services for Iran?"

"Now why would you think a thing like that?" Willy asked with a twinkle in his eyes.

The next pair of men were Western. One looked British or Scots from his clothing. The other could have been Canadian or American. The waiter hurried up with a bottle of whiskey. He poured for both men. The first put about two drops of water in his glass and sipped. The second put two ice cubes from a bowl on the table into his drink and took a healthy swig. American, then. The men settled back to chat. I looked a question at Willy.

"The one who drinks his whiskey with ice is Martin Worth, called Marty. He has a bonded warehouse at the new airport at Jebel Ali. The other one is Wilson James, a whiskey importer. Deals with most of the hotels and clubs in Dubai and is trying to move into some of the other Emirates."

"And what connection might they have with Malyakov?"

"I don't know, but I can find out."

I rolled my shoulders to relax them. The feeling in the back of my neck that somebody was watching me had returned. I turned my gaze from the table to look around the room and locked eyes with a man in khakis and a blue T-shirt sitting alone at a table near the door. Fred Atkins sketched a salute. Was he following me?

Chapter 8

I LOOKED AT my watch. It was after two. I got tired immediately. Just as I was about to suggest leaving, a middle-aged Arab wearing tailored tan slacks and a matching cashmere sweater with the sleeves pushed up to his elbows pulled out the chair beside Madame Malyakov. His sharp nose bisected a long face, tan to match his slacks and sweater. A waiter hastened up with a glass of what looked like fruit juice, and a blonde with an olive complexion and attributes only a little less extreme than Madame Malyakov's own slipped into the chair next to him and patted his hand. I couldn't imagine how much that jade-colored silk dress had cost her, but it was worth every penny. Its fabric was draped softly over her bosom and hips, subtly emphasizing both. Her green eyes were outlined with enough kohl to supply an Egyptian dynasty and highlighted by pale green eye shadow. Altogether she was a symphony in green. Money green. He looked at her briefly before returning his attention to Madame Malyakov.

"Another Natasha, this one Lebanese, and very expensive," Willy commented.

"And the gent?"

He shook his head. "I don't know," he said. "I haven't seen him before. I'll find out."

"Saudi?" I ventured.

"Looks like it."

The traffic at the Malyakov table had slowed to a stop. The band started another set, this time smooth dance music, and Willy led me to the dance floor, moving me around the floor and searching the tables.

"Willy—"

"Bear with me. I'm looking for a guy."

"Who?"

"Somebody you need to know."

"Who?"

He shook his head. Distracted as he was, Willy steered me into another couple. I turned to apologize and found myself looking at Sergei Malyakov. He looked me up and down and liked what he saw. You can always tell. We apologized, and Willy took me back to the table.

"I guess he's not here," he said. "I'll have to look elsewhere."

"Who are you looking for?" I asked.

Our waiter approached and handed me a note.

I read it, and looked at Willy. "Malyakov wants us to join him."

"Why not? From what I hear, you'll find him very interesting."

Willy paid the tab, and we started across the floor to Malyakov's table. I felt three pairs of eyes examining me as we walked. The two men were measuring me for their harems, and madame was considering me for a job. By the time we reached the table, I felt as if I had fingerprints all over my body. Malyakov kissed my hand and held a chair out for me. I sat down beside him, and Willy sat down beside me. That left madame on Malyakov's other side and the Arab next to her. Malyakov poured us vodka, and I sipped. It was superior vodka, but it needed juniper berries.

"And what brings you to Dubai?" Natalie asked.

"Just touring. Europe is so cold this time of the year, you know," I replied.

"I'm sure you're not just a tourist," Malyakov said archly. His accent was hard to place, more English than Russian.

I felt his leg rub against mine, and I kicked his shin. He winced.

"A woman as fascinating as you must have a career. Attorney? Author? I know. The star of a TV series."

"Ms. Carruthers' late husband left her well provided for. Her portfolio is quite healthy," Willy said. "She might just relax on the beach until Dubai begins to bore her. I'm Willy Soo, her investment counselor. And you are?" he asked Malyakov.

"How careless of me. Sergei Malyakov, my wife Natalie, and this is Abdullah bin Mohammed al Kabil, Abdullah for short." He stood and reached across me to shake Willy's hand.

"I've heard of you, Mr. Soo," Abdullah said. "Your clients lost nothing in the crash. You will invest the money I am transferring to Dubai." Saudi. And of royal birth.

Willy looked steadily at him. "I have all the clients I can handle, Abdullah," he said, deliberately using the Arab's personal name. "I can recommend somebody."

Abdullah reddened, and his eyes flashed. He did not like to be refused. Natalie changed the subject.

"Dubai is just a wonderful place to shop! I'm sure you must agree, Ms. Carruthers."

"I'm Lee, Natalie. Yes, it's a wonderful place to shop. I've picked up a number of things I saw in the fall Paris shows. They're just the thing for the Dubai climate. "

Natalie insisted that she would introduce me to her favorite couturier. Looking at her, I thought he might find his art wasted on my slender frame. I mentioned a few places I wanted to look into. I thought we were probably even on points. Guidebooks are such wonderful sources. After that the conversation became general. Things I must do in Dubai, restaurants, clubs. Quite suddenly my ears popped as the decibel level of the music suddenly dropped, and the band began playing "Goodnight, Ladies." I looked a question at Malyakov.

"It's three o'clock and time for them to close."

I began to pick up my purse.

"No, no," Natalie said. "The evening is still young."

I've never regarded three o'clock in the morning as young. We all stood, and Malyakov smiled. "We're going on to another club. It's in Bur Dubai, an after-hours place called The Nachtlieben. I think you'll find it quite amusing." Natalie was looking a bit bleary, so he helped her to her feet. We walked out into the hotel lobby.

"It's not a place to take your car," Malyakov said. "We'll take a taxi."

Five of us were going to take a taxi? Yes, we were. Somehow it worked out that I sat on Malyakov's lap. I took his hands in mine so that I would know where they were. The Nachtlieben was in a rundown building in a part of town that was still rocking. We stepped down two steps, and Malyakov knocked on the door. I swear a peephole slid open, and Malyakov said something. The door swung open, and smoke and loud music fell out. We went into a small room with a low ceiling. Asbestos-wrapped pipes crisscrossed it. Malyakov led us to a wooden table and pulled out a kitchen chair for me. I put my hand on the scarred top of the table and it rocked, one leg shorter than the rest. I looked at Willy. Willy's white silk suit stood out like a spotlight. Abdullah and Malyakov were casually dressed, but Natalie and I were as dressed up as Willy. I looked around and saw that half the crowd was wearing evening clothes and the other half torn jeans and scruffy sweaters. Altogether, there were twenty tables with mismatched wooden chairs. There was a dark wooden bar against the far left wall with the painting of a very large pink nude behind it. The walls were decorated in multi-color graffiti, *Juden raus* in big red letters prominent among them. I guess there aren't very many Jews in Dubai to be offended.

A waiter with a dirty white apron tied around his waist slapped five teacups on the table and left. "Drink up! Drink up!" Malyakov roared and tossed the contents of his cup down his throat. I approached mine gingerly and sniffed. Raki. I took a sip, and, as usual, it burned all the way down. My palate was certainly having an exciting night. So were my ears. The music was loud, pounding, insistent. Several couples were dancing on a small dance floor, two men with each other. Suddenly, a spotlight came on. "Cabaret" blared from the speakers as the curtain opened on a bed occupied by a naked man and two women. They began complicated sexual maneuvers. The light went out, and then came up again; a pair of men began disporting themselves. They were soon joined by a pair of women. When the couples tired of each other, they traded places and began again. This went on for one of the longer half hours I've ever watched a program. The lights came up, and I looked around. Abdullah was sitting back in his chair, his right hand in his lap, a dreamy look on his face. I wondered which one of the couplings had excited him. Malyakov and Natalie were mesmerized.

"I think we'd better go, Willy, before they bring on Catherine the Great and her stallions."

The Malyakovs stirred.

"Embarrassed?" Natalie sneered.

"I'm just not used to regarding sex as a spectator sport," I said.

I picked up my purse, and Willy and I went out the door. The street had calmed down some, and Willy's white suit stood out like the beam from a lighthouse. We backed into the doorway of a closed shop, and Willy called for a taxi. One came in five minutes, but those minutes were interminable. We were driven back to the Arab Towers Hotel and retrieved Willy's car.

"Interesting, that," Willy said. "I was in a place like that in Singapore once. Same number of sexes, different number of races."

"It certainly went with Berlin."

"You were embarrassed."

"I'm just a simple country girl at heart. I know about cows and horses, but there are only two of them when they do it. Willy, what made him think we would like something like that?"

"They probably try it out on everybody."

"Yes, but they chose us. A test?"

Instead of turning right toward my hotel, Willy turned left and drove to Jumeirah Towers.

"I think we both need a good stiff drink of coffee," he said, "and I'll get my man to scramble some eggs for us."

Willy's apartment was full of fantastic and beautiful things, but I was too tired to take them in. We went into the kitchen and drank coffee while a lean and very British-looking man scrambled eggs and made toast. The doorman at the hotel was only moderately surprised to see me coming in at seven in the morning. Dubai being Dubai, that was probably normal.

Chapter 9

THE CHAMBERMAID HAD closed the drapes the night before, so it was still dark in the room. I got ready for bed by
kicking off my shoes, stripping off my dress, and retrieving
the Glock from the clutch bag. I fell into the bed and
turned off the light. I saw the feet under the door again.
Holding the gun in my hand, I went softly to the door and
looked out of the peephole into the hall. A guy with a
baseball hat pulled down over his face was standing there.
This is getting tiresome, I thought. Why did they want to
know whether or not I have said my "now I lay me's?" Or
did they just want to know what time I went to bed? I
must've kept this guy up past his bedtime. What I could
see of his face was distorted by the fisheye lens of the
peephole. I'm going to have to do something about this, I
thought, but he turned away and walked down the hall
before I could get the door open.

Who were they and what did they want? How did they
know I was here? Followed me from Switzerland? For that
matter, how did they know I was in Switzerland? I hadn't
paid much attention on the flight from Paris, but I had
made every effort to keep from being followed from
Vienna. I eventually went to sleep and had been sleeping

almost an hour when the phone rang. I reached out to the bedside table and knocked the house phone over. The ringing continued. Not that phone. I groped around on the floor and finally turned on the light, considering which of my languages I should curse in. The iPhone was right beside the Glock on the floor as it always was. I looked at the screen. A 703 number. Virginia! Sidney Worthington? I looked closer. It was none of Sidney's numbers. Good. I was not up to refusing to come back to the Agency right then. It was Cynthia Branson, and she was very drunk.

"Why haven't you called me?" she whined. I heard something clink against a glass. "You should call me. Where's George?"

"Cynthia, I will call you when I have something to report," I said, feeling quite virtuous for not screaming in her ear.

"You must have something."

"Cynthia, you hired me less than a week ago. I am not a magician. If George were that easy to find, you would have found him yourself."

She began to cry, huge, sloppy alcoholic sobs. My stomach cramped, and I saw the bottle on the top shelf of the closet in my mother's bedroom. "I'm hanging up now, Cynthia," I said and broke connection. It rang again as soon as she could punch in the numbers. I turned the phone off and dropped it on the floor. It was not so easy to turn off my childhood memories.

I staggered into the bathroom for a shower around noon, unable to sleep anymore. I'm getting too old for two late nights in a row, I thought. I turned on the phone, and it rang immediately. I checked the Caller ID. 703. I clicked answer and said, "Look here, Cynthia—"

"It's not Cynthia," I heard Sidney Worthington, my former mentor, say. "You're working her case. Be careful." He cut the connection.

I sat there looking at the phone. Damn him! He wanted me to come to Dubai to look for George. If there was something I needed to be careful about, you think he'd tell me. But would he? I thought bitterly of Morocco. And I already knew there was something to be careful about, didn't I? Somebody had shot at me in Switzerland, and somebody was tucking me into bed every night.

I wondered what there was in the Agency files.

Cynthia wanted action, and Sidney wanted none. I decided not to decide and went downstairs to the dining room, where I found breakfast was no longer being served. Fred Atkins joined me while I was ordering lunch.

"What a coincidence," I said and ordered a bacon and tomato club sandwich.

"Isn't it?" he said and ordered the same.

"Quit following me," I said.

"What makes you think I'm following you?"

"Just a lucky guess," I said. I stared out at the dhow docks until my sandwich came.

"The first American food I've had in months," Atkins said.

I finished my sandwich. "Nice to see you," I said, signed the check, and walked away.

Back in the room, I booted the laptop and found an e-mail from Jerry telling me to call him. After a bunch of clicks and assistants, I got him.

"CEOs sure are protected from being hassled," I said.

"It's a security company," he said.

"What do you want?"

"This Gringikov guy? What do you know about him?"

"Not much. He's a Belarusian arms dealer, a big one. He disappeared mysteriously about two years ago. When I Googled him I found hundreds of links, most of them Robin Hood stories, so I just decided to give up and get you to dig. Why?"

"Walter, my guy who reads Russian? He says the guy doesn't exist. No birth certificate, no school records, no military records, nothing."

"But that's ridiculous. No records at all?"

"Probably significant," he said.

"Oh yes. Try the Belarus records," I said.

"He did. Nothing before the end of the Soviet Union in 1991 and very little good stuff since then. He's trying to filter what you found on Google. Maybe he can put something together from that. He's really pissed that he can't find out anything about the guy. Goes to his professional pride. Meanwhile, I've pulled a string. Two, actually. No promises, but if anybody knows him these guys will."

"Anything on Malyakov?"

"Got a few things. He was born in Kazakhstan. That came up with the first Google. He owns a bunch of airlines. Walt counted five. Trans-Caucasus is the biggest, registered in Kazakhstan. Thing is, he doesn't seem to own many planes. Trans-Caucasus has two registered. He can't find any others."

"He's tried—?"

"Don't try to teach your grandmother to suck eggs, Lee. Anything new at your end?"

"Just that I saw Malyakov last night. He's adorable," I said.

"Yeah, I pulled up a picture. Looks like a TV anchorman."

"But he has tastes no anchorman can afford."

"Oh, yes? Wine or women?"

"Sex."

"You don't say. Kinky?"

"Let's just say multi-gender. See if he's got a criminal record," I said.

"Lee, he's an arms dealer," Jerry protested.

"I know, I'll bet he's got no convictions for that. He took me to a creepy after-hours sex club last night. This morning. If he's been into things like that for length of time, somebody must've caught him at it."

"How do I know what's illegal in Kazakhstan?"

"They've got an awful lot of horses there."

"I'll let you know," he said and hung up.

I called him right back. "His wife owns a bunch of planes, has a charter service. Tell Walt to see what he can find out about it. And why her husband owns airlines and only a few airplanes, and she owns a bunch of airplanes."

"His and hers? I'll get back to you."

By then it was two o'clock, and I decided if I put my head down I would go to sleep and sleep until dinnertime, so I got an introduction to the Vietnamese pirate's daughter from Ralph and went calling.

Phung Nguyen lived out by the golf course in a new development of multimillion-dollar bungalows with red tile roofs that looked vaguely Spanish. The houses had big lawns and walkways up to front porches. The streets were lined with trees, and the whole thing looked as if it had been picked up and transported by magic carpet to Dubai from Southern California. An Asian girl in a white uniform opened the door and took my card to her mistress, returning to usher me into a large room with a fire burning in the fireplace. Air-conditioning is such a marvelous thing. The settees, chairs, and tables had been young when Louis XVIII was on the throne. A large Aubusson in pale pastels drew the conversation setting in front of the fireplace together.

A slender Vietnamese woman stood by the settee, her red *ao dai* making an issue of her petite figure. She flicked her long black hair back, showing off long crimson fingernails. A star sapphire the size of a small offshore island winked at me from the middle finger of her left hand.

"Ms. Carruthers?" she asked, my card in her hand.

I bowed and said "Madame."

She waved me to a chair and took a seat on the settee. The maid placed a tray with a delicate porcelain teapot and small handleless cups on the table in front of her. I received my cup carefully. My experience with handleless cups had taught me that they were invariably quite hot. I felt that blowing would be a breach of etiquette.

The lady sipped her tea in silence while I looked around. Like Morocco, Vietnam was a former French colony, and all things French were regarded as being the height of chic. In many cases, the decor was just slightly off, the equivalent of paintings of kids with big eyes. This room, however, showed the hand of a talented interior decorator. Madame Nguyen finished her tea and placed her cup gently on the table. She sat perfectly still, one leg negligently crossed over the other, a dainty beaded slipper hanging from her foot. I had to admire the poise of this pirate girl. Tiny wrinkles at her eyes and the corners of her mouth told me that she wasn't as young as she wanted to seem and that her temper might not be as good as she wanted that to seem, either.

"How do you know Ralph?" she inquired.

What to say? That I had met him while confiscating a pile of arms- smuggling loot? "We were acquainted before he retired," I replied.

She raised the delicate eyebrow of a Chinese courtesan.

"In Djibouti," I continued.

After her eyebrow returned to its proper place, she returned to sitting without moving. I sat negligently myself, engaging with her in silent arm wrestling. When she finally moved, it released me.

"He says you're looking for Gil Brady."

I nodded. "I'm told you know him," I said neutrally.

"We have things in common," she said, equally neutrally.

"But he works for Felix Gringikov. Doesn't that constitute a conflict of interest?"

Her eyes pinned me to the chair and then released me. I started breathing again.

"When was the last time you saw him?" I asked.

"Why do you want to know?"

"His wife wants to serve divorce papers on him."

Her head swung toward me. "Wife?"

"Wife, yes," I said blandly. Her gaze returned to the fire. "She wants to remarry."

"I will never marry," she snapped.

"Queen Elizabeth discovered that not marrying was the only way to retain control of her empire."

"Queen Elizabeth?" She looked confused. "But she's married."

"Elizabeth I," I said. "Sixteenth century."

She shrugged. Ancient history didn't interest her. "I will never marry," she repeated firmly.

"Gil Brady?"

She tapped her long red nails. "He amused me for a while," she said.

I had the vision of those long fingernails on the tail of a mouse and suppressed a shudder. "How long since you've seen him?"

She flicked her nails again. "A year? More. He has not been in town, I think."

"What can you tell me about him that might help me find him?"

She stood up, which forced me to stand. "He has a flat in Jumeirah Tower Number Four." She began to herd me toward the hall. "Apartment 507."

The maid took over the herding job, and I was standing on the porch with the door closed firmly behind me before you could say Ho Chi Minh.

"He amused me for a while" and those long red fingernails. She sat in her silken web. Did she devour her mates? Or her competitors?

Chapter 10

WILLY SOO'S OFFICE was in Tower Number Four, so I had a good excuse to visit the building. I drove past the entrance and looked inside. No security? Dubai had been off-limits to terrorist attacks because so much of their money came through the Emirates, but that might not last forever, and Emiratis would be as shocked when it happened as Americans were after a mall shooting. Willy's office was on the second floor. I could stop there on my way out. They must have security cameras at least, but they were probably focused on the elevators the way they were when Mossad took out that Palestinian a few years ago. Somebody might have taken a lesson from the experience, but I doubted it. I went up the fire steps. I could see that apartment 507 was next to the stairs. There was a security camera pointing down the hall, but I could see none covering the door to the stairs. I stepped into the hall and looked at the door. Not much of a lock for a building that expensive. I turned my back to the camera and picked the lock. Slipping through the partially open door, I shut it and looked around. The living room was as impersonal as a mid-range hotel room—basic sofa, coffee table, two chairs. Neutral upholstery, carpets, and drapes. The drapes covered the door to a small balcony. Suddenly, I was hungry for the wild colors of a Jackson Pollock painting. Shelves with a collection of movies and a TV set. A DVD of *Lord of War* was on top of the TV. A touch of humor? I didn't remember George Branson having a sense of humor.

No books, no drawers, no papers anywhere. The kitchen had basic dishes and a microwave. No cooking utensils. The refrigerator contained a bottle of champagne, and some frozen dinners, well past their pull dates, had frost on them in the freezer. I wondered how long it had been since George Branson had been in the apartment. I was crossing the living room for the bedroom when I heard a key in the lock. I sprinted for the balcony and left the door just a bit open.

"Check the bedroom," I heard a man say as he came toward the door. I flattened myself against the wall beside the door just as the door slid open. I heard the man mutter about stupid people as he shut the door all the way. I heard the lock click. How long should I give them to finish their search? I looked at my watch, and then down. Bad mistake. I flattened myself harder against the wall. If it's one thing I hate more than confined spaces, it's heights. Grateful that I was only on the fifth floor of the fifteen-story building, I looked straight ahead and breathed slowly, in and out, in and out. I gave them ten minutes to finish. You want to know how many ins and outs there are in ten minutes? At the end of that time, I took my knife from its ankle sheath and turned to the balcony door. The police always say that you should have one of those lock bars for that kind of the door, because the lock is so easy to open. By the time I heard the lock click and the door slid open, I was ready to shoot the damned thing. Maybe I'm not such a good burglar as I thought I was. I stepped back into the living room and spent a few moments looking at the lovely floor and even lovelier wall in front of me before I resumed my search.

The bedroom held the bare essentials too. A bed with nightstand on each side, lamps on the nightstands. Chest of drawers. The closet held three pairs of slacks and a jacket, with a pair of dress shoes on the floor. Underwear and shirts in the dresser drawers. The bathroom was the same. Tylenol and Preparation H in the medicine cabinet over the sink. A hair dryer. What is the world coming to? The left-hand bedside table had several condom packets. Nice to know George practiced safe sex. I stood back and looked around the room. There was something there. I could smell it. I stood quite still and let the room talk to me. On the wall were two cliché paintings of Paris street scenes, the one of the Rue Madeleine in the rain crooked. I lifted it off the wall and found a small safe behind it. I don't crack safes. I looked around. George wasn't here very often. Maybe he recorded the combination somewhere. I began emptying drawers to look on the underside. Nothing but a cocktail napkin from the Caspian Lounge in the underwear drawer that I'd missed the first time I searched. It had a lip print in bright red lipstick and "love, Sally" on it. It was the only personal thing I had found in the place. Maybe Sally knew something. I stuffed the napkin in my pocket and went back into the living room. No drawers. My eye was drawn again to the DVD of *Lord of War*. George really didn't have a sense of humor. I opened the jewel box and found not a movie but a data disk. Interesting, useful even, but it didn't help me with the safe. I snapped the disk out of the box and turned it over and found a small piece of white tape with numbers on it, numbers with L's and R's—the combination to the safe.

Back in the bedroom, I tried the combination. Not only could I not crack safes. I couldn't even open them when I had the combination. Maybe it wasn't a combination. I wiped my hands on my jeans, breathed deeply, spun the dial, and tried again. Left eight, right six, left eight again. The door popped open. Nothing in there but a plastic bag of pebbles. I took a couple out and rolled them around in my palm. They weren't gravel.

Except for the safe there was not a single indication that anybody lived in the flat, much less Gil Brady.

The door to Willy's office was glass. So was the receptionist's desk, which made the laptop look as if it were floating in midair. The reception room had been bought by the yard from the very best dealers. The rest of the furniture was Bauhaus and the view was of the Gulf. A young man was at the desk, slender, long horsey face, ears second only to Dumbo's, flaxen lock of hair falling over his forehead.

"Mr. Soo, please," I said.

"Do you have an appointment?" he asked down his nose. "He's with a client."

Was the accent Oxbridge or County?

"I'll wait," I said and took a seat in a black leather sling chair. I opened a copy of *Architectural Digest* and prepared to wait. I waited and after twenty minutes spent trying to decide between a neo-Hispanic mansion in Bel Air and antebellum confection outside Atlanta, I decided that enough was enough. I stood and strode toward the office door.

"Here! You can't do that!" the receptionist protested.

I opened the door. Willy was quite alone. He looked first at me and then at the young man standing in the doorway. "Wilbur?"

"She just barged in."

"After waiting twenty minutes because you were with a client," I added.

Willy's look would've blistered paint, but it bounced right off Wilbur, who returned resentfully to the reception room.

"Both annoying and incompetent," Willy said.

"And you employ him because?"

The East End urchin emerged and he grinned. "Gives tone to the office. Title goes back to the thirteenth century."

"And?" I pressed.

"His father owes me half a million."

"Not dollars."

"No. Pounds. GBP."

I took in the office, which had been bought by the yard, too, but from a much different catalog, the one that sold to English men's clubs. The walls were paneled in dark wood up to a chair rail and then covered in leather, medium green with small crowns embossed on it in gold. A cheerful fire burned in a fireplace with a light green marble surround. Over the mantel was an oil painting of a thoroughbred horse standing at attention, with the jockey sitting easily in the saddle. George Stubbs had painted portraits of horses for the English aristocracy in the eighteenth century. If it was an original Stubbs, it was worth more than I was. I looked at Willy, and he nodded. Whitechapel had made it. A tasteful grouping of Queen Anne settee and upholstered chairs stood on a large Turkish rug. Willy's highly polished desk would have been a partner desk if he'd had a partner. If Madame Nguyen's European longings were French, Willy's were English, and much more to my taste. The only break in the English gentlemen's club decor was a floor-to-ceiling window with a view of the Gulf.

"Impresses the punters," he said blithely.

"Impresses me," I said.

He laughed. I took a seat on the settee, and he went to the drinks cabinet, raising his eyebrow.

"Some water would be good."

He poured a little whiskey in a glass for himself and opened a bottle of Perrier and poured some in a glass, which he put on the table in front of me. He took one of the upholstered chairs.

"What brings you to me, love?"

"I just happened to be passing—"

"Yeah, right."

"I just happened to be passing, and I thought I'd drop in to see if you'd found out anything about that Arab at Malyakov's table."

"I e-mailed you what I could find out quickly."

"Haven't been back to the hotel in a while."

"Abdullah is Saudi, a minor princeling, four hundred and eighty-third heir to the throne. His father has four wives and a bunch of concubines. Abdullah is the son of the fourth wife and has never been very close to his father, a man who has fifteen sons. He went to a minor public school in England, was thought not to be university material, so he came back to Saudi. The most interesting thing I found is that one of his wives is a Bin Laden, cousin to Osama. Abdullah went to work for the Bin Laden Construction Company for a while in some minor executive position, but that didn't work out. I can't tell what he does now except breed racehorses. He's here on the run from his imam and his wives, having a little sin and racing some horses. One guy I talked to said that Natalie Malyakov is not entirely retired. She still does special customers, and Abdullah is one of them. No confirmation."

"A Bin Laden."

"I've been looking into his finances, which are a mess, but I haven't found anything interesting."

"If you're looking for a connection to terrorist funding, I don't think you'll find anything. That gets done off the books," I said.

"I know. I identified the two Levantines. They're both Lebanese and both are diamond merchants. Both have offices in the Diamond and Gold Park."

"Anything known?" I asked.

"Nothing I can find. One of them, Michael Wazzan, is married to the daughter of the head of the customs office."

"My."

"Yes. Convenient isn't it?"

"Who is a cousin of the emir?"

"Exactly."

I took the baggie of diamonds from my pack and handed it to Willy. "Are these what I think they are?"

Willy leaned forward and poured some of the contents on the coffee table. He looked up at me. "Where did you get these?" he asked.

"No comment," I said.

He sat back in his chair. "A lot of diamonds have started appearing on the Dubai market recently. Unsourced, from what I can find out. Is there any connection between these diamonds and the chap we partied with last night?"

"No comment," I said.

Chapter 11

WILLY SHOWED ME out past a pouting Wilbur. As I waited for the elevator. I thought about having a look at Sergei Malyakov's offices in the Gold and Diamond Park while I was in that part of town, but good sense prevailed. Akbar Khan in the Dubai Gold Souk was next on my list. He would know what money was coming in and going out and who was doing the deals. But first I returned to the hotel to offload the diamonds into the room safe.

The Dubai Gold Souk is not the souk you see in *The National Geographic*—a crowded alley with narrow stalls where a merchant in a caftan sits on a cushion in front of his shop smoking his bubble pipe, scuffing his red pointy-toed slippers in the dust, and telling his worry beads. There are still shops like that in Dubai, but before they built the Gold and Diamond Park, the gold merchants were all located in a two-level air-conditioned building that resembles your average suburban mall, except that the shop windows glitter more. There are a hundred shops that sell every kind of gold object imaginable. Salesmen in spotless white *kurtas* and red and white checked *kaffiyas* stand in the windows among gold chains, necklaces, and belts, and sometimes seem to disappear altogether in the shimmering mass. You can also find spectacular pearl pieces. Dubai's pearl fisheries were world famous before Japanese cultured pearls destroyed the market for real ones. The pearls are now imported from elsewhere, but the skill of Dubai jewelers in marrying gold to pearls is still unrivaled.

In the old days, when I was in and out of Dubai a lot, I got to know a Pakistani gold merchant named Akbar Khan pretty well and found him engagingly honest, in a Middle Eastern sort of way. Akbar knew whatever there was to know about the movement of money in and out of Dubai, which explains my original interest in cultivating his acquaintance. Shortly afterward, however, I began to like him for himself. He was knowledgeable in matters that interested me, yes, but he was also a practiced observer of the human condition and loved to talk about it in a dry and witty way. He was also aware of my love of baroque pearls, to my cost.

Although it was probably five years since we last met, the moment he saw me, right after he embraced me and before he gave me a cup of tea, he cunningly deposited a gold filigree chain with a baroque pearl-drop pendant on a piece of black velvet on the counter in front of me and was surprised when I shuddered. I put my hand on Kemal's pearl. I may never look at a baroque pearl again. When he looked at the pearl, he saw the dark stain on it and raised his eyebrow. I shook my head. He changed the subject.

"It's good to see you, Lee," he said. "You are in disguise?"

Instead of my usual black suit, I was wearing jeans. I smiled. "I'm on vacation," I replied.

"Come," he said, putting the pearl back in the case and leading me to his office. When we were seated on the sofa under an exquisite silk prayer rug displayed on the wall in the Eastern manner, he clapped his hands for tea.

"Now, how have you been?" he asked, beginning the welcoming ritual as a boy came in swinging the tea tray from a chain.

I accepted a cup of tea and did my best to follow our ritual. "Overworked and underpaid as usual. This is my first vacation in two years. How are you?"

He laughed. "Business is terrible. It grows increasingly difficult for an honest man to make a living."

Tea in hand, the ritual complete, we were now free to chat about this and that—the subprime mortgage scandal, the investment bank meltdown, Bernie Madoff, the teetering progress of Dubai World as Sheikh Mohammed sought to convince the world that his sovereign wealth fund had enough funds.

"Samira's math exam at Cambridge is next month. She will earn first-class honors," he said, failing to hide his pride. "She will be even better at money than I am. She has learned not only my skills, but she has worked with her maternal grandfather as well."

"She will work with you when she gets back?"

"She will. Her mother wants to arrange a marriage, but she complains that Samira is already too old for marriage."

"Does Samira want to get married?" I asked.

"Not right now, I think. Too many of her friends have married professional men who claim they want women with a profession, only to find, too late, that they were wrong." He opened his hands out, palms up. "It is the religion."

"Not entirely. Western women have the same problem. The custom is ancient and very strong. You will help her?"

"In everything," he declared.

"And how is Nasir?" His son raced Formula One cars.

He pursed his lips, and then he shrugged. "Nasir is Nasir. He races. Sometimes he wins. More often he loses."

I put my teacup down. "Besides wanting to see you," I said, "I came to ask you what money is moving."

"I thought you said you were on vacation."

"I retain an interest. I've been away for so long that I've lost track. Dubai used to be the money-laundering capital of the world, but I understand the new laws are taking hold."

"So they say." He shook his head. "The emir has perceived how much of that money has been going to terrorists."

"Much of it has always gone to fund the Taliban in Pakistan and Afghanistan," I said.

He nodded. "And Al Qaeda, yes. That is so, but it's the Islamic State's advances in Iraq that have worried the whole Gulf."

"I await the day that Saudi Arabia closes down terrorist funding," I remarked.

"We all do. I know that more gold is moving, coming in and going out. The refinery in Sharjah, you know, is working at capacity." He threw up his hands. "I know where it's coming from, but I'm not sure I know where it's going anymore. I know it's not going through my hands. I think much of it is going by courier to Iran. It *is* increasingly difficult for an honest man to make a living," he said bitterly.

"What do you know about diamonds coming into Dubai?" I asked. "They seem to be big business now."

"The emir is constantly looking for new business activity," he said neutrally. "He wishes the Emirate to be as big in diamonds as it once was in pearls."

"Or in gold?"

"As you say. Diamonds are imported from almost every diamond-producing country in Africa despite the best efforts of DeBeers and the International Diamond Consortium," he said.

"Diamonds are coming to Dubai from Africa? Blood diamonds?"

He nodded. "They come in uncut; some are cut here, some made into jewelry. The rest are fed into the international system of dealers."

"Is there no way for the dealers to know where the diamonds originated?"

"Oh, yes, but why would they ask?"

My tea had gone cold. Blood diamonds. They could only come from one source. "The arms trade," I said.

"This is not like the old days of money laundering, Lee. It's a much bigger business. And the war among the arms dealers here has only produced more diamonds, as the organizations fight to sell more arms to acquire a bigger portion of the market."

"Gringikov and Malyakov?"

"Yes. But it's not just arms dealers fighting for market share, Lee. In Congo, Zimbabwe, Liberia, the Ivory Coast, there's war in the diamond fields among local factions trying to seize control of the villages to force the villagers to mine the diamonds. It's not just civil wars. The conflict over the districts where the diamonds are mined is what the wars are about. They need arms to control the diamond districts and control of diamond districts to buy the arms," he said.

"And the diamonds come through Dubai?" I asked.

"Not all, that depends on where the arms dealers are located, but many come through Dubai. Dubai's biggest business is no longer money laundering. It's scrubbing the blood off of diamonds."

I hugged him. "Samira. Remember Samira."

I looked at my watch. It was nearly seven. If I knew anything about Dubai merchants, the shops would be open until late, so I decided to have a look at the Dubai Gold and Diamond Park after all. The traffic was heavier than usual, possibly a sign Dubai's evening rush hour started at seven. I hacked my way through Jumeirah until I found the Gold and Diamond Park, a large three-story building with an entrance tower in aqua decorated with abstract palms. I was right. The parking lot was full, and the shops were open, their windows displaying goods much like the Gold Souk windows in Deira but bigger and better. The jewelry displays were stunning in the dictionary sense of the word.

Their contents stunned. My Puritan conscience was revolt-
ed by the vulgar display, but it did look like big bucks. I
strolled along until I found a directory. The retail gold and
diamond shops on the first floor were getting most of the
traffic. The jobbing shops were on the second floor. There
you could buy gold and diamonds in bulk. Businesses that
didn't advertise what they did, including Malyakov Enterprises, were on the third floor. I took the escalator to the
third floor and strolled along looking at the offices. Many
were still open, although most of them were showing signs
of closing down for the day. The lights were lowered in the
offices of Malyakov Enterprises. It was closed for the day,
but I could see as far into the reception area as some
Swedish modern chairs and tables, and a desk with a computer monitor. My fingers began to itch to go and have a
look, but I couldn't imagine what I could find in Malyakov's
office quickly that would be of any use, so I just looked
and returned to the second floor. There wasn't anything
there for me either. On the first floor I considered trying
to pose as a buyer for department store, but I couldn't figure out what good that would do either. In fact, I couldn't
figure out what good the whole visit had done me. I returned to the parking lot where a handsome man with
blow-dried hair and capped teeth was being ushered into a
black stretch limo.

The only profit I got from the entire visit was the sight
of Sergei Malyakov leaving for home.

Chapter 12

BACK IN THE room, I discovered a huge bouquet of orchids on the desk beside my laptop. On the card was an invitation to dinner from Sergei Malyakov. My first thought was to dump them in the trash, but then I called the chambermaid. She was a slender South Asian.

"Madame?"

I handed her the vase. "Please take these away," I told her.

"But they are so beautiful."

"They are unwelcome," I said.

After she left, my cell phone rang. The Caller ID showed Sergei Malyakov. I turned the phone off. I would have to be awfully hard up.

I booted the laptop and Googled blood diamonds. I found pretty much what Willy and Akbar had told me with a few more details. There were repeated references to Nicholas Cage's movie *Lord of War*. George had more of a sense of humor than I had remembered to save his docs in that DVD case.

Somehow blood diamonds had flown under my radar while I was chasing terrorist money.

I turned to George's disk. It contained the financials missing from his file: spreadsheets listing shipments going from here to there and diamonds going back. Money deposited in Gringikov's bank accounts in Luxembourg and Geneva. Nothing in the Caymans. Were their money-laundering laws actually working? I knew the bank in Geneva, a quiet little private bank owned by a family who had known Calvin or at least his grandson. I had a look. The account had an extremely healthy balance, which I was tempted to send off into cyberspace just for fun. I grabbed hold of myself. This is not fun, I chided myself. Then I found a healthy account in George's name in Dubai. Salary? There were regular deposits to the account until just before his death. Where had he been and who had been paying him? Not Gringikov. He was missing. The depositor was identified only by a number. I started to work on it, but I decided that was a job for Jerry's man.

And where did he get the diamonds in his safe? Had he been skimming? George had been executed and allowed to float ashore in Dubai. *Pour encourager les autres?*

Some of the stones I found in George's safe were of considerable size. Their worth depended on what they were like after they were cut, of course, but the total still must be substantial.

I rubbed my eyes. I sat back. Diamonds. No gold transactions. Did that mean Gringikov worked exclusively for diamonds?

I closed the computer and went to bed without even looking to see if my feet were in the hall.

I was just back from breakfast when my phone rang. The Caller ID showed 703.

"Sidney . . . !"

"Lee, it's me. Cynthia Branson." She sounded rocky. Was she drunk again?

"What do you want?" I demanded brusquely. I really must develop a better bedside manner if I'm going to work for civilian clients.

"I'm in Dubai."

How did she know about Dubai?

"You have to come over here now. I'm at the Hilton, and I just saw—"

I heard a gasp.

"Cynthia, which Hilton?"

"The blue one. Lee, I just saw—"

I heard a gurgle, and the phone hit the floor. I ran. The blue one. A block back toward the airport. I watched the elevator lights stopping and starting and stopping and starting and then doing it all over again. I gave up and ran for the fire stairs. I didn't try to get the car. I just ran. I'm sure it will be on the nightly news, somebody running in Dubai. Two police cars passed me, their sirens blaring. When I got to the blue Hilton, the uniforms were pushing viewers back from a crumpled form on the pavement. I looked up and saw curtains blowing gently out of the balcony window on—I counted—the fifth floor.

Fire stairs again. I flung myself up the stairs and by the time I reached the fifth floor, I was regretting five years of sitting on my fanny in front of a computer screen. I stopped to catch my breath and looked through the window of the door. Two men stood outside a room. I'd never seen either of them. A tall blond man was standing with his hands on his hips. The other was a squat man who looked like a paratrooper. The buzz cut of his dark hair suggested that he was military at least. I opened the door a crack so I could hear what they were saying.

"I tell you there's no key in there," insisted the paratrooper.

"You idiot! She had it on her," snapped the tall guy.

"She was wearing a nightgown. She didn't have it."

"Did you touch her?"

"No. She backed away from me and went over the balcony rail. She just fell."

Cynthia Branson and a key. I had better move myself before they concluded that if Cynthia didn't have it, she might have given it to me. George sent it to her from Istanbul. That's where I needed to be.

Fifteen minutes later I had packed, cleaned out the safe, and was on my way down the service elevator to the parking garage. I had left Vienna using my second passport and was registered in the hotel under that name, but Ralph and Willy knew my real name, and I was sure that Con Owen would tell it to anybody who asked, if they asked hard enough. My real passport would require a crooked passport control officer. I sat in the car park at the Abu Dhabi airport and looked up flights. The first flight in the direction of Istanbul was an Olympia flight to Athens that left in an hour. I booked a flight on it and charged it with my real credit card. I locked my gun and my knife in the glove compartment of the car and felt naked. I had nothing to protect myself with but my hands, and my left shoulder was unreliable to use as a fulcrum.

Cynthia Branson was dead. Theoretically, my job was over, and I had a bag of uncut diamonds as payment for my services. I could just go home to Paris and be out of the thing, whatever the thing was. There were two problems with that. Paris wasn't my home anymore, and that key would drive me nuts until I found out what was in the safety deposit box. The key. The key Cynthia gave me.

I photographed the key and sent it to Willy.

"Willy, love, can you identify this key?"

"I can see that it's old."

"The clue is Istanbul," I said.

"Ah. Try the Atatürk Bankasi. It's the oldest in town. I don't suppose you're going to tell me what this is about."

"Not today, love. Bye."

I called and left a message for the Istanbul lawyer who would help me with the safety deposit box for a fee. The only problem was likely to be getting a power of attorney forged in a hurry.

Putting a folded hundred-dollar bill in my passport, I went into the airport. The only difference between airports these days is the amount of glass in front. Inside they're all the same. I walked down the line of passport control desks as if looking for the shortest line instead of a venal officer. I chose a man with a round discouraged face and slumping shoulders who looked as if his feet hurt and stood in his line. Approaching his desk, I said, "I have a problem," and handed him the passport.

He opened it and looked at me quickly. Would he or wouldn't he?

"Madame?" he asked.

"When I entered Abu Dhabi four days ago, the passport control officer neglected to stamp my passport."

"Ah. That will not be a problem." He changed the date on his stamp, searched for an empty space, and stamped it. Then he returned the stamp to today's date and stamped my exit on another page. He handed my passport back, and we smiled at each other.

Waiting at the gate across the concourse from my Olympia flight gate, I used the laptop to make a reservation at the Sofitel Hotel at the Athens airport. The flight from Athens to Istanbul wasn't long, but I needed time to think and a place to do it in without somebody with feet and an ear making sure I was going to bed. I watched people gather for the Athens flight and saw nobody I recognized, so I went to the end of the line and boarded last. The flight was comfortable, considering that I had a key that somebody had killed to get: the food was good, the attendants were attentive, and there were no screaming kids.

The Sofitel is an upscale businessman's hotel, the kind of place where I never stayed, except in Dubai, where there isn't any other kind. The charges on my credit card were stacking up. Maybe they would take a diamond in payment? It was another hotel room with an aircraft carrier bed. I shucked my boots and lay down. Aircraft carriers were never that soft. I wrapped myself in the quilt and slept soundly for the first time since that guy shot at me in Switzerland. I slept for twelve straight hours and then ordered an omelet from a blessedly twenty-four hour room service. I finished it, booked a midday flight to Istanbul, and then I went back to bed and slept some more.

The hall in the Atatürk airport was as empty as ever. A small group of people hovered around the passenger exit waiting for family or clients. The rest of the place was empty. I've never understood how the merchants make a living. The sky was lowering, and there was a nasty wind blowing from the sea as I waited for the shuttle to the Rent-A-Car places, so I went back into the hall to see if I could find something warmer than what I had worn from Dubai. It's a good thing Turkey has plenty of sheep. I bought a nice heavy wool sweater, hat, scarf, and gloves in one shop, and the sales clerk directed me to a shop that sold jackets, where I bought a sheepskin vest. I left the shop feeling like Charlie Brown being shoved out into the winter.

I was just barely warm enough as I left the shuttle to the car rental building, where I rented a car and began the short drive to town. The traffic on Kennedy Cadessi was heavy, and just before we reached the walls of old Constantinople, it began to snow heavily. That confounded the traffic. It does snow in Istanbul but not often. I gave up my plan to go up the back way to Deniz Zeki's office. The side streets were still cobbled, and I didn't like the idea of driving on them. This meant that I had to swing around the walls of Topkapi Palace, drive past the train station to the docks by the Golden Horn before I could turn left and, heaven help me, begin to climb Divanyolu to the top of the second hill where Zeki's office was. The street was like glass, to coin a cliché, and cars were sliding at will. It occurred to me that it would be ironic to end my days in a car accident in Istanbul after so many people had tried to kill me. I saw the alley to the right across from Zeki's office and turned into it. It was seriously against the law to park there, so I abandoned my car and picked my slippery way across the street. His office was on the second floor behind a huge sign that said "*Avocat*." The French, Italian, and Turkish word for lawyer—*avocate*—always made me think of salad.

Deniz Zeki greeted me with reserve. It wasn't a sign of a bad relationship. He greeted everyone with reserve. He had changed little since I first met him almost a decade ago—a tall, thin, tubercular-looking man with a long face. What hair he had left was tightly plastered to his skull. His suit was a lugubrious dark gray, and his tie was an even more lugubrious black. He looked more like an undertaker than an attorney, but he was the best defense lawyer in town, if you could pay his fees. He had other skills, too, and I had found him useful before.

He had very little patience with involved Ottoman politeness, so he got right to the point, which was just as well, considering his hourly rate.

"I had no trouble identifying the owner. Box number 38 at Atatürk Bankasi is held by a man named Karl Spiegel, with an address in Beşiktaş. It's an apartment house," he said. "A very expensive apartment house. He opened the account three years ago in October, using a Central American passport for identification." He patted his skull to make sure his hair was still in place.

I raised an eyebrow. Several Central American countries raise a large portion of their yearly revenue issuing passports to the needy with the proviso that they never be used to enter the issuing country. "And when did he last access it?" I asked.

"Two years ago on August 19th."

"I need to get into it. I'll need a power of attorney."

"I thought you might. I began the process of acquiring one as soon as I had the information. It will be ready tomorrow. Expedited, of course." I was going to have to sell a diamond or two to pay that bill. I could give him a down payment in dollars, but I doubted that he took Visa. He would want the rest in cash before he handed over the power of attorney.

"I got them to fax me his information. I prepared a copy for you." He passed me a sheet of paper.

I recognized the man in the picture. He was George Branson.

Chapter 13

IT HAD STOPPED snowing while I was in Zeki's office, but the skies still looked unfriendly. I retrieved the car from the alley where it had escaped the attentions of a meter maid and began to make my way carefully down Divanyolu, which was more slippery on the way down then it had been on the way up. Normally I liked to stay in the little boutique hotels that ran down the hill to the Hippodrome, but that day I felt in need of a large international hotel, one with a lot of people around, good locks on the doors, and multiple exits. Those hotels were all in Beyoğlu across the Golden Horn from old Constantinople, which meant going down the hill to the Galata Bridge and then going up the hill to the Taksim square area. Bridges freeze before roadways. The bridge was slick, and traffic was trying to hack around two fender benders that had been pushed to the side, one on each side, which meant a lane and a half were clear. By the time I was up Galata Hill into the center of modern Istanbul, I had a good deal of time to contemplate George Branson's sins. One: George Branson was dead in Dubai, carrying a false US passport. Two: he had a parcel of diamonds in a safe in his flat. Three: he had rented a safety deposit box under the name of Karl Spiegel, using a false and highly dubious passport. Four: he sent the key to the box to his wife Cynthia, whom he had not otherwise contacted in two years.

Cynthia was now dead in Dubai, as well.

George Branson/Karl Spiegel was somehow connected to Felix Gringikov, the Belarussian merchant of death, who was missing under mysterious circumstances.

It was full dark when I handed my car over to the parking attendant and took refuge in the warm, bright, luxury of the hotel. I hoped they could be induced to take a diamond or two in payment.

Mehmet Osman was my man in Istanbul. He was a cargo handler at Atatürk airport, a petty thief, and a good man, big all over, with a gut that was a testament to his wife's cooking, and a mustache that would make a bandit proud. He lived in, Tarlabaşı, my favorite slum. It was cold, but it stopped snowing, so I walked down Tarlabaşı Boulevard, which runs down Beyoğlu Hill from the fine old Ottoman mansions slumping into collapse at the top to the rotten wooden buildings of the poor at the bottom. Walking was easier than trying to find a parking place or coming back to the car to find it dismantled. Tarlabaşı is a den of thieves but is under siege from the gentrification squad, and some of the houses near the top of the hill already sported gleaming new paint and flowerpots on the steps. My destination was back in a warren they wouldn't get to any time soon, a two-story wooden Ottoman house that had not seen any paint since the reign of Abdul Hamid the Damned. It listed gently against the house next door, which was listing gently against the next, and so on down the street, like a slow-motion collapse of dominoes.

When I knocked on the door of the ramshackle place that housed his extended family, Mehmet opened it cautiously and peered out. It's not a friendly neighborhood after dark. It's not entirely friendly in the daytime. I had to speak to him before he recognized me. It had been a while.

"*Merhaba*, Mehmet," I said. "How have you been?"

He opened the door wide and pulled me inside.

"*Merhaba*, Lady. I am well, thanks be to God. And you are well?"

"I am, thanks be to God."

He fussed around the small room, pulling up a chair and dusting it off and calling out for tea. I could not believe that his wife would want to make tea for me.

"Ayla!" he shouted.

A woman fully as large as Mehmet, but shapeless in her dark gown, emerged from the back of the house.

"Tea!" he demanded. "Tea for the lady!"

She made a sound suspiciously like a snort and disappeared. Ayla and I had never been close. She didn't mind his petty thievery—a man had to make a living after all—but she knew the jobs he did for me were not just illegal but sometimes dangerous to boot. No, we weren't friends.

With Mehmet it was not necessary to begin the neverending questions about the health of everybody within three degrees of separation. With Mehmet it was politics. His wife might wear the hijab, but Mehmet was Kemalist to the core and didn't mind who knew it. He displayed one of my favorite pictures of the Ghazi on the living room wall, the one of him in winter uniform and wearing an Astrakhan hat.

"How are things?" I inquired.

As I expected, he launched into a political harangue. "Well, he's done it this time! He's fired half the cops in the country and transferred half of the magistrates to jobs in Erzurum."

Being banished to Erzurum was not just being sent to pound a beat on Staten Island, it was the moral equivalent of being transferred to the moon. "Erdogan? But why?"

"Because of the scandal!"

I clearly hadn't been paying attention. "What scandal?"

He continued to fulminate.

"What scandal?" I repeated loudly.

"An investigation into corruption. Even Erdogan's son was questioned!"

"About what?" I pressed.

"Illegal sale of gold to Iran."

"But I thought Turkey was selling gold to Iran legally."

"I don't know. They won't say, but cabinet ministers have resigned. Delegates are leaving his party. And then he began firing people and yelling it was a plot. He forced a bill through Parliament giving him more control over the appointment of judges." He smiled. "Big fistfight in Parliament. One guy got a broken nose. Another had to go to the hospital." Then he calmed down. "The judges are the only ones standing between us and *them*. Without the judges, we'd be cutting off the hands of thieves and stoning adulterers to death!"

Sniffing, Ayla put the tray with the tea and some pastries on the table with a thump and poured out. On her way out, she glared at me. "They deserve it," she said. Mehmet lifted his mustache to slurp his tea. The pastries were sticky with honey and delicious. I just hoped that Ayla hadn't poisoned them.

"Only the judges? What about the army?" I asked. He slammed his hand down, making the tea tray rifle.

"They won't do anything. He's cut their balls off."

I might have said emasculated them, but I couldn't argue with the sentiment. I changed the subject.

"Mehmet, I need a gun. Glock 26, spare clip, box of hollow points." I got out a stack of lira.

He looked embarrassed. "The price has gone up," he mumbled.

"A lot of that going around," I said and added another small stack.

He left the room and returned with a box containing the gun. I took it out and loaded it. It felt good when I seated it in the holster. It cut off that cold wind that had been blowing on my right hip.

"Have you got work for me, lady?" He smiled in anticipation.

"Right now, I need some information. What do you know about an arms dealer named Felix Gringikov?"

"Unh," he said. "He's bad, that one, but nobody's seen him lately."

"How long since anybody's seen him?" I asked.

He rubbed his chin, making a rasping sound, and shrugged. "Year? Maybe two. Been a while."

"And his company?"

He poured us some more tea. "I don't know. It's still in business. Maybe his wife? There's a new guy."

"I hear his headquarters are here."

"Yeah. He owns a bunch of clapped-out Ilyushins. In and out all of the time. Land, pick up cargo, off they go."

"Pick up cargo? They've got a warehouse?"

He scratched his ear. "You know, I don't know. I suppose so."

"Find out. If they have a warehouse find out what they store there. Anything you can find out."

Ayla returned with a kettle of hot water.

"We do not need the money." Her tone was sharp. She glared at me as she refreshed the teapot.

"Go to bed, woman!" Mehmet ordered.

"Humph," she replied and stomped out.

"Pay?"

"Standard rates plus danger money if you have to go inside."

"To do what?"

"To see what he has in there."

I finished my tea and stood up. "Oh." I stopped. "Do you know this man?" I showed him the picture of George Branson on my iPhone.

"Sure, that's the new guy Karl, Karl something."

"Spiegel?" I asked.

"Yeah, that's his name. Word is he's been running the outfit since Gringikov disappeared."

Chapter 14

GOING BACK TO the hotel, I stayed close to the buildings, but I still attracted attention. At that hour, a woman could have only one reason for being on the streets. A couple of young guys who smelled of raki and tobacco backed me up against the wall and tried to hire me.

"Hey, baby. How much?" They smirked and grabbed.

"No. Really?" I said. I leaned against the wall, shoved the left guy away with my foot, and showed them the gun. They looked surprised and then uncertain. "Go," I said. They went.

What were they thinking of? It was cold enough out to freeze even a sailor's lust and unwrapping me would take a while. Holding the gun by my side, I walked placidly all the way back to the hotel.

When I woke that morning, the day was clear and so bright the light hurt my eyes. It was too soon to expect the power of attorney to be ready, but I had Spiegel's address. The Spiegel who was Branson who was dead and who worked for Gringikov who was missing. Gringikov hadn't been heard of in two years, and Spiegel/Branson—I stopped myself. In Istanbul George Branson was Karl Spiegel. Karl Spiegel hadn't accessed his safety deposit box in the two years before he washed up dead in Dubai carrying a passport in the name of Gil Brady, the name he went by in Dubai. Where had he been in those two years? Mehmet said Spiegel was running Gringikov's business. Where from? He hadn't been seen in a couple of years, had he? What did he keep in that safety deposit box, and why did he send his wife the key?

I decided to see what I could find out about Karl Spiegel, and then go and toss his apartment. An Internet search turned up several dozen Karl Spiegels, one in Wiesbaden who looked good until I discovered he was eighty-five. The one in the South African Defense Force didn't look likely. Neither did the rest of them. That's the problem with the Internet: too much information. At last I found the right man tagged in a picture dated a year and a half ago, looking chummy with Mrs. Felix Gringikov, the well-known society hostess. HMM in capital letters.

I switched the search to Gringikov—Istanbul. He might not have any records in Belarus, but Felix had quite a profile in Istanbul. Dozens of pictures, one showed him looking doughy beside a blonde wearing lots of diamonds. My Turkish is slim to nonexistent and the Google translating service sometimes presented me with strange text, but I could squeeze enough information out to learn that the Gringikovs moved in at least middle society, sponsoring charity events and attending galas. They funded several childcare centers in the slums. Strange for a heavy merchant of death, very strange. Other photos showed him among local businessmen at conferences and at a Rotary club meeting. There was no mention of the nature of his business. He was listed in the Yellow Pages as Gringikov Enterprises. While Sergei Malyakov entertained like a mafiya don in Dubai, Felix Gringikov seemed to have assumed a mantle of respectability in Istanbul. I sent an e-mail to Jerry to have somebody dig deeper into Gringikov in Istanbul.

Karl Spiegel's apartment was in a group of high-rises in Beşiktaş out past the new US Consulate. The underground parking garage was card access and so was the entrance to the lobby. I was just trying to figure out how I was going to get in when a tall man in a well-tailored suit carrying a little yapping dog held the door for me before putting the mutt down to do his business. He looked exquisitely embarrassed.

Spiegel's flat was up in the high-priced zone on the tenth floor. Maybe the real estate was expensive, but strangely enough the locks were not. The door opened directly into a living room remarkably like the living room in Gil Brady's Dubai flat, a generic living room bought by the yard from an inexpensive decorating firm. No papers, no magazines, no suggestions that anybody lived there. The kitchen was complete with standard appliances and the cabinets held equipment for four. A couple of pots. In the refrigerator, a six pack of Heineken. The freezer held six frozen meals from a private catering firm. Just like Barnes'. Spiegel either ate out a lot or the apartment had catering.

The bedroom was just as generic as the living room. I was beginning to feel sorry for Karl Spiegel/Gil Brady/George Branson. It must have been like living in a dentist's waiting room without the magazines. I went through the chest of drawers. Underwear, socks, shirts. The closet. Slacks, jeans, sports jacket, running shoes. No low quarters. I was just heading into the doubtless generic bathroom when I heard a key turning the lock and the door open. Feeling entirely ridiculous, I rolled under the bed among the dust bunnies and pinched my nose to keep from sneezing. I closed my eyes and withdrew my favor from the goddess of the search. At least this time I was on the floor and not staring out into space with the firm conviction that I was spinning off to the left. I heard a vacuum cleaner start up, then thumping sounds and footsteps coming in my direction and on past to the bathroom. Water running. Surely there was no need to clean a place that hadn't been occupied for who knows how long. I tried to distract myself from my predicament by analyzing George Branson's various metamorphoses, but the vacuum cleaner running two inches from my nose made concentration difficult and stirred up the dust. Finally, the vacuum stopped and after a few more thumps I heard the door close. I rolled back out from under the bed. I couldn't decide whether to giggle first or sneeze. I sneezed. I looked around. There must be *something* in the place. I lay down on the bed and put my hands behind my head. There was something here. I could smell it. Closet, chest, mirror, chair, in the closet? No. Painting. Painting? Off-center on the left wall was a generic painting of Paris in the rain. Not again. This place really *was* like Brady's flat in Dubai. I got up and lifted the painting off the wall and found a small safe there, the kind you open with a key. A key. I went back to the chest and went through the drawers again. I had missed the small key in among the underwear. I opened the safe and found that it contained a small book with what looked like addresses written in Cyrillic, dammit. And an oval enamel disk about the size of a nickel featuring the Blessed Virgin surrounded by angels on the front. On the other side was a red star and hammer and sickle.

I put the medal with its chain in my watch pocket and felt something paper. I pulled it out. Sally at the Caspian Lounge. I put it back. The little book went into my pack, and I took a cursory look into the bathroom. Karl Spiegel's apartment was identical to Gil Brady's, identically without personality. It was as if neither man existed. All I had was George Branson's body and a false passport to prove he had ever lived. I went down in the elevator to the lobby and out to my car. Pulling quietly away, I parked on a side street and checked my iPhone for the Gringikov address. It was not far away in Beşiktaş, so I decided to have a look at it while I was in the neighborhood.

The Gringikov house was not just a house; it was a mansion. A mansion among other mansions, early Republican style, with a ten-foot wall around it and a uniformed guard in a little house by the gate. I drove around the block to the alley and followed it down to the Gringikov place. There was a wooden door in the middle of the back wall, six feet tall to the wall's ten feet. I got out and tried it. It had a latch, but the door was barred on the inside. I looked around. There was always a neighbor. Climbing it was night work. I hoped there was no dog.

After having some lunch, I called Zeki. I was right. It was too early for the power of attorney to be ready, but he would have it by the next morning. His fee rattled my teeth, but I had George's diamonds from Dubai. I considered paying him with a few, but that would make him suspicious and possibly greedy. I didn't know what they were worth, so I returned to Tarlabaşı Boulevard to a small antique shop where some Ottoman jewelry was displayed behind a dirty window. I pushed the buzzer in the doorframe and stood where I could be seen. The door clicked open, and I entered a small musty-smelling shop. A young man in blue jeans stood silently behind the counter.

"Where's Omar?" I asked.

"My uncle has retired."

Not dead, then. "I have some business to transact with him." He lived above the shop last time I was here. "Only with him," I said firmly.

The young man looked me over carefully and went through a door to the rear. Several minutes passed before a bent man with a white beard appeared. He squinted at me through round metal-rimmed glasses and grunted. The young man stood behind him.

"My business is confidential," I said.

Omar gestured, and the young man disappeared into the back. I placed three small diamonds on the counter. Omar looked at me over his glasses and reached for a jeweler's loupe. After examining the diamonds, he looked up at me and mentioned a price. I tripled it and smiled. He came up a bit, calling to the back room for tea. I took a seat on the stool beside the counter and waited. The young man appeared with the tea tray and served us tea in minute glasses. We sipped, and I came down. We went back-and-forth, Omar quite enjoying himself and me not. You have to be born into a dickering society to like it really well. After he stuck at a price for a while I accepted, and he unlocked a cash drawer.

"In dollars, please."

"That will cost you five percent in the exchange."

I nodded. I had expected ten. I counted the bills, and he wrapped them in tissue paper before putting a rubber band around the package.

"You will be careful, lady," he said.

"Always."

The local toughs expected people coming from his shop to be worth robbing. I swept my sweater and vest back until he could see the gun, and the young man let me out the door.

I had not gone more than fifty meters when a middle-aged man with a five o'clock shadow moved away from the wall where he was lounging. I showed him the gun, too, and he went back to lounging.

Nothing much happened for the rest of the day. I considered the idea of calling the numbers in the address book, but I gave it up. Somebody answering the phone in Belarusian wouldn't be much help. It looked like being a long night, so I decided to take a nap and went to sleep trying to figure out why I was going to break into the Gringikov mansion.

I was dressed to go and was reaching for my watch cap when the phone rang.

"Lady! Lady! They're leaving the warehouse!"

"Mehmet. Mehmet, slow down. I can't understand what you're saying."

"Somebody is emptying the Gringikov warehouse! Big trucks!"

"Where are you?" I asked.

He described the route from the highway. "Hurry!"

I tucked my hair under my watch cap and went down to P2 to collect my car. I love to wear a watch cap. It makes me feel so professional. I made good time to the airport, but it still took more than half an hour. When I pulled up at the gate to the Gringikov warehouse, Mehmet stepped from the shadows and got in the car, shivering. I turned the heat up. There were two large unmarked trucks being loaded at the docks, the bright lights there throwing the rest of the yard into shadow.

"I think those are the last," he said, rubbing his cold hands together. "There were six others loaded with large wooden crates."

"Where did they go?" I asked.

"I don't know, but they turned that way," he said, pointing to the left.

We sat with the engine running and watched. Finally, the drivers got into the cabs and started the engines. I backed farther into the shadows, facing the car in the direction the trucks had to go.

"I'm going to follow them. You get inside and see if you can find out what was there." I handed him small lot of dollars. He nodded and got out, pushing the money inside his jacket. I followed the last truck, hanging back with my lights off until we reached the on ramp to the motor route. Then I turned on my lights and followed. There was enough traffic to mask me, and the trucks were big enough to be seen at some distance. When the trucks swung around to the east and crossed the Bosphorus Bridge, I knew we were headed for the new airport at Sabiha Gökçen. The trucks led me to the cargo area and drove directly onto the tarmac, where men began loading the cargo to a conveyor belt that led directly into the belly of a Trans-Caucasus Ilyushin. From Gringikov's warehouse to Malyakov's airplane.

My phone rang as I was turning back to the European side of the city. It was Mehmet.

"They cleaned it out," he said. "Nothing left but some packing material. From the marks on the docks, I'd say that it took more than six trucks to carry it away."

All the Gringikov stock in Istanbul. That made it more important than ever to get inside the Gringikov mansion.

How could I get to Mrs. Gringikov without terrifying her? Did you know that Spiegel is dead? Did you know that Malyakov has cleaned out your warehouse? I needed to talk to her about the little book I found in Spiegel's safe. After my visit earlier in the day, I had concluded the only way I could get to the house was to go over the back wall. I had intended to do that much earlier, but Mehmet's call changed that. Now she would be asleep. How was I to wake her? The auto route to the second bridge went to Beşiktaş. There was a fire burning on the hill where the Gringikov mansion was. I drove swiftly up the hill and was stopped by police at the fire lines. I could see that it was the Gringikov place that was burning.

"English?" I asked the nearest cop. He shook his head and waved to a colleague.

"Lady?" he asked.

"Is Mrs. Gringikov safe? Did you get her out?" I asked frantically. "She's a friend of mine. Is she safe?"

He shook his head and went toward the fire engines. He returned with a frown on his face.

"They have found nobody, lady. They have not seen her."

I gave a little sob and turned back down the road. The sob was not entirely false. I drove around to where I could see down the alley behind the house. It looked as if the fire was mostly confined to the front. At any rate, I saw no flames and, better yet, no firemen. I drove down to the door in the back wall and got out of the car. I tried the door, but it was still bolted. I reached up and hooked my fingers over the top, but I couldn't pull myself up. I must think about lifting weights when I get finished with this case. I got back into the car and drove it as close to the wall as I could get. I got out and climbed on the roof of the car and threw my legs over the gate. I dropped to the ground. If there was a dog, he'd gotten out when the firemen opened the gate. I started up the path to the door and collided with a running woman. She screamed. It didn't do me any good either. I grabbed her and clapped my hand over her mouth. She struggled. I had to yell to be heard over the noise of the fire.

"I'm a friend!"

She still struggled. "I'm a friend," I yelled again, "and we have to get out of here. *Now!*" I dragged her to the gate, and opened it, but we couldn't get out. Great! The car was up against the fence. "Stay there," I commanded. Some of the madness had gone from her eyes. "Okay?"

"They're trying to kill me!"

"I know." I took the bar and used it to help me walk up the side of the car until I could get on its roof. From there I could get to the driver's side of the car. I pulled forward so she could get out of the gate. She joined me in the car, and I walked down the alley to the street in front of the house. The fire equipment was still there, so I returned to the car, backed out the way I had come and drove away as rapidly as I thought appropriate.

The fear returned. "Where are you taking me?" she asked.

"To my hotel," I replied. "We need to talk."

She chewed on her thumbnail. "About what?"

"Sergei Malyakov," I replied. "Did you know his men emptied your warehouse tonight?"

She shivered, and I turned up the heat.

Chapter 15

IN THE HOTEL room she continued to shake, and hysteria wasn't far behind, so I wrapped the quilt around her and gave her a healthy slug of the minibar brandy. I had a little gin myself. It'd been a busy night, and it wasn't over yet.

In person, Marina Gringikov was even more beautiful than she was in her photographs. A classical face with no trace of Slav was framed by naturally blonde hair with just enough curl to make it interesting. I didn't think she was Greek, but the Greek genes come out in the Balkans sometimes. She wore no cosmetics. Dark brows framed brown eyes, and her lips were full and red. She was about five and a half feet tall. Dressed in jeans and a sweater, she looked like a model who had eaten a few good meals. Sergei Malyakov looked like a cleaned-up mafiya don, and his wife looked like a tart. Felix Gringikov had looked like a young Khrushchev, but his wife looked like a lady. By the time I finished my gin, she had stopped shaking. I ordered a pot of coffee and some sandwiches from room service, and we sat in silence, looking out over the Bosphorus to Asia. The waiter put the food on a low table between us, poured the coffee, and put the pot on the desk. She ate hungrily, as if she had missed a meal or two. I was hungry myself after the night's activity. When we had finished the sandwiches and were sipping the coffee, she said, "They were trying to kill me, you know. They set the fire to kill me."

A thought that had occurred to me.

"Who are they?" I asked. "Business rivals of your husband?"

She looked startled. "What kind of rivals could Felix have? He deals in supplies for refugee camps, Africa, the Middle East, you know."

Supplies for refugee camps?

"I don't know who they are," she said. "They just came after Felix disappeared. All of the servants left, and new people came. They said Felix sent them, but he wouldn't send people like that. They wouldn't let me go out alone. They always came with me. They wouldn't let me drive myself. The driver said my car's brakes were broken, and he would drive me in the big car until he got them fixed, but he just kept driving me. And another man came along with him. The houseman took all of my calls and told people I was away. They held me prisoner."

I looked at my watch. Two a.m. I pulled the medal and chain from my pocket and handed it to them to her. She gasped.

"Where did you get this? Where did you get it? This is Felix's!"

I didn't answer her. "What is it?"

"It's a medal his old army unit had. This"—she pointed to the front—"is the shield of Minsk and on the back is the symbol of the Soviet army." She began to cry. "He's dead, isn't he? He's dead. He never took it off! Where did you get it?"

I showed her the picture of George Branson on my iPhone. "Do you know this man?"

"That's Karl Spiegel. He's running the company while Felix is away. Why do you want to know?" She clutched the medal "Where did you get it?"

"From Karl Spiegel's safe," I replied.

She looked stunned. "He killed Felix?" she asked.

I paused. She had to know eventually. She had known, hadn't she?

"Either that, or he knows who did."

I handed her the little book. "I also found this in the safe. What is it? I can't read it."

She leafed through it. "It's Felix's address book." She looked more closely. "This man's not in Vienna anymore. He's dead. And this one is not in Varna. I think he's in Kinshasa. Why would this be in Karl's safe?"

"For the same reason your husband's medal was, I imagine. Tell me about that flight from Minsk that your husband was on. The one that never arrived here."

"Who told you that?" she asked.

"Somebody in Dubai," I answered.

"Dubai? Why Dubai? The flight was from Varna. That's in Bulgaria?" She looked at me, and I nodded. "Felix's headquarters are really in Varna. We have a big office there, several warehouses where they store the supplies before they fly them out."

"What kind of supplies?" I asked.

"Oh, you know—tents, food, medicine, blankets."

"But you have an office and warehouse here, too."

"Felix didn't like Varna. He liked to live here. I like it, too. Liked." She looked frightened again. "Until this . . ."

"Men got into your warehouse tonight." I looked at my watch. "Last night."

"What!"

"Took the cargo to Sabiha Gökçen and loaded it on an Ilyushin belonging to Trans-Caucasus airline."

"Trans-Caucasus? I never heard of it."

"No? It belongs to Sergei Malyakov."

"Who?"

By now it was three a.m. There was only one bed in the room. Big as an aircraft carrier, but it was the only one. I turned the covers down on the right side of the bed. She looked startled.

"There's only one bed, and I'm not going to sleep on the floor." I went into the bathroom and changed into a caftan, muttering because I'd forgotten to pack a night-gown again. I should glue one to the suitcase. She was still standing in the same place when I returned. I put the Glock and the phone on the floor beside the bed and got in it. She took a long breath.

"Somebody's trying to kill you, remember? Good night," I said and turned out the light.

I don't know about her, but I didn't sleep well or enough.

If Malyakov was trying to kill her, I didn't think it was wise for her to show herself in the dining room, so we had breakfast in the room. I put out the Do Not Disturb sign and set her to translating her husband's address book. It was time for me get into Karl Spiegel's safety deposit box.

The day was bright and warm, laughing at the idea of snow. Divanyolu was thick with traffic and parked cars, but I presented myself at Zeki's office only half an hour late. We dispensed with the tea and chatter. I put a small stack of hundred-dollar bills on the desk for him to count. He looked up in surprise.

"You are two-hundred dollars short," he said.

"You and I and the power of attorney are going to the Atatürk Bankasi. If I get into the box you get the last two hundred."

He looked displeased.

"You don't take me for a fool, do you, Zeki?"

"No. No." He put his coat on, and we went down-stairs. The bank was only two blocks away, so we walked. It was well named, that bank. It had been built early in the Republican period. I could see Kemal himself cutting the ribbon to open it.

The banking room was marble-floored and paneled in dark wood. The chandeliers were brass, and the teller's stations had little brass grills. Altogether it was the very model of a trustworthy and secure institution of a century ago. Zeki led me to the safety deposit desk. The dark-suited young man there looked as if he still wore a fez. He rose and shook Zeki's hand.

"What can I do for you today, Mr. Zeki?" he asked.

Zeki introduced me. "Ms. Carruthers has Mr. Karl Spiegel's power of attorney to get into his box, box number thirty-eight." He handed the document to the young man and gestured to me for the key. I held it until the young man had finished perusing the power of attorney and nodded. I produced my key, and he produced the other. I turned to Zeki.

"Thank you, Mr. Zeki. I believe that will be all." I turned my back to the desk and gave Zeki the rest of the money, which he received with a grimace.

The young man had seemed comfortable with Zeki, but he wasn't sure about me. If only he knew. Box number thirty-eight was one of the smaller ones, about eight inches deep. In it I found another baggie of uncut diamonds, rather larger than the one I found in the Dubai flat. The diamonds were accumulating. Perhaps that was why he was dead in Dubai. There was also a flash drive. When I accessed that I might find out why George Branson had sent the key to his wife. She seemed to play such a small part in his life.

Back at the hotel, I found Marina almost finished translating the book entries. She had three pages of hotel stationery with names, addresses, and phone numbers in small writing. Some of the contacts were in Dubai. I called Ralph.

"Who is Arkady Federov?" I asked.

"Lee, where are you? What's going on?"

"Never mind. Who is Arkady Federov?"

"He works for Malyakov. Why?"

"Thanks," I said and ended the call.

When Marina finished translating the last entry, I photographed the pages with my iPhone and burned them in the bathroom sink. It left a stain. I threw the book cover into the trash can. I couldn't conveniently destroy it, and it wouldn't tell anybody anything anyway. The flash drive proved to have photos of a number of men. I scrolled through them until I found Arkady Federov. Perhaps the drive carried files of at least some of the men in the address book? I attached the cable to the computer and transferred the files to my iPhone too. Then I jerked the drive from the computer and stomped on it, shattering it. I put the pieces in my pack to dispose of later.

"What are you *doing*?" Marina demanded.

I deleted files from the laptop and hoped no bad guy was an IT specialist.

"Come on," I said. "We're going to the office."

"I'm not going anywhere until you explain what you're doing and why," she insisted. "Why are you going to the office?"

"To find out who's there," I replied.

"Somebody's trying to kill me!"

"And it's time to find out who," I retorted.

Marina didn't look convinced.

"Either come with me or stay here," I said. She came.

The offices of Gringikov Enterprises were on the eighth floor of one of the high-rises not far from Karl Spiegel's flat, a ten-story tower faced in blue glass. As we got into the elevator, Marina asked, "What was Karl doing with Felix's medal?"

"You can ask him," I replied.

"He killed him. Felix. He must have. Felix never took that medal off."

"You can ask about that, too."

She stiffened her back and ceased to be the helpless damsel she had been since I rescued her from her burning house. I could see that she was getting agitated. She took

Felix's medal from her pocket and held it in her hand like a talisman.

Gringikov's office looked as if it had been designed by the same guy who did Malyakov's in Dubai: glass and modern furniture and a delectable receptionist. Marina swept past her and walked into the office without knocking. The man at the desk looked up angrily.

"What is this?" he demanded. "Who are you?"

I knew we were in trouble.

"Where's Karl?" Marina demanded angrily. "And who are you?"

I knew him. He was Roger Findley from the CIA station in Dubai. He saw me and flushed.

"What are you doing here?" he demanded.

"That's my line. What are *you* doing here?"

He reached for a drawer, but I was quicker. Pulling the Glock and holding it steady, I said, "Keep your hands where I can see them." To Marina I said, "Get out! Now! Run!" I heard the door to the reception room slam. Findley tried for the drawer again, I shot close to his hand, and he flinched. I turned and ran after Marina. I heard a buzzer sound as we made it to the fire stairs. I heard people coming after us. We were two or three flights below them, but they were gaining. I pulled Marina inside the fourth-floor door and watched two burly men in uniform swing around the landing and continue down the stairs.

"Come on," I panted. We ran to the stairs at the other end of the hall and ran down to the parking garage. I eased my head gingerly around the door and saw one of the men standing by the far door and one looking out the exit to the street. My car was parked halfway along the third row. If we could get to it. If we could get into the first row of cars we had a chance. We crept bent over and reached the first row without attracting attention. So far so good, but I couldn't see either man. I led Marina along the aisle between the second and the third rows until I saw the car ahead. I darted across, with Marina just behind me, safely I thought, but the man by the gate had seen some kind of movement and yelled, "Hey!"

I jerked the car door open and started the engine while Marina got in the other side. I screeched from the parking place and headed to the end of the row. One of the guards was standing in the way, legs spread with his gun in firing position. I clipped him as I turned right, and he fell. By the time I got to the gate he was on his feet again. He squeezed off a shot as I slammed through the gate. He got off another shot as I raced up the incline to the street. He hit something, because I heard the ping.

"Who were they?" Marina asked.

"The men who are trying to kill you," I answered grimly.

Chapter 16

I TURNED LEFT and right at random until I found an alley and backed into it. My heart was pounding, and my palms were sweaty and slipping on the steering wheel. I wiped my hands on my jeans, and, slowly, my respiration returned to normal. I sat there considering our options. Findley knew I was in Istanbul and with Marina Gringikov. It wouldn't be long before they had the airports covered.

"Where's your passport?" I asked Marina.

"In my purse," she replied. "Why?"

"They've taken over your Istanbul office. What about Varna? Do you have people in Varna?"

"I told you. Our main office is there," she replied.

Not surprising. Varna was the point of departure for a lot of the arms going out to Africa. I sat trying to get my bearings. I squinted at the map on the iPhone. There didn't appear to be a road that went up the coast to Varna. Route 032 to Edirne seemed the best bet. I pulled out of the alley and headed for the auto route.

"Where are we going?" Marina asked.

That's one of the reasons I like to work alone. I don't have to answer questions. "Varna," I replied.

"But why are we driving? It's only an hour's flight."

"Because they will have the airports covered before we can get to either of them, and I want to keep my gun."

I stopped to gas up just before the highway and bought a map. It looked like four lane as far as Edirne. The rest of the way was short hops between cities. The Bulgarian frontier was about fifteen kilometers from Edirne. I put the car in gear and hoped they sold visas at the border. It was after three. We should be able to make it beyond Edirne before stopping. I handed the map to Marina.

"Figure out what the next city after Edirne is," I said.

Traffic was heavy around Istanbul, but once we left the urban area, it was mostly long-distance trucks doing a steady seventy-five kilometers per hour, which forced me to do the same unless I wanted to be the baloney in a truck sandwich. I kept trying to fall back to get away from them, but I couldn't. The muscles in my shoulders began to curdle. Driving in a truck convoy is serious business.

Marina looked up from the map. "Stara Zagora looks like the next place of any size after Edirne. It looks like one hundred and fifty kilometers," she said.

"Four hours to Edirne?" I asked.

"About that," she agreed.

"And to Stara Zagora? Two hours?"

"I think so."

Nine hours. Could we do that?

"Can you drive?" I asked.

"Not this kind of car," she replied. "I can't shift gears."

That made it me. Could I do nine hours? We needed to get to Varna before they figured out where we were going.

"From Stara Zagora?"

She started measuring with her finger. "It's a crooked road. Perhaps two hundred and fifty kilometers."

"Three hours plus, if the road doesn't get worse."

"Yes."

"Plus time to talk to the people in Varna. We better try to get to Stara Zagora tonight," I decided. "We don't know what we'll find in Varna."

"Why should there be anything wrong in Varna?" she asked.

"Because there was something wrong in Istanbul," I replied.

The highway bypassed Edirne. It didn't matter. I wouldn't have time to see Sinan's best mosque anyway. The border crossing was huge. Dozens, maybe hundreds, of trucks were parked or lined up to go through the Turkish border control. Cars were shunted to another post. There was a long line there too, and it wasn't moving. After waiting ten minutes, I got out of the car and walked to the car in front.

"English?"

"Yes," the driver said.

"What's going on?" I asked.

"The Bulgarian border control people are staging a work slowdown," he said.

I returned to the car and drummed my fingers on the steering wheel. We had to get to Varna, and this wasn't helping.

"Stop that," Marina said.

"Stop what?"

"That noise you're making."

We moved ahead a car length and then stopped and waited. We moved ahead another car length then stopped and waited. I got out and walked along the line of cars counting them. Fifteen. I got back in the car and looked at my watch. Should we turn back to Edirne? We could spend the night there and get a fresh start in the morning. The Bulgarian border control people would probably be having a work slowdown tomorrow too. It was over an hour before we reached the Turkish border control, and an officer was standing taking passports, checking our faces, and stamping them. The bar was up, probably had been up for hours. We crossed the five hundred meter space to the Bulgarian border control officer. He took our passports and looked at them. He said something, and I looked at Marina. She shook her head.

"English?" I asked.

He left the car and entered the building, returning with another officer.

"No visa," he said.

"Can't we get one here?" I asked.

He waved us out of the line to a parking place next to the building, and we went in. The officer behind the desk took our passports and passed the identification pages through a scanner. Then he looked at each and every page in both passports. Obviously, the work slowdown extended to the office. After a long wait, he took our money and stamped the passports and waved us through. We had lost precious time crossing the border.

The tractor-trailers rejoined us. About ten kilometers from the border post it began to snow. Now we were on a slippery highway among massive trucks.

"We need to stop," I said.

Immediately, all signs of civilization disappeared, and it began to snow harder. Then I saw an exit. The sign was in Cyrillic. Before Marina could translate it, I took it. We were on a narrow country road leading to a village. A small village. Marina saw a beer sign, and we stopped at a small wooden two-story building. We entered a room smelling of spilt beer and tobacco. Five men dressed in dirty jeans and work boots stopped talking to look us over. No point in being shy.

"English?" God, I was getting tired of saying that.

The man behind the bar answered, "Yes?" His squint could have come from the smoke in the room, but I couldn't tell which way he was looking.

"Where can we find a room for the night?" I asked, hoping there was a nice bed-and-breakfast just down the road.

One of the men sniggered, which did not give me confidence.

"Here is a room," the barman replied.

Marina and I had the same thought. With bedbugs? Would it be better than sleeping in the car? We took the room. The man came out from behind the bar and limped to a steep flight of stairs, which led to what had originally been a loft. He gestured for us to go first. We declined the honor and climbed the stairs behind him. When he turned on the light and limped inside I saw he had a slight hump to his back. Mildly hysterical from the drive, I thought, "Igor, walk this way."

He went out and shut the door behind him. We looked at each other. We could clearly hear the men downstairs laughing.

There was no lock on the door.

We shoved a chest up against the door and looked around. No convenience. I looked under the bed and found a chamber pot.

Neither of us slept well. I kept itching, although I found no sign of bites when I got up in the morning. Our host had coffee and bread and homemade cherry jam for us before we left. It was seven a.m., and we calculated we had at least seven hours of driving in front of us. The road had frozen overnight, and the highway was full of trucks again. I began to wish I had risked the airport back in Istanbul. I could always get another gun.

It took us nine hours.

Varna is a good-sized place, the third largest city in the country, according to what Marina read on a sign. Its architecture is a mixture of Balkan Baroque and Stalinist Realism. The Soviets certainly could design depressing apartment blocks. Marina didn't remember the way to the office, so we had to drive around the business district in the slush for a while before she recognized the building.

"I'm sure this is the place. There." She pointed to a broken tile by the staircase. "I remember that tile."

In the lobby, the business directory showed no sign of Gringikov Enterprises, but there was an empty space on the directory, no listing for the fourth floor. For lack of an elevator, we walked. When we reached the third-floor landing, we heard footsteps coming down. We sprinted to the back of the hall. Two men stood on the landing and watched us. Quickly I opened the first door I saw, and we slipped inside an office with maps and pictures of large trucks on the walls. A thin blonde woman with her hair scraped back in a bun looked up from her computer, a question in her eyes.

Marina covered her mouth with her hand and said something in what might have been Bulgarian. The woman nodded her head and went back to her computer. I looked around the edge of the door. The men were gone, so we continued up the stairs to the fourth floor. The offices on both sides of the hall were empty of people but full of everything else: desks, chairs, filing cabinets. No computers. I took out my lock picks, and while Marina watched incredulously, I opened the first door on the right and held it for her to enter.

"But these are the offices. I know they are." She looked confused. "Lee, what is happening?"

All of the other offices were the same. The sign had been scraped off the window of the door at the end of the hall, but we could trace G and a K in the first line and "prize" in the second. The confusion on Marina's face was quickly replaced by fear.

"Where are all the people?" she asked anxiously.

It looked as if Malyakov's men had gotten here before us. If Roger was working for Malyakov. I went inside that office and started on a filing cabinet. It had file folders, but they were empty. Marina joined me and started on another cabinet. It was empty too, but there was a shredder, and it was jammed.

"I think we should have gotten here last night. There are warehouses," I said gently. "Are they at the airport?"

She nodded miserably. "I guess."

There was a cold wind blowing, and the remains of the snow were beginning to freeze. The cargo area of the airport was large, and I didn't want to ask anybody where the Gringikov warehouses were, so we drove around looking for them. Since Marina had never been to the warehouses, she couldn't help. After a half hour, we found a group of three warehouses with a "to let" sign pasted over another sign on the chain-link fence. I got out and scraped some of the paper away and discovered a G. The gates were open, a sure sign the warehouses were empty, so I drove up to the stairs by the loading dock of the first warehouse. I could see a sign from the car. Somebody had tried to chip it away, but "Gringikov" was still there. I climbed the icy concrete stairs. Marina joined me as if afraid to be alone in the car. I picked that lock even quicker than I had picked the one at the office. Shocking security for a warehouse. There was nothing in that office either, not even any file folders. A door led to the warehouse proper. The only thing there was torn tarpaulin.

Back in the car, Marina said, "There's nothing left. Nothing."

I put the car in gear and drove back toward the passenger terminal.

"No, there isn't. They've cleaned you out both here and in Istanbul. Now we have to decide what to do next. Leaving would be a good idea."

I parked and pulled Yahoo Travel up on the iPhone. After a bit of grinding, Yahoo told me that they had never heard of Varna. Tut, tut, I thought, how narrow-minded of them. Travelocity told me that the last flight out had left twenty minutes before, and there wouldn't be another until a flight to Sofia at ten the next morning, so I booked two seats on it and began looking for a hotel. I was traveling under my own name, and Marina, of course, was too. Roger Findley could find us if he thought to look in this direction. I got us a double at an airport hotel. The clerk was surprised at our lack of luggage. Suspicious, even.

"Lost," I explained as I handed him my credit card. "Somewhere between Minsk and here."

That or the credit card satisfied him. The room was up to the standard of the Holiday Inn, even to the paper strip across the toilet seat in the bathroom. At least there were two beds.

"Marina, we need to talk about what you're going to do after we get to Sofia."

She looked at the floor. "I don't know. Maybe I could come with you?"

Just what I needed: the widow of a merchant of death for a pet. I should tell her the widows of merchants of death didn't have much of a life expectancy in my company.

"Do you want to go home?" I asked.

She shook her head vigorously. "No. They've disowned me."

"For marrying Felix?" I asked.

"No. For what I did before I married Felix," she said defiantly.

"Everybody's got a make a living somehow," I said. "You don't need to go home. You can make a new life for yourself anywhere in the world."

"I don't have any money."

I removed one of the baggies of diamonds from my pack. I found it in Spiegel's lockbox. I figured it belonged to Gringikov and thus to Marina. I emptied it on her bed.

She looked at me in surprise. "What?"

"Uncut diamonds. They belonged to your husband. Now they belong to you."

I let her look for a while. She touched them, pushing them this way and that.

"They're diamonds?" she asked. "They are so ugly."

"They are diamonds, believe me. I don't know how much they're worth, but they're worth a lot. Enough to keep you in luxury for a long time. Maybe you'll remarry. You'll be rich. You can marry anybody you want to."

"I don't want another man!" She gave me a fierce look, and I remembered what she did before she married Felix. Maybe not.

"I know a man in Paris who will give you an honest price for them. You'll like Paris."

Any woman with a baggie full of diamonds would like Paris.

Chapter 17

I WOKE EARLY and debated what to do next. Who had George Branson/Karl Spiegel worked for—Felix Gringikov or the Agency? Somebody at Langley wanted to know why he was dead, which might mean they didn't know who he worked for either. The diamonds might be the reason he was dead. Somebody wanted the key to the safety deposit box badly enough to kill Cynthia Branson for it. Did they know about the address book? Was Spiegel really running Gringikov Enterprises after Felix disappeared? Was he doing it for the Agency? Had he been working for the Agency all along, or had he gone bad?

Then the penny dropped. That guy in Switzerland shot at me after Cynthia Branson gave me the key, so it was them, whoever them were, shooting at me and not the Pure Warriors of Islam looking for payback. But nobody had bothered me in Dubai, and Roger Findley knew I was there. Actually, somebody was keeping tabs on me. Or at least when I went to bed, weren't they?

When Marina woke, I showed her the photographs from the flash drive.

"I know him," she said, pointing to the picture of a man with the high cheekbones of a Slav. "I once saw him having an argument with Felix."

"What's his name?" I asked.

She shook her head. "I don't know."

Had Felix Gringikov really shielded his wife from any knowledge of his true business? I looked at her speculatively. Was she playing me? She looked so innocent, but she "did things" before she married Felix. Did she know more about the business than she claimed? What had been her relationship with Karl Spiegel? They were photographed together looking pretty friendly at a fancy party.

At the airport, I had a serious discussion with the car rental clerk when I went to return the car, because I was supposed to have returned it in Istanbul. I calmed him by paying a hefty fee for my transgression. After returning the car, I went into the ladies room in the terminal and waited in a stall until the room was empty before I ditched the gun in one trashcan and the mag in the other. I had to do it, but when I did, I was truly alone, and I felt that cold wind down my back again.

Waiting for the Sofia flight, I considered Marina again. I had known some very dangerous women who looked so sweet it made your teeth hurt. Somehow I couldn't see Marina Gringikov in that role, but I've been wrong before.

"Marina," I said. "You have to decide what you're going to do before we reach Sofia." She'd gone back to helpless again. "I've got work to do, and you can't come with me."

"I don't care what I do," she said listlessly.

"Then go to Paris. You can make other plans after you sell a few diamonds."

"All right," she agreed.

This allowed me to call Raoul Dupree, a Paris antique dealer with a taste for diamonds.

"I'm sending you a client, Raoul. She'll arrive sometime tomorrow with a baggie of diamonds," I said. I turned to Marina. "Do you speak French?"

"No." She looked as if she didn't care.

"And she doesn't speak French. English, yes, but not French. I'm sending you a picture." With a click it was done.

I got her a seat on the flight to Paris that left two hours after we got to Sofia.

"Go to Raoul's first. Take a taxi from the airport." She nodded. "Raoul will send you to a hotel." She nodded again. He would after I called him again.

The flight to Sofia was bumpy, and we were both out of sorts when we got there. We picked up her ticket and boarding pass and went to the gate to wait.

"What am I going to do in Paris?" she asked fretfully.

"Anything your heart desires," I replied.

The Paris flight was late getting in, and Marina showed signs of changing her mind.

"You can always stay here," I suggested.

"No! Any place but here!" she replied sharply, and I wondered where she did what she did before she met Felix. The flight came in, and we waited impatiently for it to board. Marina looked over her shoulder as she went down the ramp as if I had abandoned her to the cold, cruel world. Maybe I had.

A man in line behind her looked familiar. I went to a café with tables outside and ordered lunch. Who was he? Did it matter? As far as I could tell, nobody had the faintest interest in us. Getting paranoid, girl, I thought. And paranoids sometimes have enemies, I replied to myself. With my eye on the passing parade, I booked a flight to Athens on my phone. It didn't leave until seven p.m., which gave me lots of time to get more paranoid. I dawdled along the concourse window shopping. I needed something to wear. I always carry a shirt and underwear in my pack, because one morning I woke up in Paris and went to bed three days later in Bucharest, but the things I had gotten in Istanbul were pretty grungy. A new pair of jeans would be nice. The ones I was wearing could stand up by themselves. I shrugged my shoulders and gave up because I couldn't find a pair without rhinestones. I did find a T-shirt that didn't say "I ♥ Sofia."

In and out of stores, in and out of restrooms. So far as I could see, I was clear. I bought a bodice ripper at a newsstand and sat down to wait my flight. I started to read, but the book didn't hold my interest except as an example of what an experienced author could do with the Kama Sutra. I returned to the question of Felix Gringikov and his enterprises. He had disappeared almost two years ago. Karl Spiegel, who was George Branson who was also Gil Brady and worked for the Agency, had been running the company in Felix's absence. Was he also sleeping with Mrs. Gringikov? Irrelevant, probably. He had stashed baggies full of uncut diamonds in his safe in Dubai and his safety deposit box in Istanbul. Where did he get them? The key. Cynthia was dead because of the key. I got up and dropped it in the nearest trash can. The hamster on the wheel started over again. Where did he get the diamonds? Spiegel also had a book with a list of names and phone numbers that Marina said was her husband's. Where did he get that? The entries were in Cyrillic. Somehow I couldn't see George reading Cyrillic.

Spiegel/Barnes/Branson also had a medallion that Gringikov never took off. Where did he get that? Was Gringikov dead? Did Spiegel have something to do with it? Because Spiegel was dead in Dubai.

Twenty minutes before the Athens flight was due to take off, I transferred to the gate slowly and cautiously and felt like a fool. Nobody was paying the slightest attention to me. The flight took off on time. I would be in in Athens in time for a good dinner, bottle of good wine, and a good night's sleep. I looked out of the window and watched Sofia disappear. I didn't get to see the town, but I'd been to Bucharest and Kiev, and Varna, for that matter, so I knew what it looked like—Balkan Baroque and Stalinist Realism. I dozed, not really sleeping because my brain would not let go of the problem. Suddenly, I snapped awake. What if Marina had given me a list of false names and phone numbers? I had destroyed the original pages and had no way to check. I could check the phone numbers. How do you say "wrong number" in Russian?

I checked into the same airport hotel, and the clerk welcomed me back by name. I did have a good dinner and a good bottle of wine. I did not have a good night's sleep. After dinner I worked on the telephone numbers, using the hotel's list of country and area codes. The numbers were all reasonable: Varna, Kiev, Minsk, Kazakhstan, Gringikov's office number in Istanbul and another Istanbul number, probably the warehouse. Some Dubai numbers I didn't recognize, and all of the African holes that were currently hellish. If she had falsified the names, which she might have, would she have had time to make up false numbers? Sure. All she would've had to do was scramble the digits in the real numbers. I considered calling a random batch of the numbers but gave it up.

I finished the last of the wine. The debate over what to wear to bed was solved in the usual way. I put jeans and shirt beside the bed in case the hotel caught fire. I deeply regretted not having the Glock to put with the phone beside them. I went to bed wearing my skin. It fit. I turned out the light and was about to turn over when I glanced at the door. A pair of shoes showed in the crack under the door. I sprinted to the door in time to see a guy moving away in the fisheye lens of the peephole.

I sat down on the bed and put my head in my hands. All that fancy footwork, and they knew where I was all of the time, didn't they? They had me on a leash, a long leash, but they had me. All they had to know was the name of the bank in Istanbul. They didn't even have to know that. After they were sure I was going to Istanbul, all they needed was my phone number. If they found me in Athens, they knew I was going back to Abu Dhabi. Into how much danger? Roger Findley was cleaning out the Gringikov office in Istanbul. Unless he had gone rotten, the Agency was involved. And the Agency wanted to know why George Branson was dead in Dubai.

It was a long night. I stared at the ceiling contemplating how I was going to work alone against the largest intelligence agency in the world.

Chapter 18

THE DESK CLERK at the hotel in Dubai was pleased to see me, relieved that he did not have to sell my belongings to pay my bill.

"I'm sorry. A crisis you know, with no cell phone coverage."

"There are messages, Ms. Carruthers." He handed me a fistful of envelopes. Who writes messages in this day and age? When the elevator came, I stuffed them into my pocket and stepped aside for a couple to get out. A middle-aged man with a middle-aged suit and middle-aged face joined me, and we sorted ourselves out, one to each corner. I took the car keys from my pocket and inserted the longest one through my index and third fingers, but he got off on the floor below mine, so I didn't have to try to poke his eye out. I opened my room door and was inside before I saw the two of them. One of them was the squat man who looked like a paratrooper from Cynthia's hotel room. He was pointing a gun at me. The other guy stood to the side.

"Give me the key, bitch," the squat man said.

"I don't have any key, bastard," I replied.

"Cynthia Branson gave it to you. Search her," he ordered the second man.

I held my arms out as if ready to be searched, and the second man reached toward me to pat me down. I stomped on his foot, whirled, and hit the side of the neck as hard as I could, and he dropped. It's a killing blow, but I'm not strong enough to kill with my hands. He'd know he'd been hit tomorrow, though. I stepped aside and looked at the paratrooper. He walked toward me, emphasizing the gun he had.

"I said, give me the key, bitch."

"You don't want to kill me," I said.

"I'll kill you and take it off your body," he replied.

CIA trained? Paratrooper was enough. I took the keys out of my pocket and held them out. He had learned nothing. He stepped toward me, and I dropped them. Automatically, he bent over to pick them up, and I hit him as hard as I could in the back of the neck, bringing my knee up to his nose. He went down on his knees with his hands over his bleeding nose. I kicked his gun away and pulled mine.

"Get out of here, the both of you, or I *will* kill you and say you attacked me," I ordered and gestured with my gun.

They got out. I slammed the door shut and threw the bolt. The paratrooper had killed Cynthia and could just as easily have killed me. I ran into the bathroom and threw up. Afterward I leaned against the bathroom wall and shook my hands. They were going to be swollen. I rinsed out my mouth. I'm getting better. Hit the toilet. I went into the bedroom and threw myself on the bed. I'm really going to have to find a new way to react to stress.

When I stopped shaking, I took the notes from my pocket. There was a whole stack of them from Sergei Malyakov. I had missed the rotting flowers, four large bouquets of orchids. I rang for the housekeeper. Some of the others were from Willy and Ralph, who had given up trying to reach me on my cell phone. There was one from Phung Nguyen inviting me to tea, and a fairly stiff note on fairly stiff paper requesting my presence at the consulate yesterday.

The housekeeper came and took away the dead orchids.

My e-mail was clogged with offers to increase the size of my penis and several commands from Sidney. I really must go off the grid more often. People miss me so. Sidney first. I looked at my watch. According to my calculations, Sidney would be sound asleep. I dialed his home number. After several rings, somebody picked up. Then there were thumps and curses. Sidney waking up.

More thumps. "Carruthers, what the hell? Do you know what time it is?" he demanded.

"No, Sidney, I don't. What time is it?" I asked with all the innocence I could muster. "You asked me to call. What can I do for you?"

Rustlings replaced the thumps, and I heard the click of his cigarette lighter.

"Smoking is bad for you, Sidney."

I heard a long exhale and pictured the smoke dribbling from between his lips. "So are you. What have you gotten yourself into this time?"

"I'm trying to discover why George Branson washed up dead on Russian Beach carrying a passport in the name of Gil Brady."

"Your client is dead."

"So she is," I said equably.

"So what are you doing?"

"Trying to find out why George Branson is dead."

"And what have you found?" he growled.

"Inquiring about either man stirs up a hornet's nest," I replied.

"Don't go enigmatic on me, Carruthers. What have you discovered?"

"That he was running Felix Gringikov's Istanbul office under the name of Karl Spiegel after Gringikov disappeared. And then we . . ." I stopped. "I also discovered that you have some connection with that office."

"We do?"

"Unless Roger Findley has gone to work for somebody else, we do. He was there a few days ago closing down the office."

The silence extended as Sidney thought. "I wondered what it was," he said.

"What what was?"

"What made them tell me to pull you off the case."

"And who are they?" I asked.

"I don't know," he replied.

"You also told me that you didn't know who told you to put me on it."

"Right."

"And now you tell me you don't know who wants you to take me off the case."

"Yes," he snapped. "Get off the case. It will get very dangerous if you don't." He cut the call.

Do tell, I thought. I looked at the phone as if it could tell me something—like what's going on. Sidney was obviously just the messenger. I had clearly stepped on somebody big's toes. So what was the message? In the beginning, someone up the chain of command had wanted me to keep Cynthia Branson quiet by looking for her husband. When I began to find out things, Cynthia was killed. Now they wanted to stop me from finding out anything else?

They hadn't read my personnel file very closely.

The consulate was still open for business, so I decided to let the local boys tell me to stop snooping too. I called the man who had requested my presence.

"I'm sorry, Ms. Carruthers, but Mr. Manning has left for the day. I know he wanted to see you," said a personal assistant in a pleasant voice. I knew she was a personal assistant because nobody has secretaries anymore. "Perhaps you can come in tomorrow morning?"

"Certainly," I said. I couldn't wait.

"About ten?" she asked.

"How about ten thirty?" I asked. "I've just gotten in from Athens, and I'm bushed. That is, I'm very tired. I'm hoping to sleep in a bit."

"That's fine," she said generously. "Just tell the receptionist that you want to see Humphrey Manning and have somebody bring you around."

The messages from Malyakov were all invitations to dinner. I tore them in half and threw them in the trash can. I guess the Malyakovs have an open marriage.

I had a steak and a bottle of Burgundy from room service and let Ralph yell at me for a while for not picking up my calls. I asked him how to get in touch with Fred Atkins. Reclaiming the Glock had not entirely cured the draft down my back, and finding two thugs in my room didn't help. If I was going to fight the CIA, I needed some company. I arranged to have dinner with Ralph the next night. He had some things he wanted to tell me. I told him that unless his information was that I was going to be shot in the next fifteen minutes, it could wait. I was going to bed.

I did tooth brushing things and when I was ready for bed, I wrote a note saying "I'm going to bed" and posted it on the door.

The guy at the consulate gate ran my passport under a scanner before lifting the bar so I could drive inside. I went through a metal detector to prove that I had left my gun and knife locked in the car. My phone rang. It was Raoul in Paris. What did he want? I let it go to voice mail.

The receptionist called a recruiting poster Marine to escort me to Manning's office. I was surprised when we turned right and not left toward the station. My escort led me down the hall, past closed office doors, past portraits of former secretaries of state. He knocked on an unmarked door once, not twice, and ushered me into an office the likes of which no chief of station ever saw. The conversation area held a loveseat and two upholstered chairs around a table too tall to be a coffee table. They were probably copies of antiques, but they were good copies. GSA has gone upscale, I thought. But it was more likely that I'd never been in the office of a man of Manning's rank before. The man standing beside a mahogany desk was lean with graying brown hair and a face as starched as his white long-sleeved shirt. For office casual he had turned his cuffs two painful turns up and looked as if he feared being ejected from his dining club for not wearing a tie. He extended his hand to shake mine.

"Humphrey Manning, Ms. Carruthers. How do you do?" His handshake was firmer than I had expected. Somehow he didn't look the tennis type. Racquetball? We went through a greeting ritual as regular as any Arab's, though mercifully not so long.

"Perhaps you might like some coffee?" he inquired.

"Coffee would be nice," I answered.

He pressed a button on the desk, and we sat and waited for the coffee. I thought that I much preferred to be among the unwashed in the station. They could at least come to the point. Of course, they did tend to call a spade a damn bloody shovel. We chatted in the stilted way one chats before the coffee comes. Yes, I had been in Dubai before. Yes, the weather was much cooler this time of the year. Yes, it was a fantastic place. No, I had not been up the Burj Khalifa, the recently finished tallest building in the world. The coffee came, and we continued the minuet through the whole range of conversation a diplomat has at his disposal until we finished our coffee. That, at least, hadn't changed. Manning put his cup down on the saucer with a click and cleared his throat.

"Ms. Carruthers," he said formally as if announcing a decree from on high, "I have been instructed to inform you that any further inquiry into the Branson affair would be viewed with grave displeasure."

Fighting a strong urge to giggle, I rose, which surprised him and made him rise.

"How very kind of you to give me coffee, Mr. Manning," I said and offered him my hand, regretting for the first time that white gloves were out of fashion. He shook my hand and crossed to the desk, where he pushed that button again. He stood looking uncomfortable, and I wondered if I should talk of Michelangelo. The decorative Marine took me back along the hall and out the door to my car. I felt as if I had just received a note from Queen Victoria's Foreign Office.

Chapter 19

BACK AT THE hotel, I went into the café and had a sandwich while I determined what to do next. Being natively contrary, I mulled over steps I could take that would annoy both the CIA and the Department of State, but to do anything I needed more information. I needed to get into Roger Findley's personnel file. I went to the room and flipped through my Agency phone numbers until I found Matthew O'Brien. He would do. It was a little early to call Langley, so I called the number Ralph had given me for Fred Atkins. It went to voice mail, and I left a message. Then I settled down to transfer the address book and flash drive files to my computer and encrypt them. Some of my stuff is encrypted, some isn't, but it's the Agency system, and Roger Findley could read my encrypted notes if he had my key. I made a note to myself to get another system. I had to compare George's files with Roger's when I got the chance. Time to call Matt. I called Langley on a burn phone I picked up at the Abu Dhabi airport.

"Hi, Matt," I said when he picked up. "Lee Carruthers."

"You're gone. I'm not even supposed to talk to you," he said nervously.

"Don't be that way, Matt. How have you been?"

"Fine, just fine. What do you want?"

"That place near Scott Circle still in business?"

"How do you—?"

"I'm a spy, Matt. I collect information."

"You're not a spy, you're an analyst. Were an analyst."

"But I collect information," I said smoothly. "Now I need some."

"I can't do anything for you. You're outside. You don't have access."

"But I have you, Matt, and you're going to send me Roger Findley's personnel file."

"I can't," he squeaked. "I can't do that! I'll be caught! They'll fire me."

"You'll just have to make sure you're not caught then, Matt, won't you?"

"I can't."

"Did you ever tell Walker about that little trouble you had in Bangkok?"

"No." He gulped. "No."

"He wouldn't be pleased to learn about it, would he, Matt? His daughter was fourteen about that time."

"Please, Lee," he pleaded. "You can't."

"I can and will, Matt, unless you send me Roger Findley's personnel file."

There was a long pause. Then he surrendered. "All right," he said faintly.

"Promptly, Matt."

"Okay, okay, but that's the last thing I'll ever do for you."

"Wrong, Matt. Until you tell Walker about Bangkok, I own you, body and soul."

Perhaps I was a trifle harsh with Matt, but he had been indiscreet enough, or unlucky enough, to get caught in a raid on a Bangkok whorehouse between two fourteen-year-old prostitutes.

I turned back to the laptop and found that the George Branson files from Sidney had arrived. I downloaded them into a READ file on the desktop, where they joined the files from Gil Brady's safe and the list of names and files on men I got from Spiegel's lockbox. The total amount of stuff I was going to have to process was deeply depressing. Wasn't there some way I could get Jerry to do it? I shut down the laptop and went out into the sunshine. It was always a joy to cross the street between the hotel and the dhow docks. Despite the best efforts of ingenious Dubai drivers, I arrived safely. Tourist gewgaw kiosks had multiplied since I was last there. I've always wondered what a person did with a five-foot long scale model of a dhow. It reminded me of the guy I once saw put a farmer's carrying pole and its two large baskets in the overhead compartment of a Dragonair plane in Guilin, China. I bought a frozen yogurt and strolled along, admiring the new motor dhows with their scrolled tracery. Walking as far as possible from the loading and unloading to avoid being brained by flying cargo, I stopped to watch a pile of plastic-covered mattresses being loaded one by one onto the deck of a shiny new dhow alongside a stack of boxes containing flat screen TVs. I wondered how dry the mattresses would be when they arrived.

Sinbad's ship was docked down at the far end along with the other creaky old sailing dhows. Sinbad believed that there was no point in buying gasoline when Allah provided wind for free. When I pointed out that motor dhows could make three or four round-trip voyages to Sinbad's one, he replied that there was too much greed in the modern world.

I hailed the boat, and a man with a brown and wrinkled face looked over the side, pulling the patch over his left eye into place. His remaining one twinkled as he helped me aboard and clasped me in a huge hug. I hugged him back, despite the fact that nothing but seawater had touched his body in some time. He buys new clothes occasionally.

"Allah be praised!" he exclaimed. "You are well?"

"I am well, thank God. And you?" I replied. "You are well?"

"I am well." He sat me down on a crate and went below to get the raki. How is it that all my disreputable friends force raki on me? That stuff will ruin your palate for gin. Enough of it would ruin you, period.

"How's business?" I asked after my tonsils recovered from the first swallow.

"Not bad," he admitted. "Business across to Qeshm Island is always good. If the US ever lifts its sanctions on Iran, I'll go broke," he said with an evil smile.

"What's going across?" I asked. "What I've seen loading is just domestic stuff."

I prevented him from pouring me another drink, so he consoled himself with pouring another one for himself.

"That's what you see loading here. The rusty old buckets docked down at the mouth of the creek load a lot of unmarked boxes. I've carried some of that stuff myself," he admitted.

"What kind of merchandise?" I asked.

"I don't know. Heavy crates. Unmarked."

"You said you carried some of those crates. What was in them?"

He shook his head.

"You don't expect me to believe you didn't open one of them, do you?"

He grinned. "One of them had what looked like some kind of pump. I don't know what they wanted pumps for."

I didn't either. Does a nuclear program need pumps?

"I don't think I ever asked you how you are paid."

"Gold, Maria Theresa thalers, US dollars. Anything but rials. Can't use them anywhere but Iran."

"I've never seen a Maria Theresa thaler. The Austrians are still minting them? Since the eighteenth century?"

He reached into his pocket and handed me a heavy silver coin.

"They are still minting them. This one says 1780."

"Feels like money," I said. I hefted the coin in my hand and gave it back to him. "Do you hear anything about diamonds?" I asked.

He grunted. "Hear a lot. Never seen any."

"What do you hear?"

"Just that there are lots of them around recently. Have to turn them into gold before they're worth anything in the trade to Iran."

"Surely they are useful elsewhere."

"Yeah. Saudis snap them up. Some of these emirs like them, too, but mostly not to spend. To save, like."

I was envisioning a casket full of diamonds in a Saudi harem when my phone rang. It was Raoul. I let it go to voice mail.

"The specie coming from Tehran?"

"Specie?" Sinbad asked.

"Gold. The gold and thalers."

"Yes," he answered.

"How does it get there?"

"The gold? They say from Turkey. Some of it comes from here."

"Did you ever carry any?"

"Nah. Goes by courier."

Turning diamonds into gold. Taking gold into Iran. The world sanctions must be biting. The Iranians had no banking facilities in the outside world, did they?

"You say you get paid in gold?"

"Or in the Maria Theresas, yeah."

"Does the bank just take them? Gold bars or silver coins?" I asked curiously.

"What bank?"

I looked at him seriously. "Then you've got a security problem."

He looked crafty. "Not me."

We parted with the same formality that we had used when we met, and I went back to the hotel and returned Raoul's call.

"Hi. What's up?" I asked.

"Don't you ever answer your phone?" he asked crossly.

"I was busy," I replied vaguely.

"You know that woman you sent me? She was dead when she got here. Had a heart attack in a taxi on the way in from the airport."

"What?!"

"The driver found her dead in the back seat. And if she was carrying diamonds, they weren't on her when she got here."

Surely it was too convenient for Marina to die like that. Who did I know in medico-legal? Nobody. What cop did I know at the Quai des Orfèvres? None who was speaking to me. I'd have to settle for a reporter. I flipped through my contacts until I found Elise Buffon. She worked at the tabloid *Canard Enchaînè*, and Marina was a duck.

"Yeah?" I heard the clicking of the keys on her keyboard.

"Lee Carruthers with a duck," I said.

"Ha. Ha. What have you got?"

She did not praise Allah or ask about my relatives, praise Allah.

"An acquaintance who was found dead in a taxi in the Marais. They said a heart attack, but she was carrying an object of great value which is not mentioned in the newspaper article."

"Name?"

"Marina Gringikov."

"What article of value?"

"No comment," I said.

She grunted. "How do you know?"

"Because she had it with her when I put her on a plane in Sofia."

"Sofia? In Bulgaria?"

"That's it," I said firmly and cut the call.

Poor Marina. Merchant of death widows don't last long in my company. If they knew I was going to Athens, they knew she was going to Paris. That guy behind her boarding the plane in Sofia? I knew I'd seen him somewhere, but who was he? Did he belong to Malyakov? To the Agency? Somebody was cleaning up Gringikov's offices and inventory. Malyakov or the Agency? Somebody was tidying up loose ends. The Agency or Malyakov?

I could no longer avoid working the files. I decided to do the personnel files first. My life passed before my eyes just looking at them. I decided to make a list of the places where George had been stationed, starting with the most recent. Dubai, of course. Under his own name? Istanbul, ditto. In between stops here and there, he had been in various African states but not at our embassies there. From the reports he filed, he traveled in murderous company. Payment was into Citibank accounts. Citi was a bank with branches all over the world, even in African hellholes. Two years ago, the reports and the payments stopped.

Roger Findley had always been stationed at an embassy or consulate. It was curious how often he was in the same place George was. I ran George's aliases through both files and found nothing.

I stood up and stretched. The skies still had a memory of the sun but the red rosy line was sinking. It was possible to track George through various assignments. He had presumably been Gil Brady in Dubai and Karl Spiegel in Istanbul. Where had he been George Branson?

My cell phone rang. It was Fred Atkins returning my call.

"I find I need a partner, after all. Are you still available?"

"I thought you didn't want a partner?"

"The circumstances have changed."

"How?" he asked.

"Now I'm working against the CIA. Can you handle that?"

"Hoo-rah," he answered.

Oh, God. A Marine.

"Meet me at Ralph's."

"When?"

"Now," I said.

It was early to go to Ralph's, but he would be there. I needed the assistance of Walter W. Willoughby, and he might be sober at that hour. A tanned man in a blue suit wearing horn-rimmed glasses got in the elevator with me on five, and we sorted ourselves into opposite corners. A man with high cheekbones and thin lips got on at four. He was sunburnt across his nose and didn't really need the sunglasses. We sorted again, the newcomer in the center of the rear. Paranoia made me push the button for the ground floor instead of the parking garage. I didn't like the thought of the parking garage with either of them. At the lobby, we all moved toward the door. Mr. Sunglasses bumped me with his hip without apology as he went out the door past me. He was carrying a gun. The blue-suited one stepped out behind me, and I stepped aside to let him pass. I went into one of the cafés and ordered a cup of coffee. Sunglasses had taken his seat across the lobby. He sat with his feet flat on the floor and his hands on his thighs, not even pretending that he wasn't watching me. Blue suit was out of my line of sight. I toyed with the coffee until it got cold and then decided to take a taxi to Ralph's. I didn't like the odds in the garage.

I looked back as my taxi pulled away from the curb. The two of them were in the taxi just behind me, making no effort to hide the fact that they were following me.

If I'd had a cell number I would have texted them my destination.

Chapter 20

THE NIGHT HADN'T started properly at Ralph's yet. A pair of early drinkers sat at the bar, and the DJ was testing his sound levels. Ralph was in his office studying a paper through a pair of half glasses that had slipped down his nose. He jerked them off when he saw me standing in the doorway.

"Don't do that for me. I know you're over forty. Here I am to pick your brain, wagging my tail behind me. Actually two of them," I said, "one in brown and one in blue."

"Two tails?" Ralph asked.

Fred Atkins was leaning against the filing cabinet, his arms crossed, one ankle crossed negligently over the other, looking like the Marlboro Man. He raised an eyebrow. Whoever saw the Marlboro Man with a raised eyebrow? I have just hired a Marine with a Bad Conduct Discharge to have my back. Who was going to protect me from my protector?

"Two tails?" he asked.

"Thank you, you're hired. In the same taxi," I replied. "I think they're watching each other as well as me."

"We'll see about that," Atkins said.

"No, we won't. Whoever they are, they know where I'm staying. All they have to do is go back to the hotel and wait. I'm more interested in the guy who takes the next shift. Eventually, we're going to get down to somebody I know."

Ralph shifted Atkins and picked up a camera from the top of the filing cabinet. "I just as soon have a picture of them, anyway." We both followed him to the entrance. He walked over to the waiting car, jerked the back door open, and stuck the camera in. I saw the flash go five times before he slammed the door, and the taxi scratched off.

"Subtle," I said.

"I don't do subtle," he said. "Here," he said. He handed me the camera, and I scrolled through the photos he had taken. "These are the guys?"

I nodded. There they were—Mr. Sunglasses and the guy in the blue suit. The pictures weren't very good, but I recognized them, and, with a little tinkering, somebody else might too. He opened his photo editing program and fed the photos into it. After brightening them and raising the contrast some, they were recognizable but would never win any prizes. Atkins came and looked over my shoulder.

"Recognize them?" I asked him.

He shook his head. "Unh, unh."

Ralph looked at his watch. "Willoughby should be here . . ."

The door opened, and Willoughby walked in.

". . . about now," Ralph finished.

Willoughby looked at me. "I've seen you before."

"Give that man a cigar," I said.

Then he looked at Atkins, and Atkins looked at him, and the air froze. I had a vision of two big bucks locking horns. Willoughby scowled. Atkins scowled back

"There's money in it," I said.

Willoughby turned to look at me again. "How much?"

"That depends on how sober you are." Willoughby looked like a man who was never entirely sober, but he was standing up and neither shaking nor leaning. "I want you to look at some pictures and identify the men in them. I want to know who they are, who they work for, and what they do. Start with this guy." I handed him my phone with George Branson's picture.

"That's Gil Brady." He looked at the picture closely. "Taken a while ago. Has more gray in his hair now."

"And?"

"Works for Malyakov, sort of a troubleshooter. Travels around making sure things are going okay."

I sat him at the computer with the photos from the flash drive that I found in Spiegel's lockbox. "I need to know who these men are and who they work for."

"I need a beer," he replied.

I looked at Ralph. Ralph looked him over and gave him a beer. Of the thirty men pictured, five of them he knew worked for Malyakov, but he didn't know their names.

"I've seen 'em around. They do a little of this, a little of that, y'know? This one," he pointed to a bald man, "Arkady Federov. He's some kind of dispatcher."

Five of them he had also seen around. They did what he called "odd jobs." Then I saw the man behind Marina in the line at the Sofia airport. He was one of the odd jobs men.

"Names?"

"Don't know. They're not the kind of guys who advertise."

"What do you mean by 'odd jobs'?" I asked.

He shrugged. "Like I said, they do this and that."

By that time, Willoughby had consumed three beers and was maintaining the level of intoxication he'd come in with. He closed the picture file and the pictures of my tails came up.

"These guys I know," he said. "Russians—mafiya, I think. Where did you get these pictures?"

Ralph answered, "I took them just a few minutes ago. They were tailing Lee."

"Bad dudes." He finished a beer and reached for another.

"Who do they work for?" I asked.

"Anybody who wants wet work done," he replied and belched. "That all?"

I looked at Atkins, and he shook his head. I handed Willoughby a bill, and he walked a straight line through the door.

I looked at Atkins again. "Still want in?"

He smiled his lazy smile and said, "Why not?"

"Not much information for the money," Ralph said.

"Yes. Only one name, and he works for Malyakov. Willoughby has the idea that some more of them do 'this and that' for him. I wouldn't want to meet any of them in a dark alley. Ralph, you said you had some information for me," I said.

"Yeah. That plane of Gringikov's on the ground in Bangkok? It took off a few days ago." He grinned. "I guess the money came through. But what's interesting is the word has it that the plane landed in northern Laos, up near the Plain of Jars."

"What? Where? Who's there that wants guns?"

"It's Hmong territory. Haven't heard anything about them in years, but it sounds like they're going home."

"The Vietnamese won't like that," Atkins said.

"No, they won't," Ralph said.

I looked from one man to the other. "What?"

"Just another gallant little bunch of people we betrayed in one of our foreign adventures," Atkins said.

"Vietnamese? You know, maybe our little pirate girl knows something," Ralph said.

"Our pirate girl?" Atkins asked.

"Yeah. A little Vietnamese doll who sells guns to the highest bidder."

The club was beginning to fill up with the early crowd of mostly late middle-aged tourists who had given up try-ing to be cool.

"I want to have an early night, Ralph," I said. "I have to think tomorrow."

"Now that's bad. Are you sure you have to?" He smiled.

I returned the smile. "'Fraid so. I've put a lot of miles on the carcass since we last met. The synapses aren't all firing."

I was staring out the window at Dubai Creek the next morning, trying to make sense of all the information I had. Names with faces. Names without faces or places. Why did Karl Spiegel have a file with pictures of men who sometimes did "odd jobs" for Sergei Malyakov? Along with an address book belonging to Felix Gringikov and a bag of diamonds? Why did he send the key to that lockbox to his wife? And why, blast him, was he dead?

I was just deciding that I had to call the phone numbers of the men on the list when my phone rang. It was Willy.

"Well. You're answering your phone now, are you?"

"Been away."

"And you don't check your calls?"

"I was using that key," I said.

"Was I right?" he asked.

"You are right," I replied.

"Feel like lunch with a pair of bankers, doll?"

"Persian bankers?" I asked.

"One's Persian, one's Pakistani."

"Associated with the Dubai–Persian Bank?" I asked.

"You got it. I think you'll recognize them. Can you look like a rich woman with money to invest?"

"Can you doubt it?" I asked. "Both men are Muslim?"

"Yes. Why?"

"You'll see."

"I'll pick you up at one o'clock."

"Banker's hours."

"Banker's lunch hours," he returned.

Willy looked at me with approval when I met him in the lobby. I was wearing a burgundy suit with a loose jacket and a rather tight and low-cut matching sweater.

"Trying to freak them out? You don't look much like an investor."

"You'll see when I bend over at lunch. I'm a recent widow. My elderly husband died and left everything to me. It's too bad I'm not a blonde."

"That would be overkill," he said and led me out to his car, which was being watched over by an alert parking attendant. It was one thirty when we entered the restaurant next to the Dubai stock exchange and were ushered into the room where women were allowed. I regretted that the sweater wasn't cut lower. Willy led me to a table where two men were sitting. I remembered them. They had been at Malyakov's table at the Berlin. They looked more comfortable in their well-tailored suits than they had in leisure suits. Abdel Fawaz, CEO of the Dubai–Persian Bank, was about five foot six and slender. He didn't resemble what I thought an Iranian man should look like. Although he had a slightly olive complexion, his face was classical, right off a Greek coin. I wondered how much time Alexander the Great had spent in Persia. Rajiv Kumar, the Pakistani who ran the online section of the bank, was livelier and had a mustache, but he had the same classical profile. Alexander and company had left a lot of genes in a lot of places. They both felt able to shake a woman's hand, which I thought was decent of them, but they shied a bit at my sweater. Still, all in all, they took me rather well. Willy jovially ordered fruit juice for them and martinis for us. The routine seemed to be to talk of this and that, order lunch, and return to this and that. There was a delectable Persian rice dish that I adored on the menu, but I thought that my character would not be that adventurous, so I stuck with a modest steak with green salad, no potato. After all, I might want another mature husband.

The food was good. I've noticed that before. Money men do themselves well. After the coffee was served, the briefcases came out. Fawaz cleared his throat and took out a prospectus in nine-point type.

"Oh, Mr. Fawaz," I chirped. Yes, chirped. "Mr. Woo does all that for me. I mean, I don't know anything at all about money," I confided. "That's why I have Willy." I beamed at him. "I go by faces, you know. I mean, I think you can just tell if a person is trustworthy by looking at his face." Willy quickly wiped the incredulous look from his face and patted my hand. At that moment my phone vibrated, and I looked at it. The caller left a message. I looked back at Willy and then at Fawaz. "That's why I needed to meet you."

Willy speared me with a look and took over. "Mrs. Carruthers is, of course, very interested in the investment potential of Dubai-Persian. Dubai-Persian is only one of a number of investment possibilities that I have shared with her."

Fawaz and Kumar sat up straight in their chairs and looked trustworthy. Fawaz picked up the prospectus and carried on anyway.

"What we're offering you is a chance to invest in a desalinization project we're financing in Oman. I'm sure you're aware of the value of fresh water in this part of the world. I assure you the return on your investment will be substantial."

"How much?" I asked innocently.

Fawaz looked at Kumar and back at me.

"We estimate the return will be substantially over ten percent."

Kumar looked at Willy. "Of course, we can't promise anything like that."

"Of course not," Willy said, "but the plant you financed in Bahrain two years ago returned twelve percent, so I think that at least ten percent is not outside the ballpark."

"Ballpark?" Kumar asked.

"At least ten percent is a good estimate," Willy explained.

Fawaz handed me the prospectus, and I leafed through it, looking confused. There were lots of pretty pictures.

"You and Mr. Woo can discuss this at your leisure." He almost said, "Don't worry your pretty little head about it."

I usually slug big, brave, strong men like that, but I nodded brightly, and he proceeded. "There are very few shares in this project left, so you will have to decide very shortly."

I squared my shoulders, managing to make the neckline of my sweater dip. "But I'm sure I need to read this brochure," I said bravely.

They both spoke again. I heard "not really necessary" and "just some additional facts" before Willy tanked over them.

"I'm sure you don't need to understand all these details right now, Mrs. Carruthers. Any project financed by the Dubai–Persian bank would be a solid investment, I assure you."

I look chagrined. Kumar gave me another "little darling" look and started to speak.

"I do need to know one thing," I broke in. "I mean, I don't want to be offensive or anything, but you are Iranian." I looked from Fawaz to Kumar.

"Yes, I am Iranian," Fawaz replied. "Mr. Kumar is Pakistani."

"Oh. Well, is it legal for me to buy this stock? I mean, we—the US and the UN—have a lot of sanctions on doing business with Iran."

"That's true, Mrs. Carruthers, but the Dubai–Persian Bank is not an Iranian company. No, it is chartered by the Emirate of Dubai. There is a large Iranian population in Dubai."

"Oh. I didn't know that."

"Yes. Many of us are in exile from our homeland." He looked sad. I looked sad with him. "It is these Iranians who have put their money together to form this bank. We have nothing to do with Iran at all. Our business is with the rest of the world. We scrupulously abide by the sanctions as the emir directs," he finished piously.

Well, he was a banker after all. Willy gathered the reins of the meeting into his hands, and soon the party broke up, with the best of wishes on my part and the desire for my money on theirs. After Willy got me in his car, and we were on our way back to the hotel, he said, "Damned if I ever introduce you to a banker again."

I smiled demurely.

"The ownership of Dubai-Persian is obscure. I think half belongs to the Iranian Revolutionary Guard, but I can't prove it. The other half belongs to a company chartered in the UK. I can't find out any more except for the names of a couple of nominees listed in Companies House filings." Willy looked at me as he stopped for a red light. "I recognized one name from some due diligence I once did on an investment for a client. The investment smelled of a money-laundering scheme, so we dropped it. As far as Dubai-Persian is concerned, let's just say that the emir wouldn't be entirely pleased with the business D-P does."

"Or, as the case may be, would be delighted. Helps to make Dubai the international economic node he's trying so hard to construct."

"Tch. Tch. What a cynical girl you are. Sergei Malyakov has a lot of money deposited there."

"Can you trace some of his business? Transactions with companies in the Caymans or Luxembourg?"

"Or suing somebody in Moldova?" he said with a laugh.

Typical shell company money laundering. "Yes. Like that."

He stopped at the hotel door and prepared to go in with me.

"Don't bother," I said. "You've lost enough time already today."

"I'm chalking it up to entertainment. 'I can just tell when a man's trustworthy by looking at his face.'" He put his head down on the steering wheel and laughed so hard tears came to his eyes.

Chapter 21

NOBODY I RECOGNIZED in the lobby looked at me when I entered. That only meant that I didn't know what this shift looked like. I took the stairs. Getting plenty of stair step exercise these days, but did I want to be alone in an elevator with a guy who does wet work? I heard somebody coming up the stairs behind me; I stepped into the second-floor hall and found the door to the housekeeper's room open, so I ducked inside and stood behind it. A man carrying a tennis racquet opened the door to the fire stairs, walked halfway down the hall, and entered a room on the left. Paranoids not only have enemies, they get a lot of exercise climbing stairs.

The chambermaid had pulled the drapes when she left, so the room was dark and cool. The bed was tempting, very tempting. What had I learned so far? Persian and Pakistani bankers looked just like every other banker I'd ever seen: well-tailored, smooth and trim, with the cold eyes of a shark smelling blood. I changed from the "I am a darling little idiot with a lot of money to invest" wardrobe to my usual "credit cards are paid up but that's all" wardrobe of jeans and a shirt. It's amazing how tiring trying to look rich is.

I had forgotten to ask Willy for somebody at the Diamond Exchange and was getting ready to dial his number when the phone vibrated in my hands. I made a note to call him and answered.

"Nothing in it," a woman with a raspy voice said abruptly. The Duck calling.

"What do you mean?"

"Nothing hinky, just a simple myocardial infarction."

"That doesn't sound simple," I remarked.

"It's not, but it's natural. That's the cause of death. Case closed." She coughed in the phlegmy way of a longtime smoker. "So nothing there, and thank you for nothing."

"Can't hit it out of the ballpark every time," I said.

"What?"

That makes two people who've never heard of the ballpark. "Never mind." Before I could say thanks she cut the call.

Which reminded me. I punched in Raoul's number. "The autopsy was a dead end," I told him. "There was nothing in it. Just a myocardial infarction. How do you cause a myocardial infarction?"

"I don't know. An air bubble in an artery?"

"That would mean using a needle. I just don't see it."

"Maybe it was natural," he said.

"Anything about the diamonds?" I asked.

"The diamonds. Yes. Yesterday evening just before closing time, one of our local bad boys offered me two uncut diamonds—not the sort of young man to have diamonds."

"Payment for something. You think he has all of them?"

"Possibly payment, yes, but he is not clever enough to cause a heart attack in somebody without instructions. If you're talking about foul play, it must have been done just before she got in the taxi."

"Or just after, and the taxi driver either did it or saw who did."

"And just happened to know that she was carrying a bag of diamonds?" Raoul sounded unconvinced.

"And just happened to have a needle with him." I wasn't convinced either.

"How about he was driving the taxi?" I suggested.

He grunted. "And was sent to pick her up, kill her, and retrieve the diamonds. I like that better."

"Occam's razor. It's more economical. Surely he wasn't paid in diamonds."

"Unlikely. For one thing, two diamonds is too much. He probably stole those. We'll never know. He was pulled out of the river this morning. According to the police report, all he had on him was his *carte d'identité.*"

"You think he had all of the diamonds?"

"For a short time, maybe. But they probably intended to do away with him from the beginning."

"Not nice people," I said and hung up.

Who killed Marina? If they knew I was going to Athens, they knew where she was going. Whoever it was had to have contacts in Paris. You can't just fly into town and conjure up somebody to cause a heart attack, but you could send one. The man who followed her onto the plane was in the photographs from the Karl Spiegel lockbox. He worked for Malyakov? For Gringikov? I gave it up. Not enough information.

Phung Nguyen's note was written in the elegant hand still taught in French convent schools. I paused to contemplate Madame and Monsieur attending parents' day. Especially if he had a patch over one eye and a cutlass between his teeth. Probably these days Vietnamese pirates had weapons more modern than cutlasses. RPGs, for instance. The invitation had been for three days ago. I hoped she hadn't taken offense. Several Oriental gentlemen might arrive to wire cement blocks to my ankles if she had. I dialed the number on the note.

"Madame is not in," said the woman who answered the phone in impeccable French, so I switched and asked the question that should never be asked.

"Not at home or not at home to me? I have just returned to Dubai and found her kind invitation to tea."

"Madame is truly not in. She left word that if you called, I should ask you to come at five for drinks. She says she has information."

By that time it was well past five. "Shall I come along now?"

The answer was yes, so I called Atkins and told him to change into clothes fit for interviewing a lady pirate. I showered and changed into navy cotton slacks and a blouse. I met Atkins in the lobby. He was wearing a shirt and khakis and shoes that were actually polished. Since he was with me, I felt safe going down to the parking lot to get my car.

The small Asian woman who answered the door showed us into the same room where I had tea with Madame Nguyen. That evening the pirate lady was dressed in an ivory silk outfit whose flowing lines emphasized her tiny figure. Atkins stopped just short of whistling. She made me feel as if I had just gotten out of a dumpster. Her long black hair was twisted up into a pile on top of her head with decorative pins thrust through it. She looked ready to defend her honor on any subway in the world. She stood on the hearth with a martini in her hand.

"This is my partner, Fred Atkins," I said.

She nodded and gestured for us to sit on the sofa. The Asian woman provided me with a martini.

The pirate girl had Atkins pegged. "Perhaps Mr. Atkins would prefer beer?"

Atkins looked relieved, and the Asian girl left and returned with a bottle of Heineken and a glass. She poured the beer with a practiced hand.

The pirate lady continued to stand, although she had no need to. She would dominate any room just by being in it. She drank quietly, the ticking of the clock very loud in the silence of the room. I composed myself to Asian patience. I looked at Atkins. He drank his beer in Western impatience. Madame Nguyen's only movement was to raise her glass to her scarlet lips. Her long nails matched her lipstick and provided her only other dash of color. We finished our drinks in silence. At last, she put her glass on the mantel and came to sit in the chair beside the sofa. She reached into a box on the coffee table, took out a Russian cigarette, and fitted it into a long jade holder. No, really? The Asian woman reached around her to light the cigarette. I was beginning to feel that I had strayed into a Steve Canyon comic strip. She drew deeply on the cigarette and let the smoke drift from her lips. It was an impressive performance. Two more drags, and she dropped the cigarette into a cloisonné bowl. Patience was about to kill me, and Atkins was about to burst, but I did admire her tactics.

At long last, she broke the silence. "You have been away, Anh said."

I bowed my head. "Yes, for a week. I regret that I could not respond to your kind invitation earlier."

She flicked her long fingernails, and Anh poured each of us another drink and found another beer for Atkins. She sipped hers. I sipped mine. The cold gin against my teeth was quite agreeable, but I was beginning to find her manner a bit much. Western impatience, no doubt.

Atkins moved, and I capitulated. "Your woman said that you have information for me," I said.

She put her glass down with a decisive click. "You are interested in Sergei Malyakov's operation."

I nodded.

"There is beginning to be talk . . ." she paused, "among those of us in a similar line of work." She raised one eyebrow, an eyebrow that had been plucked into perfect shape.

I nodded. I didn't feel like getting into doing eyebrows with her. She was obviously world-class.

"Strange things are happening." She looked sharply at me and then at Atkins. "You know his operation is very well-conducted?"

"So I've heard," I said noncommittally.

Atkins shifted in his chair. He was having trouble staying out of the conversation.

"He takes diamonds for the merchandise he sells to certain groups in Congo?" The eyebrow went up again. I nodded. "The diamonds are taken to Kampala, where they are exchanged for the merchandise. These are then taken to Sharjah?" The eyebrow was going to have muscles of its own pretty soon.

"Where they are taken to the Dubai Diamond Exchange, yes," I said.

She nodded. "Something was wrong with the last arms shipment." A look of dissatisfaction crossed her face. "There was shooting at the compound in Kampala. I cannot determine exactly what happened. The purchasers are army men, you know? Congo army men. They force the villagers to dig the diamonds for them. They are very cruel," she said primly.

Like the Muslim terrorists she sells to are saints?

"They were ready to exchange the diamonds for the arms, which were being unloaded. The boxes were opened as a precaution." She lit another cigarette, this time without the holder or assistance. "It was when they opened the boxes that the shouting began. My friend does not understand the Congolese dialect they were speaking, but the black men were lifting the rifles in the air, dropping the magazines, and throwing the rifles this way and that, snatching the ammunition and then throwing that away too. Malyakov's men were trying to explain, but the blacks would not listen." She paused again for me to nod. I was beginning to feel like a bobble doll.

"The only ammunition in the shipment was 9 mm hollow rounds."

Atkins could restrain himself no longer. "The AK uses 7.62s."

"Yes. The firing pins were missing from some of the rifles too," she said.

"The whole shipment?" I asked.

"No. But there were problems in every crate."

Atkins was looking very interested. "Shooting. I'm not surprised. How many were killed?"

"None. Several of the colonel's men were wounded, but it's what happened to Malyakov's men that is shocking!" This from the daughter of a prominent pirate. "They were taken away to the camp of the blacks. My friend said there were the most horrible screams all night, and then it suddenly went quiet. My friend went to sleep. The next morning the blacks were gone, and where their camp had been there was nothing left but bones. The three Malyakov men had been tortured, killed"—her voice lowered to a whisper—"and eaten. They ate them."

For a moment, I thought I was going to vomit, but I choked it down.

"The cartridge boxes were marked '7.62,'" she said.

"With 9 mills in them?" Atkins asked.

"Yes," she said.

"Sabotage," I said.

She nodded.

Now that Atkins was in the conversation, he stayed in. "The rifles would've been test-fired before they were shipped."

"Mine are. You can't trust the suppliers. They're selling off inventory, and there's no telling why the items are still on the shelf."

Atkins pressed her. "Every piece?"

She shifted in her chair. "Only one or two from each box. It would take too long to test-fire them all."

"So even if they were test-fired, odds are faulty ones could go through," he said. "Belarus and Ukraine don't make rifles without firing pins. This took a lot of time and work to set up."

We looked at each other, and I made a decision. "Can your friend find out where the flight originated? The flight that delivered the guns?"

"I suppose," she said reluctantly. "Why? I don't want him to expose himself."

"True. Not if they're still hungry. Let me know what you hear."

She looked dubious. "What good can that do?"

"It might help me learn who killed Gil Brady," I replied.

The maid showed us out.

"That shipment will finish Malyakov in Congo," I said as I pulled away from the curb.

"And in a bunch of other places too," Atkins agreed. "It took a lot of work to pull that off."

I stopped for a red light and glanced at his face. "Somebody is after Malyakov."

"So who?" he asked dubiously. "It can't be Gringikov. He's dead."

"Maybe, but I saw his office and warehouses in Istanbul being closed down, and his office in Varna was empty and the warehouses cleaned out." I pulled away from the green light as some charmer behind me leaned on his horn.

"How do you know?" he asked.

"I was there."

"Who by?" he asked

"The guy who was doing the Istanbul office is a CIA man."

"How do you know?" he asked.

"Let's just say I know," I replied. "I don't know who cleaned out the Varna office and warehouse. They were empty when I got there."

"So all you've got that says CIA is a guy in Gringikov's office in Istanbul?"

Said like that it didn't sound very convincing, except it was Findley—and somebody sent a couple of goons after me.

"The stuff from the Istanbul warehouse was loaded into a Trans-Caucasus plane at Sabiha Gökçen airport." I pulled into the hotel parking lot. "Trans-Caucasus belongs to Sergei Malyakov."

"You need to tell me what this is all about," Atkins said. "What you've just told me doesn't make any sense to me."

"It doesn't make any sense to me either." I looked at my watch. By then it was nearly midnight. "No wonder it doesn't make any sense. I need some sleep. We'll talk about it in the morning. Meet me for breakfast."

Chapter 22

SO WHO DID the sabotage of Malyakov's shipment bene-
fit? Gringikov. But, as Atkins said, Gringikov was probably
dead. Karl Spiegel who was Gil Brady who worked for
Malyakov who was George Branson who worked for the
CIA, was also dead. And Gringikov's inventory in Varna
and Istanbul had been appropriated. Atkins was right.
None of it made any sense. But Roger Findley was alive.

And Phung Nguyen's story? The creepy feeling returned as I got ready for bed. Cannibalism struck an ugly
chord inside me. I know there are much worse things evil
men could do to the human body before the spirit left it,
but cannibalism still remains taboo.

The next morning Atkins came to the table with
scrambled eggs and bacon and toast on his plate, despite
the wondrous variety of food in the buffet.

"Don't like olives for breakfast?" I said.

"I'm a traditionalist," he said. "What's this about the
CIA being involved in your case? Our case?"

I pushed my empty plate aside and poured myself some
more coffee from the carafe. "I'll start at the beginning."

He spread some grape jelly on a piece of toast. "Always
a good idea."

"Sarcasm will get you nowhere at this time of the day," I said. "About two weeks ago a woman named Cynthia Branson came to my apartment in Paris and asked me to find her husband George, so she could divorce him. I know George. He's a CIA officer. That was not the first time somebody asked me to find George. Just before I quit the Agency, my boss asked me to go to Dubai and find out why George Branson had floated ashore carrying a false passport. At that time, I refused, but I decided to take Cynthia's job."

"Why?" he asked. He signaled the waiter and asked for some ketchup.

Ketchup? "I didn't have anything else to do. I had to get out of the apartment anyway, because it belonged to the Agency. It'd been raining in Paris for two weeks, and the weather would be decent in Dubai. Besides, I had to figure out what to do with the rest of my life."

He put the ketchup on his scrambled eggs.

"Quaint custom."

"In Afghanistan, you put ketchup on everything. Drowned the taste of the sand. Go on."

"I went to Switzerland to do a little skiing, and while I was there somebody wearing a ski mask shot at me."

"Somebody trying to kill you. Who might want to kill you?" He looked at me curiously.

"I thought at first it might be blowback from an operation in Morocco that went south. I had killed some terrorists while escaping from them."

"At first?"

"I decided I didn't need to ski anymore, so I took a milk run to Vienna continuing to Paris. At the same time I bought a ticket to Abu Dhabi. I picked up a tail in Vienna. No, not in Vienna. He was on the flight from Switzerland. Not an Arab, a Caucasian. He might be connected to the Moroccan terrorists, he might not. He followed me to the gate for the Paris flight, and I hoaxed him into getting on it, and then I came to Abu Dhabi."

"Why not Dubai?"

"He might not know I was headed to Dubai, and I wanted to lose him. I went to the consulate and talked to Roger Findley, the guy who had identified George. George had been carrying a passport in the name of Gil Brady, and Gil Brady is the name he is known by in Dubai. Ralph told me that Gil Brady worked for Sergei Malyakov, a local arms dealer, but I made Findley show me his CIA file, and that said he worked for Felix Gringikov, another arms dealer. You know about the conflict between them?"

He nodded. "It's an open secret in town."

"That's about it. Oh, and some guy's been coming to my door just as I'm going to bed. Has happened every night since I've been here."

"That's maybe something I can take care of. Those photographs you had Willoughby identify. Where did you get those?"

"I searched Gil Brady's apartment and found a flash drive there. The photos were on it."

He looked at me curiously. "Searched his apartment?"

"I'm not just a pretty face."

"What else did you find?"

"Nothing," I said.

We had finished the coffee. "Any more coffee and I'm going to turn brown," I said and put my key card down for the waiter to see.

"But that's not all, is it?" He put a key card down for the waiter too.

"You're staying here?"

"It would be hard to have your back staying somewhere else. Where to?"

My room? Outside. "Let's take a walk," I said.

We went out the front door, and I led him across the avenue to the dhow docks, where we sat on a bench and watched guys loading cargo.

"When Ralph first introduced us, you refused to hire me. What changed?" Atkins asked.

"My client was murdered. Went off the balcony of her hotel room."

"And?"

"And I went to Istanbul. That was the last place either Cynthia or the Agency had heard from him."

"And?"

"That's when I found Roger Findley closing up the Gringikov office there. And somebody transferred the contents of Gringikov's warehouse to a Trans-Caucasus airplane."

"So?"

"So Trans-Caucasus belongs to Sergei Malyakov."

He thought about that. "The combination of the CIA and Malyakov made you hire me."

"I felt a draft," I said. "Can you look like an aviation bum?"

"I can look like any kind of bum you want," he said.

"I want you to go to the Sharjah airport and bum around Malyakov's hangar. He's got a lot of airlines but not many planes. See what you can find out."

"Do I want a job?"

"Use your own judgment, but you can't have my back if you're tied down to a job."

"What are you going to do?"

"I'm still trying to get bios of these guys. Gringikov's records seem to have been erased."

"What do you mean?"

"I mean my guy can't find any. A Belarusian that age? He had to have been conscripted into the Soviet army, but there aren't any records. He doesn't exist."

Chapter 23

WE PARTED AT the hotel entrance, Atkins to get his car and me to go upstairs and stick my head in the computer again.

There was a message from Jerry telling me to call him. I checked my watch and called him.

"What have you got?" I asked.

"Hello to you too," Jerry said.

"Next time I'll call collect. Hello, Jerry. How are you, Jerry?"

"I'm fine, but my guys aren't. My contact at Fort Meade is still drilling. No oil."

"That's ridiculous. Gringikov must've been in the army."

"You're right. My guy is very unhappy. Neither one of us can imagine what Gringikov could've done that caused them to destroy his records. There's plenty about Malyakov, though, and a bit of it has to do with Gringikov. You want it?"

"Just the key points. You can e-mail me the rest," I answered.

"Okay. Sergei Alexievitch Malyakov was born in 1965 in Kazakhstan, in Tselinograd, which was the center of

Khrushchev's Virgin Land Program. You remember the Virgin Lands Program?"

"Khrushchev had them plow up the Kazak grasslands and plant wheat. Wasn't a great success."

"Not so much. Malyakov's parents were Russians, sent to Kazakhstan in 1954 at the start of the project. His father was a policeman, and his mother was an agricultural engineer. They married in 1960. Sergei was born 1965, the year after Khrushchev admitted the failure of the Virgin Lands Program, but, of course, the program didn't end just because it was a failure."

"Why should failure have anything to do with it? Do we change our foreign policy just because it's a failure?"

"Don't get me started. Sergei grew up mildly privileged because his parents were Russian, but he wasn't a little Soviet prince getting the best of everything—that status was reserved for the children of high party functionaries. His family did eat meat fairly often and could buy at the party stores, an important privilege in Tselinograd, but Tselinograd was still in the back of beyond, a forgotten town in a forgotten project in a forgotten corner of the Kazakh SSR. The nuclear testing site at Semy and the missile site at the Baikonur Cosmodrome got most of the goodies Moscow was sending to Kazakhstan."

"So Tselinograd is dying on the vine. I suppose there was no hope of the Malyakovs going back to metropolitan Russia?"

"Are you kidding me? You needed the permission of the local party chief just to travel to the next town. You probably needed permission from God to move."

"And a new work unit. You're right. What was I thinking?"

"Anyway, Sergei was conscripted in 1983. He showed a talent for languages and was sent to the Military Institute of Foreign Languages in Moscow, which prepared cadres for military intelligence and the espionage network abroad. When he graduated in 1986, he was posted to Afghanistan."

"Like everybody else," I commented.

"Like everybody else, except that he was trained in Arabic."

"They will do that," I said. "It's so easy to interrogate people who speak Dari and Pashto using Arabic."

"I took the word of a blogger that his unit designation meant that he was in military intelligence. The blogger cheerfully described Soviet interrogators driving nails into the skulls of prisoners to get information."

"If you drove the nail in too far, I would think your results would be sparse."

"Right. Sergei got out of the army in 1989 at the end of the Afghan war and returned to Tselinograd to his parents' home, but there wasn't much to do there, and he missed the bright lights and action of Moscow. After a couple months he even missed Kabul."

"How do you know how he felt?"

"Artistic license. His parents were retired, and they stayed in Kazakhstan when it became independent in 1991, maybe because pensioners had it a little better there than in metropolitan Russia. Sergei was probably bored and restless, so he went back to Moscow and hung out. Now Natalie comes into the picture. You know Natalie?"

"Yes, I do. I saw her covered in diamonds just the other night."

"Sergei met her in Moscow. He didn't have a job, but she did, so he moved in with her and lived on her earnings. He spent his nights drinking in bars where the Afghan vets met to ventilate their anger, until it was late enough for him to go home to the one-room flat where Natalie took her customers."

"This is all very interesting, Jerry, but I said just the highlights."

"Here's where Gringikov comes in. It was at one of those bars where he met Felix Gringikov, who was looking for men of talent who weren't too worried about how they made a ruble, so long as they made one. By that time,

Gringikov had turned his Afghan supply contacts into gold."

"What Afghan supply contacts?"

"I've got my guys looking into Soviet logistics in Afghanistan. Maybe they can find him there, maybe work backward. When the Soviet Union fell apart, Gringikov helped loot the former Soviet arsenals that were lightly guarded and run by men who were either natively corrupt like all good supply sergeants or hadn't been paid in six months and had bills to pay."

"What is in this that had to be expunged?" I asked.

"Besides, why would they bother? We won't know until we find it, will we? Anyway, what he needed was some-body tough who could look smooth and speak something besides Russian and had military contacts Gringikov didn't have. Malyakov still had his GRU contacts. He took to the arms trade from the first. The army had intended him for service in Muslim lands, so he had very good Arabic. Gringikov sent him to Africa to the old Soviet client states, now engulfed in permanent conflict, and his GRU contacts provided him with an entrée to the highest levels. He learned more languages as he went along. Gringikov and Malyakov were complementary, and the two of them seemed to be perfect partners.

"Gringikov sent Malyakov to Dubai, where he and Natalie married in deference to Dubai sensibilities. The Malyakovs were very popular with the Beautiful People who partied in Dubai."

"*That* I can believe," I said.

"Oh?"

"Not relevant. Go on."

"Then something went wrong between the two men, and they ended their partnership in mutual recrimination."

"I can follow them once they get here, Jerry," I said.

"Okay. I'll send you the rest of what I have by e-mail. I've got the guys into logistics in Afghanistan, trying to find Gringikov and working backward. I'll let you know."

I sat back and looked out the window, considering the map of the Black Sea area. Gringikov set up shop in Istanbul. He had warehouses there. Why? It might have been the Bosphorus, but arms went by air, even something as large as an attack helicopter. I couldn't figure it out.

I set out to do my share of the work, searching the local sites. Natalie showed up first. She began with a travel agency, Go Dubai. It did business exclusively with the countries of the former Soviet Union, running package tours that ranged from the ultracheap to the very expensive, as well as private escorted tours. Her prices were competitive, and the cheap tours were a little cheaper than most, with lodging in small hotels in back streets in Deira and Bur Dubai. Willy said that's how she got her 'escorts' into the country. Dubai required tourists to have a sponsor, but the sponsor could be a hotel or travel agency. Tourist visas were good for fifty-five days with one extension of a month allowed. Overstaying a tourist visa was no big deal unless you got in trouble with the police. Natalie could do a good business in tourist visas alone.

Next came her escort service. The service's website was a bit coy, but to a person with any imagination at all, there was no question what services were being offered. Her staff was listed in alphabetical order by first name only, with sexy pictures and sexier specialties—different kinds of massage, singing, and belly dancing, although one could do Arabic poetry. Arabic poetry? Most of them looked Slavic, except for a few exotics—an East Asian, a couple of Turks, and an Egyptian. The Turks and the Egyptian provided the belly dancing; the Egyptian doubled in Arabic poetry. The list of men she employed was shorter, and there was no catalog of masculine specialties, leaving me to wonder which sex was catered for. Probably both. I checked out the Arabic language version of the website. At first, it seemed to be more circumspect, but the list of specialties included words I didn't know and probably would not find in my dictionary. Still, in comparison to some other sites I had viewed while I was monitoring the flesh trade, they were quite discreet, and there were no children, at least on the website, even on the Arabic version.

Madame Malyakov had opened the plane rental business about the time Gringikov disappeared, and she owned more than just a couple of clapped-out Ilyushins. That's what she started with, but her business expanded rapidly, and these days she had an executive jet as well as the large cargo planes at Sharjah airport. Last October, she announced the beginning of helicopter taxi services in the Emirates to begin January the first. The two Bell 206B3 Jet Ranger helicopters were presumably for that. Where had she gotten the capital for such a large inventory? And how could the Soviets have kept all of that capitalist energy suppressed for so long?

Malyakov himself appeared shortly after Natalie. At first, his office was at the Sharjah airport in the same building as Natalie's aircraft rental business, but when Gringikov disappeared, he moved his headquarters to the new Gold and Diamond Exchange. His business expanded exponentially after Gringikov disappeared, and soon the only name on the glass doors was Malyakov Enterprises. Trans-Caucasus was only one of his airlines. As of the previous week, he had seven airlines registered in four different countries. They had more anonymous names, like KBA and RER. Anything brief enough to be painted out on short notice. All of this was in the public domain. I wondered what else there was in the Agency files. I didn't like having to work the streets without my usual resources.

The articles about Malyakov's businesses had begun to appear on the Internet about two years before Gringikov disappeared. What was it that Willy had said? Malyakov had been a partner of Gringikov's, but they had fallen out. What caused the split?

It was getting late, and I hadn't heard anything from Atkins. I picked up my phone and realized I didn't have his number. Did he have mine? This working with a partner was more complicated than I had expected. I had not only to keep up with myself, I had to keep up with Atkins. Where was he?

Chapter 24

BY SEVEN O'CLOCK I still hadn't heard from Atkins. I debated going downstairs for dinner but decided on room service. Room service is one of the chief delights of staying at a hotel. I ordered a bacon, lettuce, and tomato club. You don't get club sandwiches in Paris. While I was waiting for it, I looked at the menu to see what other kinds of American-friendly foods were on it. Maybe I could catch up on a number of culinary deficiencies. Mac 'n cheese. Hmmm.

After I finished eating, I still hadn't heard from Atkins. We were going to have to talk about reporting. Then I remembered he probably didn't have my phone number, either. Another thing to deal with. Working alone is so much easier. I had taken off my blouse and the gun and holster when somebody rapped on the door. Out of the peephole I saw two men who had "cop" written all over them. It doesn't matter what race, creed, or color they are, it shows. The set of the shoulders? The projected authority? I went hurriedly to shove the gun and holster between the mattress and springs on the bed. I put the knife in the desk drawer. He pounded on the door again. I opened it, leaving the safety latch on. One guy was tall with a mustache and thin beard framing fleshy lips. The other, like

168

Jack Spratt's wife, was chubby with a dimple in his chin. Plainer clothes I have never seen.

"Yes?" I asked.

"Ms. Carruthers?" the chubby one said. Funny, I would've said it was the tall one who had rank.

"Yes?" I repeated.

"You need to come with us."

Hunh? "Why?"

"The inspector wants to see you."

"May I see your credentials, please?" I asked pleasantly.

The tall one showed me creds that looked official, but what do I know? Could the guys who were following me put up a pair of guys with authentic-looking Dubai police credentials? Will the sun come up in the morning?

"What's this all about, officer?" I asked of a man whose credentials said he was a detective.

He put a little steel in his voice. "You need to come with us," he said and shifted his weight.

Would the hotel charge me for a replacement of the door?

"Just a minute," I said. "I'll have to get dressed." I shut the door and put my blouse back on. I picked up my pack and went out the door with it over my left shoulder.

The tall one held his hand out for the pack. It would do me no good to refuse. In fact, it could do me a great deal of harm, so I handed it to him to search. Satisfied, he handed it back to me. The three of us went down in the elevator, the two cops flanking me. We turned heads as we marched through the lobby and out the door the same way. At least the car lacked a Plexiglas shield between the front and the back seats or a bar to handcuff me to.

We drove back toward the airport to the police head-quarters. It was a new building, brightly lighted, all blue glass and white concrete, but it was very hard to read. Towers and wings, curves and squares, it was plainly Architecture. I wondered if function followed the form. I have often observed that Architecture doesn't perform at all well in the real world, being a Concept rather than a place where people carried out their daily activities. It was a good thing that I had the detectives to guide me, for the architect had squared the circle with his towers. The major form was a circle, which we went around. At intervals in our journey, we saw halls leading to towers and to whole wings, but after a long walk, we reached a simple set of rooms. The man behind the desk was a cliché Arab, thin and light beige with the hawk nose. He turned some papers over on his desk and nodded to the detectives, gesturing me to sit down. He studied me. I studied him back and wondered just how nervous I should be.

"And what did the CIA send you to Dubai to do this this time, Ms. Carruthers?" he asked.

No "hi, I'm Inspector Whatsis," just right to the bare knuckles. I should be either very nervous or not nervous at all, but innocent people are often nervous under police interrogation. Did not being nervous mean I was guilty?

"I'm not employed by the CIA."

He looked at a paper on his desk. "You have been employed by the CIA since August 2000."

"Let me rephrase my answer. I am no longer employed by the CIA."

"What has the CIA sent you to Dubai to do?"

Men never listen. "You need new sources. I have not been employed by the CIA for six months. I am here in Dubai on vacation to escape the Paris rains while I decide what to do next with my life. A friend in Boston wants me to come to work with him in his IT business, but I'm rather tired of computers."

"You've been asking questions."

I nodded. "I have, yes. A colleague of mine was found dead on Russian Beach with a bullet in his head after having been missing for almost two years. I admit to certain curiosity in the matter."

"That is a police matter, Ms. Carruthers." He spoke as one speaks to a child. Did he really think that tone would impress a CIA officer? Or even a CIA analyst? It's because I'm a woman. Again. Should I give him a little woman routine? I could do it, but I am so damn sick and tired of being the little woman in Arab lands. It's a big part of the reason I quit the Agency. I'll have to find something to do with the rest of my life that doesn't involve Arabs. But if I did, then what would I do with my master's in Islamic civilization?

"I'm sure it is. And what have you determined? Do you know who killed him?" I asked.

"It is an ongoing police investigation," he replied stiffly. "I am not at liberty to discuss it."

"With civilians in general or me in particular?" You're going too far, I told myself. I so often do.

"You have no authority to investigate this killing, Ms. Carruthers," he snapped.

I might as well go all the way. "This is a killing? Do the Dubai police often classify the death of a man shot in the back of the head as a 'killing?'"

His face darkened. "I have the authority to deport you," he threatened.

I nodded. "I'm sure you do."

He slapped his hand on his desk. "And I will if you don't stop asking questions!"

"Yes," I said. He didn't ask if that meant that I would obey him or just that I recognized he could throw me out of the Emirate. I wondered if he threw me out of Dubai whether I could work out of Abu Dhabi. I mean, what could he do? Station a police cruiser at the border?

He left the room abruptly, shutting the door behind himself. I sat there quietly for five minutes, but then I began to get antsy. I looked at the papers on his desk. I wondered what they were and was leaning over the desk reaching for them when he returned. I sat back down. Had he seen me? He picked up the receiver of an old-fashioned rotary telephone and dialed two numbers.

"That will be all," he snapped. "You'll find life more comfortable here if you do as I say and leave this case alone. Our jails are not so nice for women. Take Ms. Carruthers to her hotel," he said when my escorts returned.

Another person trying to pull me off the case. It was getting monotonous, interesting but monotonous, and, as Sidney said, probably dangerous. At least nobody had shot at me since I'd been in Dubai, which was a plus.

On the way out of the door I saw "MUR" painted on the window, but I never did learn his name.

We threaded our way back around the building, once again experiencing Architecture over Man. It wasn't far back to the hotel. Instead of just letting me out at the hotel door, they insisted on escorting me through the lobby, where another batch of guests could watch. I suppose I should be glad I wasn't in cuffs. Maybe I should sell tickets. They delivered me to the door of my room. They should have waited. Then they'd have seen the mess the searchers left. They didn't care if I saw them following me, and they didn't care if I knew they searched my room. It looked like the aftermath of a tsunami. Clothes thrown all over the floor, and the sheets and blanket ripped off of the mattress, which had been pulled off of the springs. At least they hadn't broken anything. They could've made a right old mess if they had stirred the cosmetics around on the mattress, I thought as I returned clothes to the closet and the cosmetics to bathroom shelf. At least I can return the room to normal and not have to pay damages to the hotel. Suddenly, I remembered the laptop and ran to it in panic. I opened it and hit a key. They had booted it but found most of my files encrypted. Roger Findley would be able to read them, but only if he had my key code, which wasn't written down anywhere. After I left the Agency, they stopped bugging me about changing my key code, which was only one of the blessings of returning to the real world.

Who had done this? I wondered, as I heaved the mattress back on the springs. Who told the police I was in town and asking questions? It was not necessarily Roger who ratted me out to the police, although he was the best bet. I suppose the police could've found out all by themselves. They keep a pretty close eye on the tourists and everybody else. Who else could be? Inspector MUR had kept me a suspiciously short period of time in his office, just long enough for somebody to trash my room, but why should he bother? He could send his people in anytime he wanted to. The easy answer was that somebody was sending me a message, but I didn't need a message, did I? I knew I was being watched, and everybody kept telling me to leave the case alone. So many people, in fact, that it made me wonder. I had finished tucking in the blanket and was throwing the quilt over the remade bed when I realized something.

My gun was gone and so was the holster.

Chapter 25

MY FIRST THOUGHT was damn, I had that holster made in Morocco. My second thought was all I have left is the knife. My third was I've got to get another gun.

Sinbad. How quickly could he get me a gun? I put on jeans and a dark sweater. I took the knife from the desk drawer, resisted the urge to carry it in my hand, and strapped it to my leg. I took the service elevator down to the ground floor. It made a change from the fire stairs.

The kitchen was still noisy, but everybody was so preoccupied that I could slip by without being noticed. There were a couple of guys in cooking garb smoking cigarettes on the loading dock and talking football. They spared me a brief look before going back to discussing Dubai's need for a striker. The surest way to get noticed is to creep out looking suspicious, so I strode out of the alley as if I had every right to and crossed the street at the usual risk of life and limb.

The dhow dock was dark, with pools of light illuminating piles of cargo still being loaded. I walked in the shadows along the far edge, but long before I reached Sinbad's boat, I was in the dark, the quarter moon giving me only enough light to keep from falling down but not enough to see the three guys before they jumped me. Startled, I shook myself loose and knelt down, flicked the snap holding my knife in the scabbard on my leg, and came up with it held low and thrusting. It surprised them into backing away a little. I swiped it in a wide arc, and they jumped back in respect. Theoretically, I know how to fight with a knife. Theoretically, I know how to build an atomic bomb. The face of my instructor, Georgi, flashed through my mind before I shut it down. Thinking about anything but fighting is a sure way to get yourself killed. We circled, one after another of them coming up and trying to grab me. I slashed at the first one and heard him hiss. A hit. They stayed back after that, and the dance went on, the men keeping just out of my reach, me keeping them there. All they had to do was wait until I tired, which I was doing rapidly. I took three sudden steps forward and kicked one of the men into the creek. That didn't improve matters any. It left me with one in front and one in back, and my arm getting very heavy. One more turn of the wheel and one of them would have me.

I heard a man say, "Your back."

I was surprised into dropping my knife, and the guy in front grabbed something. It snapped as I dove into the creek to escape. I swam out toward the middle and saw first one and then the other of the remaining men tossed into the creek. I swam back to the dock, and my rescuer reached down for my arm and pulled me up.

"I contracted to take orders from a woman, not a fool," Atkins snapped.

I wrung as much water as I could from my hair and stood there dripping.

"Partners work together," he snarled as he pulled me along the dock. "One of them does not go waltzing along a dark dock asking to be killed."

"I had no idea where you were. Partners report to each other," I retorted. "Somebody stole my gun. I was on my way to Sinbad's to get another."

"In the dark."

"In the dark. All I have is a knife. I don't have that anymore, do I? I dropped it when you came up."

He pulled me across the street to our hotel, up the service elevator, and into my room.

"Get out of that stuff and into the shower," he ordered, and I obeyed. He was right, damn him. I had walked along that dock as if I were strolling along a Paris boulevard. I was shivering, and it wasn't just from my swim in the creek. The hot shower didn't stop it, and the terrycloth robe the hotel provided didn't either. I went back into the bedroom drying my hair and shivering. He handed me a glass.

"Here, drink this," he commanded.

I did. It was brandy. It burned all the way down, and I felt a little better. He pulled back the covers of the bed.

"Get in," he ordered.

I got in the bed and continued shivering. He muttered a string of curses, kicked off his boots, and got in beside me, putting his arms around me. After a while my shivering stopped, and I went to sleep. I half woke in a man's arms. *Kemal's alive.* I pressed myself into his body and felt a response. Sleepily we began to make love. Suddenly, I woke up all the way. There was something wrong. Wrong.

"No!" I said. "No. Get out! Get out of my bed!"

He turned the light on. It was Atkins, and he was furious. He buttoned his jeans, put on his boots, and went out the door, carefully refraining from slamming it. Kemal was dead. I felt for his pearl to give me comfort. It was gone, lost in the fight. The last vestige of him was gone. I got into a hot shower and scrubbed myself raw, my tears mingling with the water. Then I got back in bed and curled up in a ball. There was a lingering taste of cinnamon on my lips, but my heart was as cold as the grave.

It wasn't a good night or a short one.

Atkins was there when I went down for breakfast. He looked me up and down, his eyes cold. I knew I had dark circles under my eyes. I had seen them in the mirror and the tear marks that makeup wouldn't cover as well. The waiter brought coffee, and I drank some.

I said coldly over my cup, "This is only going to work if you stay out of my pants."

His look was even colder. "It seemed to me that you were trying to get into mine."

My face flamed, and I looked down. "I thought you were somebody else." I looked up. "He's dead. For a moment I thought he wasn't." I shoved the cup away. "Come upstairs when you're finished."

Atkins' face was still stony when he came to the room. I handed him a stack of bills.

"Two weeks' pay in lieu of notice."

He put the bills on the desk. "You're firing me."

"This is not working, Marlboro. It's not going to work. I work—"

"Yeah, I know. You work alone. The fact that you nearly got yourself killed last night doesn't mean anything to you?"

"Marlboro, I have the right to get myself killed. I don't have the right to get anybody else killed."

He slammed his hand on the desk. "I can take care of myself, thank you very much. It would work if you weren't so damn stubborn."

I turned away and walked to the window, staring blindly at the creek. *They won't revoke your manhood if you have backup*, I heard Kemal say, and I saw him bleeding out in the sand. I rested my forehead on the cool window, trying to hold the tears at bay. You always do this, I said to myself fiercely. If there's a man anywhere near it you screw it up. My eyes were wet when I turned back to Atkins.

"I can't do this. I can't."

He was leaning against the door with his arms crossed. "You can jump off mountains and shoot bad guys, but you can't do something so simple as share the work? It's easy.

You do the thinking, and I do the heavy lifting. Twice as much work in half the time."

"Marlboro, you're fired. Now take the money and get the hell out of here," I said.

He went to the bed and lay back on it with his hands behind his head. "You haven't heard my report on the Malyakovs yet. You paid for it. You might as well listen to it."

I was either going to have to listen to him or club him and drag him into the hall, so I pulled the desk chair over to the end of the bed and put my feet up. "Go on then."

"I drove over to Sharjah to the airport and found the hangar that belongs to the Malyakovs. It's good-sized, with a Gulfstream and a couple of Ilyushins with no identification numbers parked on the pad."

"No helicopters?" I asked.

"No. Three guys who looked like mechanics were inside."

"Russians?" I asked.

"Looked like it. Slav anyway. One of them was working on an engine that had been pulled from one of the Ilyushins. I walked in, and nobody looked up. Not much going on, but then a Suit arrived, and everybody got busy. The Suit walked around jawing at them, and I went for the car. When the Suit left, I followed him. He led me to the Luxe Hotel on Jumeirah Beach. I lost him while I was parking, but I went into the hotel and looked around. The hotels on Jumeirah Beach go from Holiday Inn clones to those with suites costing five thousand a night. The Luxe tops them all. You can easily spend ten thousand a night there."

"Dubai often makes me want to throw up. That's one of the reasons why."

"Yeah, in contrast, you want to see your average village in Afghanistan. The conference rooms at the Luxe have meetings going on, but nothing is listed on the boards. It's

like they're private, you know? I hung out in the hall leading to the rooms—"

"They didn't see you?" I asked anxiously.

He gave me a "what do you take me for, a fool?" look.
"All the people going in were guys except for one woman.
Guys in late forties, early fifties. Suits hand-tailored but a
bit flashy, you know."

"Large diamond pinky rings?"

"Yeah. It's like they're from a gangster movie."

"Maybe they are. The woman?"

"Dumpy, gray suit off the rack, short cropped hair.
Looks like a dyke. Must be important, though, because the
men were crowding around her, and it wasn't for her sex
appeal. I hung around until they came out for a break, cart
with coffee and pastries, you know? The Suit from the
Malyakov hangar was there. Let me see those pictures you
showed Willoughby yesterday."

I brought them up on the phone, and he flipped
through them.

"This one," he showed me, "this one is the Suit."

"So one of Malyakov's men was at the meeting.
Crooks? Mafiya? They were Russian?" I asked.

"Looked it. Not just one of Malyakov's men. There
were a couple of the odds and ends boys there too. Interesting, no? You've been thinking CIA. How about the
Russian mafiya instead?"

"The Russian mafiya can be having a meeting here
without any connection with Malyakov," I said.

"True, but one of his men is sure connected. There's
going to be a big banquet tonight. I thought we might have
a look at it. Have dinner in the restaurant. They have a
famous chef, so we could look like foodie tourists."

"And we get lost and wander into the banquet room?"

"Sarcasm doesn't become you. The hotel's built in a
square around a what-do-you-call-it?"

"Atrium?"

"Yeah. The restaurant's across from the banquet room. If we got a table up front we'd have a good view of the people going in."

"You're talking as if we are a 'we.'"

He got up from the bed and walked to the door. "We are," he said and started out the door.

"Hey," I said just before he shut the door, "I need a gun and holster."

"What do you want?" he asked.

"A Glock 26."

"Not a 19?"

"The 19 is too big for my hand," I replied.

"I didn't know you were delicate."

"My mind is indelicate. The rest of me is delicate. I need it soonest."

"You're in your hotel room. You've got enemies?"

"Just get the gun," I said.

Chapter 26

I BOOTED THE computer to have a look at the rest of the Dubai Malyakov files. There was a website for Malyakov Enterprises, just a homepage with Dubai high-rises for a header and the Diamond Exchange address.

Jerry said Malyakov didn't have very many planes. Did he rent them from Natalie? How many planes did she have?

I was getting ready to shower when Atkins returned with a gun for me.

"How much?" I asked.

"Don't worry. I'll put it on my expense account."

Another complication of having a partner. Expense accounts.

When I walked into the lobby at eight o'clock wearing a black dress a little low in front and a little slit on the side, Atkins pretended to stare.

"Somebody has kidnapped my boss."

"And left an android in her place. You clean up pretty good yourself."

He did look pretty good in a blue blazer, khakis, and a white shirt.

"A bra holster?" he asked.

"I want a Glock in my décolletage?"

"Might make hugging interesting. Then what?"

I handed him my clutch bag, and he almost dropped it, because he wasn't expecting weight.

"Slip your hand inside right end," I told him.

He did and felt the gun butt.

"You pull down on the clasp and the purse falls away. Bring your other hand up and bingo."

"Cool," he said.

He offered me his arm.

"Somebody stole my partner," I said in surprise.

"And left an android in his place," he said.

We debated whether to take a cab or the car and decided to take the car. You never could tell. The Luxe Hotel, like all Dubai hotels, had been designed by an architect to be Distinctive, but once inside you found that it was just a hotel. It was built around an atrium that reached up twenty-five stories to a glass roof. The balconies on each floor were constructed in a series of interlocking half circles. Our restaurant was on the fourth floor, facing the banquet room across the atrium. The tables were spaced far enough away from each other to provide some privacy. White cloths covered the tables, and the napkins were folded into the shape of swans. The cutlery was heavy, and the dishes were in the most up-to-date square shape. A row of crystal wine glasses stood at attention above the plates. Little posies in crystal vases completed the service.

We had a table just at the balcony's edge, which provided us with a good view of people standing around the banquet room doors. I exclaimed over the architecture and raised my cell phone as if to photograph the atrium. The guests were too far away to get decent pictures of them.

"The women came with them?" I asked.

"Most of them. The trophy wives and mistresses anyway. The others are hookers from Madame Malyakov's stable. Classy, are they? Hard to tell from the trophy wives."

"She owns an escort service. They're probably expensive enough to be called escorts."

"Escorts, call girls, hookers, whatever. They sit on the beach all day, rubbing suntan lotion on themselves, drinking drinks with umbrellas in them, and eyeing the local studs. I let them eye me for a while, but I thought I'd better talk to you about it first."

"Playing games with a woman belonging to a mafiya don sounds at least as dangerous as driving past an IED," I commented.

"At least. Maybe more. With luck you can escape the IED."

The couples standing around the door parted like the Red Sea at the arrival of the woman Atkins described as dumpy. She was all of that, dressed in a dark purple velvet evening gown. Even at a distance it looked old, as if the velvet might be rubbed thin in spots. The chatting couples followed her into the banquet room, and the waiter closed the doors.

The dinner from the celebrity chef's kitchen was not as good as the one I had bought Willy, and it cost three times as much.

"I hope this gets us something," I said. "I'm going to have to sell a couple of diamonds to pay for it."

"Diamonds?" Atkins asked.

I signed the check. "Let's go downstairs and have our coffee in the lobby. Not all of those people are staying at the Luxe."

"Diamonds," Atkins said.

We went down to the lobby and ordered coffee and brandy.

"Diamonds," Atkins said for the third time.

"I found a bag of uncut diamonds in Gil Brady's safe," I said.

Just then a number of people from the banquet got out of the elevator. The first group from the elevators included the Dumpy Lady. It looked as if she was leaving the hotel.

"Let's get a taxi, Marlboro, so we can follow her," I said.

We got a taxi, and I got him to lurk until the Dumpy Lady got into a taxi of her own.

"Follow that taxi," I said in Arabic and handed the driver two hundred dirhams. He looked at me in the rear-view mirror and pulled up behind her taxi. We followed her along Jumeirah Road, across the creek to a hotel much more modest than the Luxe, more in my price range. I paid off our taxi, and we followed her into the hotel lobby, where she met a man. I turned on my heel.

"Let's get out of here," I said and walked back outside, where I got the doorman to get us a taxi.

"What the—" he said.

"The Luxe Hotel," I ordered the taxi driver. "I know that guy. He's a friend of Malyakov's. He's Saudi and is married to a woman from the Bin Laden clan. The Dumpy Lady keeps interesting company," I remarked. "We might as well pick up the car and go home."

"So where does that put us?" he asked.

"Not now," I said.

We retrieved the car, and I let him drive.

"I see you're delicate," he said and grinned his lopsided grin.

"We're in Arab country. Guys do the driving."

"When you want me to. So we've got two gunrunning organizations, probably the CIA, possibly the Russian mafiya, and now a connection of Osama Bin Laden's. How cool is that?"

The next morning, I told Atkins, "I need you to go to the Dumpy Lady's hotel and get a picture of her so I can send it to Jerry for identification."

"And I need to know about the diamonds in Gil Brady flat," he said.

"Later," I said.

"You keep saying that. I need to know what's going on. Diamonds are serious."

"Two sets of gunrunners, the CIA, and the Russian mafiya aren't serious?" I asked. "I need that picture. And your phone number."

He looked mutinous, but he gave me his phone number. I gave him mine, and we put each other on speed dial. I booted the computer and found a message from Jerry.

"Lee, I found something in the Minsk juvie records about Gringikov," he wrote. "Just a couple of arrests for defacing public property. But, get this, he wasn't living with his mother. The woman who bailed him out was a schoolteacher, name and address supplied. My guy is working it."

Suddenly, I remembered the medal. I slapped myself on the forehead. I answered his message. "Jerry, I'm a fool. I have a medal that belonged to Gringikov. His wife said it is something associated with his old army unit. I'm attaching photographs."

How could I have forgotten the medal? I asked myself as I got it out of the safe. I photographed it front and rear and sent the photos to Jerry. I also asked him to search Russian mafiya activities in Dubai.

Chapter 27

I GOT OUT the Dubai phone numbers from Gringikov's address book. Martin Worth, with a bonded warehouse at the new airport at Jebel Ali, and Wilson James, the whiskey importer, had been at Malyakov's table at the Berlin. Jason Hildebrand, the German-Balkan Insurance Company broker, who had an office in Downtown Jebel Ali, looked interesting too.

There were a bunch of numbers without names. I really didn't want to call them. What I needed was an upside down telephone directory. I checked the Internet and, after a little bit of illegal poking around, found one. Maybe my CIA skill set would have a civilian use after all.

Most of them were cell phone numbers with names that didn't mean anything to me. When I searched the owners' names I found that almost half of them were men with businesses in the old quarter. The other half belonged to restaurants, bars, and other businesses around town. I sat back in my chair, looking out the window toward Bur Dubai. All of the phone numbers belonged to businesses, and I recognized one of them. It belonged to Ralph Prince. Why had he not told me he had a connection with Felix Gringikov? I called him.

"Ralph, why is your phone number in Felix Gringikov's address book?"

"I don't know, unless—" he paused. "You know, about a year ago some guys came in and offered to protect me from evildoers if I paid them a weekly fee."

"Who were they?" I asked. "Did you recognize any of them?"

"I don't know. Not Arabs. Looked Slavic, maybe Russian."

"What did you say?"

"Told them to fuck off, you should pardon the expression. A little while later, there was a fire in the kitchen, just a small one, easy to put out. Then the guys came back and asked me how I liked their demonstration."

"What did you say?"

"Nothing. I just went after them with the baseball bat I keep under the bar to pacify overactive customers."

"Did they come back?"

"Yeah. That time I used the bat. I broke the elbow of one and the kneecap of the other. I went armed for a while and offered to stick the gun up the nose of the next guy who came by. After a while they gave up."

I thought for a minute. "Giving up doesn't sound like protection guys."

"I watch myself, and my bartender watches my back. Why do you want to know?"

"I've got a bunch of unidentified phone numbers. I wonder if they've all been hit."

"Somebody is running a protection racket in town. I can't be the only person they've visited. There have been a couple of suspicious fires in Bur Dubai. You know what a fire will do in there. Take out the whole souk."

"Police ever catch anybody?" I asked.

"Not so's you could notice. I think everybody else paid up."

Which, from the number of businesses, would bring in a pretty penny, especially since Gringikov's phone numbers probably represented just a portion of the businesses hit.

Atkins sent me a photograph of the Dumpy Lady, and I told him to come in. I sent the photograph to Jerry for identification. When Atkins came in, I showed him the list of Dubai cell phone numbers from Gringikov's address book.

"Ralph Prince was on the list too. He tells me that somebody tried to sell him protection a while back," I said.

"Why were these phone numbers in Felix Gringikov's address book?" Atkins asked. "An arms dealer? It sounds more like something the mafiya would do."

"I don't know. Was Gringikov mafiya? That makes no sense," I said.

"Maybe it does if Gringikov was trying to destroy Malyakov."

"That makes no sense, either. What has one thing got to do with the other? Why don't you go and talk to these guys? See what you can find out," I said.

"Right," he said. "You're going to tell me about the diamonds."

"Later," I replied.

"You keep saying that," he said. "You're going to have to tell me and soon," he said over his shoulder as he went out the door.

The ringtone on my iPhone produced Willy.

"She's out of town. Don't know when she'll be back."

"She?"

"The diamond expert. She's Lebanese. Her father knew more about diamonds than anybody else in the Levant. He had no son, so he trained his daughter."

"Sexist remark? See what you can set up, will you?"

"Roger."

"Oh, God, Willy, stop it. The Russian mafiya seriously strains my sense of humor," I said.

"The Russian mafiya?"

I cut the call and looked at my watch. I had time to run out to Jebel Ali and have a look at that insurance agent before I checked out Sally at the Caspian Lounge in Jumeirah.

Jason Hildebrand's office was in Downtown Jebel Ali, the suburb being built near the new port. It was another assortment of glass high-rises designed for commercial and residential use, mostly for firms and people who had business at the port. Hildebrand was in a round twenty-story architect's delight, a good address, as they say in France, but good only on the first few floors. The shops on the ground floor didn't look like they were doing any business. The building directory next to the elevator listed very few businesses in the twenty stories. I wondered if this was one of the many money-laundering buildings in town. Hildebrand's German-Balkan Insurance Brokerage was on the top floor in one of a warren of small offices. The building was new, but it was even now sinking into sleaze, the letters on the German-Balkan door were already tarnishing. I entered the office to find a room about the size of half a tennis court, its unpainted sheetrock walls covered with curling rate charts and diagrams of loading containers. A gray metal desk was squeezed up against the only window in the room, its chair inhabited by a gray man in a gray suit and long-sleeved white shirt. His tie had narrow gray stripes. He raised his head to look at me though gray eyes cold as chips of rotten ice.

"Jason Hildebrand?" I asked.

He nodded and passed a hand over the thin strands of lifeless gray hair he had combed over the top of his head in a vain attempt to hide his baldness.

"A friend said you might be able to help me."

He looked at me as if he wasn't used to having customers walk in. I leaned against the door. He didn't have a visitor's chair.

"To insure a cargo," I added.

"What kind of a cargo?" he asked.

"Medical supplies," I answered.

Hildebrand went on looking at me. Maybe he wasn't used to having customers, period.

"Destination?"

I looked into his cold eyes. "Congo," I said.

His gaze shifted to a spot to the left of the door.

A little late, he said, "What friend?"

"Felix Gringikov."

His face a mask of fear, he stood up and pointed a shaking finger to the door.

"Get out!" he shouted. "Get out!"

He lunged forward. I could smell his sour breath as I pulled the door open and escaped. He didn't follow me into the hall, and my breathing gradually returned to normal as the elevator descended. The name Hildebrand sounded German. Had he sounded German? I couldn't tell. I should've checked out the company before coming. Gringikov's name certainly set him off. Gringikov's address book was proving to be a surprising treasure trove.

Chapter 28

BEFORE I DROVE back to Jumeirah, I called Atkins, but it went straight to voice mail again. I left a message saying that I was going to the Caspian Lounge, and that he should meet me back at the hotel.

It was early, but to a Russian it was never too early for vodka and caviar. Admittedly, the DJ hadn't arrived yet, but that meant that I could hear the clink of the neck of the vodka bottle on the lip of the glass as sunburned Russians with well-stuffed wallets anticipated sundown by several hours. I ordered the one moderately priced vodka in the house. Since Gil Brady's diamonds were paying the tab, I also ordered a moderately priced caviar. I sipped and munched and looked around. The waitresses' breasts were fighting to escape pastel tank tops and the denim of their short shorts looked fatigued from stress. Their hair, universally blonde with dark roots, was universally frizzy, either from exposure to the sun or overexposure to a peroxide bottle. Then a little blonde cheerleader strolled in and electrified the room. She was about five foot two, but her eyes were brown. Stripped, she probably weighed a hundred pounds, and I was willing to bet that stripped, she was still a blonde. She made the rounds of the tables, shaking hands, pouring vodka, spooning caviar on a biscuit and popping it into a patron's mouth. Her mastery of the room convinced me that she was more than another waitress. She was about to bypass my table when I gestured to her.

"Sally?" I asked.

"Who wants to know?" she asked in a no-nonsense voice. I put her from either South Carolina or Louisiana.

I put the napkin with the lip print on the table. She shot a hard look at me.

"I give out a lot of those," she said. "Where'd you get it?"

"Gil Brady said if I ever needed to get in touch with him in a hurry I should contact you. I need to get in touch with him," I said.

"Gil's dead," she said flatly.

Across the way, a bunch of sunburned men with rolls of stomach fat spilling over their belts began to beat on the table with their glasses. "S-A-L-L-Y!" they shouted and pounded harder.

"I've got to go," she said hurriedly and went over to the shouting men, uttering soothing phrases and pouring more vodka. She whispered into the ear of a bald man with more rolls of fat on his body than anybody else and nodded toward me. He turned to look at me and shook his head. He didn't know me, but I knew him. He'd been at the banquet the night before, right up close to the Dumpy Lady.

Sally returned. "Let's go upstairs." She waved at one of the waitresses, who took over hostessing. The clientele cheered. Sally led me through the swinging doors to the back and up a flight of stairs to an apartment.

"Live over the shop." She grinned. "Nobody but an Arab sheikh can afford to rent an apartment in Dubai."

"I'll bet." I refused more vodka. The absence of juniper berries had left my taste buds feeling unfulfilled. I did accept water and, since it was Dubai, the water was Perrier.

"Why do you want to know about Gil?" she asked when we were seated.

"I used to know him."

She looked sharply at me.

"Not like that. We went to school together." Well, we did, sort of. "I lost touch with him. I didn't even know he was in Dubai. An old friend told me he had been murdered. I couldn't believe it. The friend said you knew Gil, so I thought I'd come to see what you know about it."

"Where'd you get the napkin?" she demanded again.

"The friend gave it to me. He said you and Gil had a thing," I replied.

That seemed to satisfy her. "Gil was a strange guy," she said thoughtfully.

"When was the last time you saw him?"

"I don't know. Maybe a month or so? He came and went, you know? I mean, we weren't together or anything like that, but he'd come around after the bar was closed." She pointed to the door in the far wall. "There's an outside staircase."

"Did he stay?" I asked.

"Usually, but sometimes not. Sometimes, he was distracted, like, and then he wouldn't stay. That was OK. He wasn't any fun when he was like that anyway."

"Worried?" I asked.

She thought about it. "Not really." She hesitated. "Just like he had something on his mind, you know."

"Did he ever talk about his work?"

"No," she said promptly. "He said he wanted it to be just us." She looked off into the distance. "He traveled a lot, you know. Sometimes he would come here straight from the airport, the tags still on his suitcase."

"Do you know of anybody who would want to hurt him?"

She shook her head. "That's what makes it so awful." Her eyes teared. "He was such a sweet guy. I can't think of anybody."

"Was he different in any way the last time you saw him?"

"You're going to find out who killed him?"

"If I can," I answered.

"Maybe I should tell you, then. Yeah. He was different. Moody, like, and nervous. He left something with me. Said to hold onto it until he came back."

I sat very still. "What is it?"

"A box."

"Maybe it will help me find his killer."

She rubbed her temples as if she were getting a headache. "I don't know. Maybe." She thought about it, and I saw her make a decision. She left the room and returned with a package the size of a couple of packs of cigarettes wrapped in brown paper and taped.

"What's in it?" I asked.

"I don't know," she flared. "It was Gil's." I stood up, and she thrust it at me.

"Get it out of here."

I trotted down the stairs and was turning the corner to the parking lot when I saw two men get out of a black SUV and walk toward the bar. I backed up abruptly. It was my two minders from the other night. I was lucky to have missed them. I knew they did work for the Russians. Had they seen me?

Shaken, I called Atkins, and it went to voice mail again. I repeated the order to come in.

I drove off the lot very quietly. Driving in Dubai traffic required complete attention, but I was still shaken when I reached my room. I knew I was working against two important and dangerous arms dealers and probably the Agency and possibly the Russian mafiya as well. How could I have been so stupid as to visit a place where Russians hang out? I mentally kicked myself. The Lord takes care of fools and drunks, but I shouldn't use up all my credit. How could I have been so mindless? Situational awareness? Blind as a bat to anything but my immediate action.

I sat on one of the armchairs and looked out at the creek. I had done another stupid thing—walked in the dark and dangerous world of the dhow docks as if I were strolling along a Paris boulevard. It was a wonder I was still alive.

I got up and got the package Gil Brady or George Branson or Karl Spiegel—what *am* I to call that man?—gave Sally for safekeeping. I turned it over in my hands. It had no marks on it. It was just a box wrapped in brown paper and sealed with cellophane tape. I slipped the tip of my knife blade under the tape gently and cut it, allowing the brown paper to fall away. I opened the box and found another damned baggie of diamonds.

George Branson, to give him his real name, was like the diamond bunny, hopping around the world leaving diamonds in people's baskets. Those diamonds meant something.

Asking questions about Gil Brady could become hazardous to my health, I thought. Sidney told me that. The embassy told me that, but then I'd never been one to take advice, had I? Malyakov, the Agency, and possibly the Russians might have reason to hide the identity of George's killer. I'd never been up against corporate killers before. What did they want? Did they want me dead?

The pieces of the puzzle kept shifting around my head. Almost all of the men on the list worked for Malyakov as George Branson had, but Branson had also worked for Gringikov, hadn't he? Was Malyakov's staff rotten? I needed to talk to somebody. Ralph had been out of the business too long. The pirate lady had told me all she knew or all that she was willing to tell me, at any rate. Maybe Willoughby knew something. I called Ralph, and the call went to voice mail. I called again. The third time he answered.

"What the hell?"

I heard rustling in a murmured question.

"No, it's business."

Oops. "Sorry, Ralph, but it's time to get up. I need Willoughby. Can you get him and send him over to me? There's beer in it for him," I said.

"Look, Lee, I'm not even awake. He won't be sober for hours."

"If at all," I said.

"If at all," he agreed.

"Call him, will you, when he might be conscious? Find out when he can come and talk with me, and let me know. Texting is okay."

He grumbled but agreed.

"It will probably be hours," he said. I heard the murmur again. "He may never be conscious."

I tried to think of something else useful I might do until Atkins got back and Ralph got out of bed. German-Balkan Insurance Company could use some work. A Google search turned up several hundred entries for German-Balkan but none for an insurance company by that name. A tour company. A cultural center in Belgrade. Several dating sites. You'd think even a shell company would have a homepage.

When Atkins returned. I told him about Sally.

"Are you out of your mind?" He seemed quite interested to hear the answer.

"No, just mindless," I replied.

He spotted the baggie on the desk and picked it up. He shook two of the stones out in his palm and said, "This is where you tell me about the diamonds. You're rationing this stuff like it was—"

"Diamonds?"

He flushed. "You are going to tell me about the diamonds, or I'm going to quit, and I'll slug you on the way out the door."

"The last man who tried wound up down a flight of stairs."

"Oh. Tough girl."

"No, just used to working with men with attitude." I pointed to one of the chairs and took the other. "Sit. I told you I'm looking for George Branson?"

He sat and nodded.

"Everybody I show his picture to identifies him as Gil Brady. Ralph told me he worked for Felix Gringikov until Gringikov disappeared and then for Malyakov. Ralph said that Brady had a thing going with the Nguyen woman, so I asked her, and she admitted knowing him and told me he had flat in Jumeirah Towers. I went there and searched it—"

"You searched it. How did you get in?"

"Picked the lock, of course. I found a baggie of uncut diamonds in his safe."

"You cracked his safe?"

"Don't be silly. I found the combination. A napkin from the Caspian Lounge with Sally written on it was in his underwear drawer. I went to the Caspian Lounge and talked to Sally. Barnes seems to have spent a lot of time there, although Sally said they weren't 'together.' He gave her package to hold, and she gave it to me—"

"Why?"

I ignored that. "When I opened it, it contained that." I pointed to the bag of diamonds on the desk. "Malyakov takes diamonds in payment for his weapons. I doubt that he pays his people in diamonds."

"So where did Brady get the diamonds then? Are the diamonds the reason he's dead?"

"A question I keep asking myself."

On our way to Jebel Ali, Atkins reported on his visit to the souk. "Prince is right. Somebody's working a protection racket there."

"Europeans?" I asked.

"Yeah."

"Did any of them talk to you?"

"One of them did. Metalworker with a sick kid. I paid him more than he pays them. You owe me."

"Put it on your expense account. What did he say?"

"They all pay. Different amounts, depending. Almost the whole souk pays. One of the shoemakers refused to pay. The first time they just beat him. The second time they burned him out. That scared everybody else. A fire could wipe out the souk."

"Why didn't it?" I asked.

"Bucket brigade to the well," he said. "And the fire department got there quick."

"And the police?"

"Nobody's told them."

"This doesn't sound like a part of the Gringikov–Malyakov battle. Sounds more like a mafiya operation. I thought Dubai was neutral territory."

"Maybe it's not anymore."

Chapter 29

MARTIN WORTH'S BONDED warehouse in the Jebel Ali Free Zone Extension was not just one warehouse. It was five cement block buildings. Trucks were backed up to the loading docks like piglets to a sow. Worth's one-room office was in the building nearest the road: sheetrock walls, gray desk and chairs, what looked like shipping schedules on the walls. I remembered Worth from the Berlin, a chunky guy with brown eyes and a receding hairline. He stood when we entered.

"What can I do for you folks?" he asked, offering us chairs.

When we were seated, Atkins looked at me.

"We'd like to know what you're doing in Gil Brady's address book," I said.

He looked convincingly bewildered. "Gil Brady? Who's that?"

I flipped through the photos on my phone and showed him George's picture.

"Oh, him. Yeah. I guess he might have my number. He works for Sergei Malyakov. He comes around when Malyakov's freight comes in."

"What does he do?" Atkins asked.

"Checks it in. Makes sure it's all there. Like that. Sometimes he comes with Lavrinovych's trucks, sees them loaded, goes with them to the airport," Worth answered.

"What kind of stuff does Malyakov store?" I asked.

Worth narrowed his eyes.

Atkins shook his head at me and asked, "Seen him lately?"

Worth looked at Atkins and scratched his head. Then he flipped through the calendar on his desk. "I guess not recently."

"Can you remember the last time you saw him?" I asked.

Atkins glared at me.

"What is this? You sound like a cop," Worth said.

I shook my head. "No, I'm not a cop. When was the last time you saw him?" I pressed.

"I don't have to talk to you."

"Why shouldn't you? Unless you know Brady's dead."

"Dead?" he asked.

"Lee—"

"Murdered," I replied.

Worth stared at me. Then he put his fingers in his mouth and gave a shrill whistle. Atkins and I stood up as a pair of muscular guys holding cargo hooks pushed through the door.

"This would be a good time to go," Worth said.

We went.

Wilson James, the whiskey importer, had a warehouse over in Dubai City near the Jebel Ali Industrial Area, so Atkins turned south until he could pick up the road that led there.

"It looks like he didn't know Brady was dead," I said.

"Maybe not. Your technique for interrogation is a little rough. You stick a gun in a guy's ear and say 'talk or I'll blow your brains out?'"

"I have more experience in being interrogated than in interrogating," I snapped. "Besides, what else was he going to tell us?"

"We'll never know, will we?" he snapped back.

We turned onto a four-lane divided highway. Cars and trucks were going to and coming from the port, most of them driving about forty-five kilometers an hour. Suddenly, out of nowhere, a black SUV swerved across us and drove us off the road. Atkins struggled with the steering wheel, and we came to a bruising stop in a gully. He fell forward and the horn began to sound as the air bags deployed. He wasn't moving. I felt cut in half by my seat belt. I jerked it loose and beat my way out from under the air bag, thanking God my door wasn't jammed. Stumbling in the sand, I ran around to the driver's side and yanked the door open. Atkins looked woozy. I grabbed him by the arm and shook him.

"Help me here, Marlboro. I've got to get you out."

He moved his head to the side and looked at me. I beat my hands on the air bag.

"Come on, Marlboro. I've got to get you out of here! Now!"

He stirred. I reached in and pulled his left leg out of the car. Then I freed the right leg out from under the dashboard, and he yelled. The traffic just went on by. I got my arms around his shoulders and pulled, and some intelligence came back into his eyes.

"Help me, Marlboro!"

"Not Marlboro. Got a name," he muttered.

I pulled on his legs and managed to shift his hips so that his legs were outside the door. Then I put my arms around his body and pulled, and he came out like the first olive from the bottle and ended up standing with his arms around me. At least his leg wasn't broken. I tried to pull him away from the car, but he kissed me.

"Name's Fred." And he kissed me again, hard and demanding.

"You're hurting me," I yelped.

I shook his arms away. He staggered as I took his hand, and we dodged traffic across the highway. I sat him down by the side of the road and punched 999 into the phone just as the gas tank went. Traffic slowed a bit to watch, but nobody stopped until a shabby old truck pulled off the road, and the driver got out. He brought a first-aid kit with him, but nobody was bleeding. He looked at the fire and then into Fred's eyes. He turned to me and said something I didn't understand. He wasn't Arab; he looked Pakistani.

"Concussion?" I said in Arabic.

He nodded. People gawked at the merry blaze. By the time the cops got there he was still the only person who had stopped for us. Fred. He wanted me to call him Fred. The ambulance guy looked in Fred's eyes.

"He goes to the hospital. I don't like the look of his eyes. There's a chance of concussion," he said and put Fred on the stretcher.

Fred struggled against them. "I'm not going to any damned hospital," he shouted.

"Fred, you're going to the hospital. You may have a concussion. Be cool or I'll have them strap you down" I said.

He glared at me, but it bounced right off.

"Hospital," I said and watched as they loaded him into the ambulance before turning to the police.

What could I tell them? That a black SUV had driven us off the road? They asked if I'd gotten a license number.

Cops. "I was too busy trying to keep myself going through the windshield," I told them.

By the time I got the car hauled to the shop and got to the hospital, Fred was fighting off three nurses and trying to put his pants on.

"What are you doing?" I demanded.

"I'm checking myself out of here."

I pushed him back onto the bed. "Not if you want a job tomorrow. They want to keep you under observation overnight to be sure you don't have a concussion."

He swore. "I do not have a concussion. I've taken heavier hits in the boxing ring. *I will not stay in this damned place.*"

"I have no use for a concussed partner."

"Look, somebody just tried to kill us. There is no telling what kind of trouble you can get into by yourself."

"Got along without you before I met you. We're in deep enough water as it is," I said. "I need to be sure you're well. I'm taking a cab back to the hotel. What could possibly go wrong? Somebody's going to snatch me in front of the doorman?"

He grudgingly took his pants off and got back in bed. "I won't wear one of those damned gowns!"

"I don't blame you. Now settle down. That's the second time somebody has tried to run me off the road. The other night there was a close call while Ralph was taking me home. That might have been an accident, but this is too close to our visit to Martin Worth's office to be a coincidence."

"More like enemy action," he agreed.

"Why did he throw us out when I told him Gil Brady had been murdered?"

"Why didn't you just hit him over the head with the baseball bat?"

"Look, Mar—Fred, how could we possibly be a threat to him? A threat big enough to have us wiped out?"

He stirred restlessly. "I don't know, but there's a link between him and Malyakov and maybe between Malyakov and the Russian mafiya, between one of his men and the mafiya, anyway. That would make Worth linked to the mafiya. The mafiya is probably running that protection racket."

His eyes looked hot, and I could tell that somebody was beating a big bass drum in his head. I gave him a drink of water. He pushed the cup away when he realized he was supposed to be well.

"Suppose they're running a racket on the docks too? It wouldn't be the first time the mafiya has done something like that. You said we were up against the CIA. You say you know George Branson worked for the CIA. He also worked for Felix Gringikov. For both? You say Gil Brady is George Branson. How do you know?" Atkins—Fred— sounded tired. He looked tired.

"Because I know what George Branson looks like, and everybody I show his picture to identifies him as Gil Brady. Branson/Brady worked for the CIA and for Felix Gringikov. Gil Brady worked for Felix Gringikov, and, after Gringikov disappeared, he worked for Malyakov. Ralph said he worked for Malyakov. Worth said he worked for Malyakov. And we saw one of Malyakov's men at a mafiya banquet."

"So is this about the gun trade or the mafiya?" Fred asked.

"It doesn't have to be either/or, Fred. It can be the gun trade and the mafiya."

"And the CIA? Russian mafiya and the CIA?"

"Crime has made stranger bedfellows than that," I replied.

"It looks more like mafiya than CIA," he insisted.

He didn't know about Karl Spiegel. Did I tell him I saw Roger Findley closing up the Gringikov office in Istanbul? I couldn't remember. The CIA teaming up with the Russian mafiya. That would make a great movie, but it doesn't happen in real life, does it? Insofar as there is a real life in connection with the CIA.

"Get some rest," I told him. "I'll pick you up in the morning as soon as the doctors release you. Oh. I need a car. Give me your car keys, and I'll use yours. Where did you park it?"

"Second parking deck, second or third row, I think."

"What is it? We've been using mine," I asked him.

"It's a black Chevy SUV."

"Black SUV?"

"Yeah, the world's full of black SUVs. The keys are in my pants pocket. No, they put them in the bag with my clothes and wallet. The bag's in that closet." He pointed to a door beside the door to the bathroom. I got the bag and handed it to him, and he gave me the key ring.

"The license number's on the key tag."

I put the key in my pocket. "I'll check on you in the morning. I'm going to have to deal with the car rental company about the insurance. I'd rather deal with the CIA *and* the Russian mafiya than an insurance company."

"I think it's only the mafiya," he said, "but good luck with the insurance company."

"Only!"

Chapter 30

IT WAS EIGHT o'clock and dark when I got a taxi outside the hospital, but I could see the moon reflected in the canal as we crossed it. At the hotel, there were several vehicles in front of us dropping off passengers in evening clothes. I got out of my taxi just as the doorman was holding the door of a black limousine open. I took a step toward the revolving door and was surrounded. I looked around, and Sergei Malyakov kissed me hard. Natalie and Abdullah stroked my arms, and the group pulled me back toward their car. Suddenly, I felt somebody hit me on the back, and I went down on my hands and knees. The Malyakov party abandoned me. They bolted into their limousine and were driven away. The doorman stood with his mouth open as two chunky men pushed past us and through the revolving door into the hotel lobby.

"Oh, madam," the doorman said, "are you hurt?" He spoke into his lapel. "Security! Security!" he called, helping me to stand and brushing me off.

A middle-aged man in a coat and tie arrived quick-step and looked me over. "What happened here?"

I shook my head and looked at the holes in the knees of my jeans. "I don't know. I felt somebody push me from behind, and suddenly I was on my hands and knees."

"Are you hurt?"

I felt my back and my neck. "I don't think so." Always on the lookout for lawsuits, hotels are.

"Are you a resident of the hotel?" Security asked.

"Yes," I said and showed him my key card.

"Then let's get you upstairs."

He led me through the door and over to the bank of elevators. I was getting used to providing entertainment for the lobby loungers. The two husky men sat on a sofa near the door to the café, their hands on their knees, making no bones about watching me. They were my favorite tails. I looked right through them. The security man saw me to my door and followed me in it, checking the bathroom and the closet.

"I think you'll be all right, madam," he said. "Don't forget to use the security bolt."

I used the security bolt and sat down in the chair by the window so I could shake in comfort. What could possibly go wrong?

It seemed that my minders didn't want me to be carried off by the Malyakovs. So who do they work for? And why would Malyakov and company want to carry me off in the first place? To be their sex slave? How ridiculous is that?

Chapter 31

AFTER THE TREMBLING ceased, I ordered spaghetti Bolognese and a split of Burgundy from room service. I always need tomato sauce after getting scared out of my wits.

After the break for dinner, I looked longingly at the bed. When this is over, I'm going to sleep for a month, I promised myself. Instead, I settled down to call Jerry.

"Don't you ever read your e-mail?" he complained when he came on the line.

"Occasionally. What have you got?"

"A bunch of identifications. Your Dumpy Lady is Anya Markova Nickolai, age seventy-five, a retired Moscow magistrate. She has no criminal record, but her son was arrested in connection with the firebombing of a restaurant. Thinking seems to have been that the restaurant owner hadn't paid his protection money. Young Nickolai got off with a suspended sentence, thought to be due to the influence of his mother."

"Always useful to have a judge in your corner."

"It's what she did after she retired that's interesting. Opaque, but interesting. She moved to Sochi, and rumor has it that she had her thumb in a lot of the contracts for the Winter Olympics construction. After the Olympics were over she moved to Sevastopol. Apparently, she likes warm weather. When the Russians annexed Crimea and the war with Ukraine broke out, she left."

"War is bad for business."

"So it is, except for the armaments industry. I think she's decided to stay in Dubai. My Arabic guy thinks she's got a contract to buy a flat in Jumeirah."

"Now that *is* interesting. What's the address?"

"It's in the e-mail. Most of the guys in the pictures you sent me have criminal records of one kind or another, ranging from drunk and disorderly to manslaughter, but mostly 'grievous bodily harm.' The GBH guys seem to be enforcers. Their dossiers are attached to an e-mail I sent you. The guys who were following you, Igor Harkov and Anatoly Volsky, fall into the latter category—strong-arm men. If they come closer than tailing you, I'd watch out."

"I owe them. They just saved me from being carried off to a life of sex slavery."

"What!"

"I live an interesting life, Jerry. Do any of the men have a connection with either Felix Gringikov or Sergei Malyakov?"

"Oh, I forgot. I found Gringikov. The army unit was the connection. Interesting man, brought himself up on the streets of Minsk. Bastard, you know. Word has it that he killed one of his mother's clients. It's all in the attachment. Now what's this about a life of sex slavery? I thought I offered that to you years ago."

"Oh, Malyakov got into his head that he wanted to date me. I use the word 'date' very loosely. He kept sending me orchids and invitations. I thought I had gotten rid of him, but tonight in front of the hotel, Malyakov, his wife, and an Arab friend surrounded me up close and were walking me to their limousine when my tails busted through the line, knocked me over but rescued me from them. I need to thank them."

"Lee—"

"Jerry, don't start."

"Someday you're going to get yourself killed."

"I know, but not today. Go on."

"Most of the sources agreed that Gringikov is about fifty-five. After he became a notorious arms dealer, he acquired a reputation for being a Robin Hood, the Lord only knows how. Since no one knew who his father was, possibly not even his mother, there was no regular father figure in his life, just a string of men who lived off his mother's earnings. The only stable thing in his life was school, at which he was surprisingly good. There was a beloved teacher, husbandless like many a woman in a Russia that had lost ten million soldiers and another twelve or thirteen million civilians in World War II."

"Jerry, don't preach."

"Everybody knows how many Jews died, but nobody knows how many Russians died. She treated Felix like a son and protected him when she could, but one day one of his mother's men hit him once too often, and he hit back."

"This is all very literary, Jerry," I said.

"My guy fancies himself another Dostoevsky. Anyway. The man hit his head on the edge of a table and died, and Felix ran. They say he ran wild on the streets of Minsk after that and did what he had to do to survive. By the early 1970s, when Minsk had begun to recover from the devastation of World War II, Felix was nicely situated in the underworld as a bright young man, but he still kept in touch with his teacher, who tried to keep him out of serious trouble. In 1973 he was drafted into the army, the Soviet army, as it was. He wound up in logistics and learned how to move cargo, a knowledge that served him well when he got out of the army and returned to Minsk and his underworld connections. It is unclear how or when he got into the weapons trade. Speculation is that he was moving arms to client states like Angola, the People's Democratic Republic of Yemen, and others while he was still in the army. After Belarus' independence in 1991, the arsenal in Minsk no longer belonged to the Russians, and when Alexander Lukashenko was elected president in 1994, Belarus became a center of the illegal arms trade. With his experience and contacts, Gringikov quickly fought his way to the top. When he got there, he opened an office in Istanbul, although his headquarters are in Varna, Bulgaria. He did have a major branch office in Dubai for the same reason all the other shady characters who made it their home did: free trade zones, lax customs officials, and the world's best money laundering, but he seemed to like Istanbul."

"So do I," I said. "It's a lovely place. You ought to try it sometime."

He ignored my interjection again. "When Gringikov disappeared from the radar screen in May of 2011, nobody thought anything of it. He'd gone to ground before. But when he didn't emerge from the shadows grinning after a couple of months, people began to talk, and Sergei Malyakov began to move up, and then people really began to talk."

"Malyakov may have links to the Russian mafiya. Poke around in that, will you, Jerry?"

I downloaded Jerry's attachment. It listed the pictures with the names and their criminal records.

Roger Findley was in Gringikov's Istanbul office closing up, I thought. Did that mean he, too, had links to the Russian mafiya? Or was he still CIA? And George. He worked for both Gringikov and Malyakov and wound up dead on Russian Beach carrying a passport in the name of Gil Brady. Did Russian Beach mean anything? A hint to the mafiya? He did have the baggies of diamonds. Hint from the mafiya?

It still all depended on who was dead—George, Gil, or Karl Spiegel.

I had had a busier day than usual. I thought it was time to go to bed, but first I called the hospital to make sure

Marlboro—Fred—was still there. They assured me he was, but they were watching him carefully, and they had given the security guards his photograph, in case he called a taxi and got by them. They sincerely hoped he was going to be discharged the next day. I laughed and hung up. He was really going to be in a twist when I picked him up.

I had started the going to bed routine when I realized I had incurred a debt, so I put my boots and gun back on and went down to the lobby, where one of my minders was sitting on a sofa reading a magazine. I walked over and sat down beside him. He looked at me in alarm, and I patted him on the thigh.

"I owe you and your partner for rescuing me from the Malyakovs. And all the time I thought you were working for them. Who *are* you working for?"

He sat like an Easter Island statue.

"Not talking, eh? Well, the other options are Gringikov, the CIA, and the Russian mafiya." I waved to a waiter. "Surely vodka should be your drink?" I asked him. He didn't change his posture. "Two vodkas," I ordered. He did look at me then.

"I suppose your partner's in the garage keeping my car under surveillance. I might as well tell you that I'm going to bed, so he can come up and surveil in comfort."

I left him sitting there staring at the vodka. Before the elevator came, he had tossed both of them off.

Bedtime chores took as much time as usual, which was not long. I was turning out the light and looked automatically at the light under the door. There he was again! Dammit! I told him I was going to bed. I put on the caftan and grabbed the Glock. Jerking the door open, I raised the gun and yelled, "I told you I was going to bed!"

I had never seen the guy before. I waved the gun at him.

"Go!"

He went.

Who were these guys working for? The surveillance had started right after somebody tried to kill me in Switzerland. Except for the footsies, nobody had followed me until after I got back from Istanbul.

Chapter 32

THE NEXT MORNING, I considered what I needed to do before I went to get Fred. After I picked him up, anything might happen. I needed to find out if Madame Nickolai was really buying a flat in Jumeirah and, if possible, what she was up to in Dubai. Her previous moves suggested that she preferred a warm climate. Anybody from Moscow might. I needed to know if anything screwy was happening at the docks. I wanted to know about Hildebrand and why he was so upset at the mention of Felix Gringikov and why Marty Worth didn't know Gil Brady was dead. The phone rang. It was Willy.

"There's a run on the bank."

"The bank?" I said stupidly.

"Dubai–Persian. I heard a rumor this morning that merchants had withdrawn their funds from the bank online overnight. As soon as the doors opened there was a large mob of people trying to withdraw their deposits."

"There won't be enough money to cover them." No bank ever has enough cash on hand to cover all the deposits.

"There isn't. The bank closed its doors, but the mob broke in and ransacked the place. By the time the cops got there, all of the loose cash was gone, the officers and tellers were barricaded in the manager's office, and some guys were using a table as a battering ram trying to get at them."

"When was the last time you heard of a run on a bank? I wonder if this is more of the attack on Malyakov. He has a lot of money there."

"What attack?" he asked.

I told him about the sabotaged delivery to the Congo.

"And there have been other things. Willy, it looks like somebody's trying to destroy Malyakov or take him over."

"Who are the suspects?" he asked.

"Let's see. The Gringikov outfit—"

"Gringikov disappeared."

"I know, but the outfit's been in business until recently. How about the CIA? I saw an Agency man closing up the Gringikov office in Istanbul. Or take Fred's idea: the Russian mafiya."

"I've only just begun looking for Nickolai's money, but she has a substantial sum in the Dubai–Persian Bank. The Revolutionary Guard and the Russian mafiya. Interesting bedfellows."

"Stranger things have happened," I said.

"If it is the Russian mob, then he's seriously screwed. His money was transferred to a numbered account in Zurich online before the bank doors opened."

"What!"

"And your Madame Nickolai's wasn't."

"She's not my Madame Nickolai. Malyakov wouldn't know how to arrange a run on bank. Anyway, he wouldn't be such a fool. If the Revolutionary Guard and Madame Nickolai lost their money, he's a dead man." I looked at my watch. It was almost ten thirty. "Gotta go, Willy," I said. "If I don't pick Fred up from the hospital, the whole staff might go on strike."

"Hospital?"

"I'll explain later."

When I got there, I found that it was worse than I had imagined. I almost went on strike myself trying to get him to sit in the wheelchair so I could take him to the car.

"I can walk, dammit," he insisted.

"Get in the wheelchair, Marlboro," I ordered.

"Fred. I can walk."

"Fred. It's the insurance companies' rules. Get in the chair," I ordered again.

He stood beside the bed with his heels dug in like a Missouri mule.

"Get in the damned chair!"

The mule didn't move.

"FRED! GET IN THAT DAMN CHAIR, OR YOU'RE FIRED!"

One of the nurses giggled and put her hand over her mouth in embarrassment. Fred threw a sizzling look at her and sat down in the chair. I put the footrests out, took off the brakes, and wheeled him outside to the sidewalk and went to get the car.

When I got him in it, I said, "You got your BCD for insubordination."

I tried to drive past the bank on the way back to the hotel, but the streets were blocked by squad cars with flashing lights. Beyond them I could see a large crowd of angry men waving their fists and shouting.

"What's that?" Fred asked.

"There was a run on the Dubai–Persian Bank this morning. Those are probably depositors who lost their money. We need to find out what Sergei Malyakov is doing."

"Why?"

"The Dumpy Lady has lost a pile of money, but Malyakov's was transferred out before the crash."

"He's a dead man," Fred said.

"After you change clothes, go over to Sharjah and find out what's going on."

"After I change my clothes and eat."

"After you change your clothes and eat," I agreed.

I drove across the creek on the Al Maktoum Bridge, hoping he wasn't going to ask for a report.

He asked for a report.

"I have formed an alliance with my minders. They saved me from a fate worse than death."

He stared at me.

"Malyakov and Natalie and Abdullah tried to kidnap me from in front of the hotel last night, and my minders shook me free. On the strength of it, I bought them a drink."

"Malyakov did what? And you did what?" Disbelief warred with laughter on his face.

"Yeah. Fred, what are they up to? I'm not that hot."

He looked at me speculatively.

"Not only that, but the feet were back at the door. Haven't seen them in a couple of days. The minder wouldn't tell me who they work for, not surprisingly. The guy that belongs to the feet was one I'd never seen before. Either the minder didn't believe me when I told him I was going to bed, or I'm being followed by two sets of people."

"But which two sets?" he asked.

I let him off on the fifth floor so he could change his clothes.

Marlboro—Fred—looked a little green when he got to my room, so I called downstairs for a pot of coffee.

"And food. I swear hospital food is worse than airline food."

"Wait a minute," I said to room service. "What do you want?" I asked Fred.

"Steak, rare. Baked potato, butter, sour cream."

"Salad?"

"If I want grass, I'll ask for it. Just a large steak and potato."

Since we were eating, I ordered a BLT club. While we were waiting for something more substantial to chew on, we chewed over the case, but there wasn't much nourishment in it. As we were finishing our coffee, I cocked an eye at Fred.

"Fred, I need to know what you're doing on the beach here," I said. "You're not the sort of man to waste away in Margaritaville."

He shifted his chair and ran his hand over his buzz cut hair.

"Look, Fred, I'm in deep here, and I need to know you're not an ax murderer."

He looked out over the creek. "I refused to take my men into an area we didn't have any intelligence about. I left them in position and went myself. I was ambushed. My men came and got me, and two of them were killed, so it was all for nothing, but they court-martialed me anyway." He shot a humorless look at me. "I found a home in the Corps." His mouth twisted.

"I know. I found a home in the CIA."

We were looking out at the creek, but we didn't really see it. What we saw was our past and maybe an unsatisfactory future. Fred came to first.

"From now on, you are not going anywhere without me."

"You'd better believe it. Fred, I just don't get it. I mean, it wasn't just Malyakov, it was all three of them. It was like we going somewhere for a foursome."

"Well, personally, I wouldn't like to share you—"

Fortunately for him the phone rang.

"The Nickolai woman has bought a flat in Jumeirah, in the same tower I'm in, in fact," Willy said.

"Madame Nickolai's got a flat in Jumeirah Towers," I said to Fred. "I need to get into it."

"You're out of your mind."

"Probably. Let's go," I said and grabbed my pack. Fred was doing his Missouri mule imitation again.

"Why?"

"I don't know," I answered. "I just do."

Madame Nickolai's flat was in the middle of the corridor between the elevator and fire stairs. Fred leaned up against the wall while I picked the lock and slipped inside.

"Knock on the door if she comes," I said.

He snorted.

There wasn't much to see. The Dumpy Lady was still in the process of moving in, and boxes and crates stood around in the foyer and the salon. I went quickly down the hall, sticking my head in doors. Two bedrooms, one set up and occupied. Hall bath. Ah. Office, with laptop booted on the desk. I stuck a flash drive in the USB port and started draining the hard drive into it while I looked into the desk drawers. Nothing yet. Come on, come on, I thought. This always looks so quick and easy on TV. I went out in the hall to listen and heard a knock on the door. I ran back to the laptop and jerked the flash drive out, hoping I had not destroyed everything I'd copied. I ran and stuck my nose out the door. Fred was standing with his back to the elevator. I pulled the door quietly to and we walked toward the fire stairs. I heard a key in a lock and started to turn.

"Don't look," Fred said.

"Stop!" a woman called.

I took my keys out of my pocket and held one as if getting ready to insert it into a lock. We turned.

"Yes?" Fred asked.

The Dumpy Lady said, "Who are you?"

Fred hissed, but I walked toward her.

"Yes? Can I help you?" I asked.

She looked grumpier.

"What are you doing here?" she demanded.

I raised an eyebrow. "I *beg* your pardon?"

She stood with her hands on her hips. "You don't belong here," she said.

I stopped in the middle of the hall. "On the contrary, madam," I said in my snootiest tone. "We do, but I have never seen you before."

I turned toward a door, and Fred shielded me as I picked its lock, praying that no one was home. I opened the door, and we went inside.

Nobody was home.

Chapter 33

AFTER A FEW minutes, I peeked around the doorframe. The hall was clear, so I led Fred into the fire stairs and down two flights.

"You are out of your mind," Fred said.

"Shut up, Fred," I replied.

I sat down, opened my cell phone, and inserted the flash drive. I couldn't tell how much of the hard drive I had gotten in that short period of time, but whatever it was, it was in Cyrillic. I punched in Jerry's number and sent it along with instructions to tell me what it was and keep it safe. Then I led Fred on down the steps to Willy's office. As usual, Wilbur was as delighted to see me as I was to see him. He burbled in protest, but I walked past him into Willy's office.

Willy smiled. "Good morning, lovely lady. What can I do for you?"

"Good morning, Willy. Make me a very dry martini," I replied, "and Fred can probably use a beer."

He crossed to the bar and put a pair of martinis together. I drank the one he handed me down, gave the glass back to him, and he refilled it. He handed Fred a bottle of Budweiser.

"Glass?"

Fred shook his head and drank down a good part of the bottle.

"Strenuous morning?"

"Just a little B&E," I replied.

He looked Fred over and back at me.

"Willy, this is Fred Atkins, my new partner. Fred, this is Willy Soo. He does money."

"Whether you can take care of her is a good question," he said to Fred.

"Whether I can keep up with her is the real question," Fred replied.

Willy poured a drink for himself and joined us behind the coffee table.

"Am I to take it that you visited Madame Nickolai's flat while she was away?"

Some of Fred's beer went down the wrong way, and he coughed violently. Willy patted him on the back.

"You'll get used to it," he said. "She has an inquisitive nature. What did you find? I've always wanted to know what a mafiya doness keeps in her flat."

"Donatrix? She's not entirely moved in yet. No furniture except in one bedroom and a desk in an office. I didn't have much time, but I got this." I handed him the flash drive. "It's something in Cyrillic. Put it somewhere safe. If I turn up on Russian Beach with a bullet in my brain, use it to make as much trouble as you can."

Fred made a noise of protest.

"Give it to the CIA?" Willy asked.

"Or *The New York Times* or *Pravda*. Whatever you think best."

He nodded and slipped the drive in his pocket. Fred looked back and forth between us, not believing what he heard.

"You signed on, Fred. You can bail now, but if you don't bail now, you're in for the run of the play," I said.

He looked at me and away through Willy's window to the Gulf. Then he shrugged. "I guess I'll stick around," he said. "I want to see how it comes out."

Willy got Fred another beer, and we sat drinking companionably. Willy tipped his glass up, got hold of the olive and crunched it.

"I found some more of her money," he said.

"Don't tell me. Let me guess. Cyprus, like all other good Russian mobsters," I said.

"Right you are," he said. "She lifted it just before the crash. She put it in a numbered account in Doha. I'm sure by the time it got there it was lily white. It was the proceeds from a complicated series of security transactions. She's good. Or her accountant is. I had trouble finding it myself, and I knew it was there."

"Just out of curiosity, who did she use?" I asked.

Willy grinned his cheeky grin and gave me the name of a firm so respectable that they would do due diligence on the Bank of England. We laughed at the ways of money. Fred looked bored.

"I found out more about the Dubai–Persian Bank ownership." He left us and returned with a tablet. He pulled up a file and gave the tablet to me. The screen showed a series of photographs, a mixture of men in civilian and military dress. He pointed to the first one, a man with the face of a tormented saint. His uniform looked hand-tailored. I raised an eyebrow.

"That's General Rostam Tehrani, the Iranian Revolutionary Guards' inspector general. The man next to him is Nouri Yavari, deputy finance minister. According to a friend of mine"—he smiled modestly—"the two of them visit Dubai on a quarterly basis. They've both been seen lunching with Abdel Fawaz, and the finance minister has visited Fawaz's office with a young colleague. The young colleague stays for several days while the general and the finance minister return to Tehran."

"Auditing. It seems the Persian part of Dubai–Persian bank is owned by the Iranian government."

"Not just the government, the Revolutionary Guard," he said.

I sat and assimilated that. Like the People's Liberation Army in China, the Revolutionary Guard in Iran has its fingers in all sorts of pies. Banking would be an important one.

"Then they're wiring around the sanctions. Providing financial services to Tehran. How could the emir not know?"

"Did you ever know an emir to know anything he didn't want to know?" Willy asked.

I thought a while. "Willy, we need to know who is behind the shell company that owns the other half."

"The Russian mafiya," Fred said. "Maybe that's why Madame Nickolai has moved to Dubai, to keep her eye on their money."

"Well, if that's why she moved, it didn't work," I said. "She lost her money, remember?"

"Did she?" asked Willy. "We won't know until the dust settles. And the Revolutionary Guard? The bank will probably have to be wound up. When the capital is realized, the Revolutionary Guard and whoever really owns the other half will get what's left, and the small depositors will be left holding the bag."

"If Cyprus is any example," I said, "the Revolutionary Guard may be left holding the bag, too. A war between the Revolutionary Guard and the Russian mafiya would be interesting to watch." I stood up and picked up my pack. "Things may be clearer when I find out from Jerry what's in those files."

"Do I need to know?" Willy asked.

"Only in the most general way," I said. "If you need to know, I'll be long gone."

Fred was looking worried when we got back to the car.

"What?" I asked.

He shook his head. "You'll be long gone?"

"Always good to face the facts, Fred," I said. "You're in all the way, now."

I deleted the files from my phone.

"What! Why?" Fred asked.

"They're in two places. Three is one too many," I replied.

"You seem awfully calm about this," he said.

"About what?" I asked.

"It's like you break into a mafiya lady's apartment and steal her secrets every day."

"Not every day, Fred. In fact, today was the very first time." I cut my eyes toward him. "I have stolen some terrorists' secrets, but those were the first mafiya secrets I ever stole."

Chapter 34

I SENT FRED to Sharjah to see what, if anything, was going on at the Malyakov's place and returned a call from Jerry in Boston.

"What is this stuff you sent me?" he asked.

"Something I can't read in Cyrillic. It's probably Russian," I replied.

"It is, and it's encrypted."

"Well, decrypt it."

"Your tab is getting pretty big, Lee. What do you think it might be?"

"I got it out of the laptop of a Russian mafiya lady. It might be anything. Financial records. E-mails. Orders. Plans. Who knows? That's why I sent it to you."

"Russian mafiya encryption," he grumbled. "God, Lee. How do you get into these things?"

"It's a talent I have," I replied modestly and ended the call.

I went back to the computer, but I was restless and couldn't settle to anything. Running over what I knew again didn't help. I either knew too much or not enough. I was rescued from my dilemma by the phone. It was Willy.

"Come to lunch, lovely lady. I have something very interesting to show you. Just a light luncheon, a little lobster salad, some champagne?"

"Willy, you have saved me from despair," I said.

"The office," he said. "Half an hour?"

"For lobster and champagne, twenty minutes."

I called Fred. "What's happening?" I asked.

"Not much. I can't get near the hangar. I've been sitting in the car with binoculars on the place for nearly an hour. If anything is happening, it's happening inside, and I can't see in."

"Go see what's going on at the house. Is there any way you can stake it out?" I asked.

"From what I remember, not in the daytime," he replied.

"Then go and see what's going on at Natalie's travel agency and to the Gold and Diamond Mart. He's got offices on the third floor. After the trouble at the bank, there must be something happening somewhere. I'm going over to Willy's for lunch. He says he has something for me that I have to see."

"Take a cab," he said.

"Certainly Malyakov has more to do today to kidnap me."

"Lee—"

"I know. I know. I'll take a cab."

It was a little more than twenty minutes when I walked into Willy's office, but only a little more. Once again, I realized that it is better to be rich than not. A table was set for two beside the long window looking out to the Gulf—white tablecloth, silver, champagne flutes. Two orchid blooms, white with pale pink throats.

"Willy, I want to be just like you when I grow up," I said in envy.

He laughed and held a chair for me. When we were seated, a person who could only be a gentleman's gentleman served us lobster salad. Willy popped the cork on a champagne bottle and filled the flutes.

"Your health, lovely lady."

We clicked classes and sipped. It was just dry enough.

"Health which will not continue good if you don't stop breaking into people's apartments," he continued. "I didn't want to say it before your partner, but what if she had caught you?"

I took another sip. "I suppose I'd have had to shoot her," I replied.

Lobster salad and the champagne and a view of the Gulf carried us through to the chocolate mousse. Afterward, we took our coffee over to the settee.

"Delicious, every last bite." I said. "Now?"

Willy went to the desk and returned with a handful of papers.

"I printed them out. It seemed simpler." He handed them to me.

They looked like copies of property deeds. More than a dozen of them. I looked at Willy.

"Written in Arabic. You're spoiling my digestion," I said. "What are they?"

"The form is boilerplate. These are some of the holdings of the SerNa Corporation. Only some of them, and all but one in Dubai."

I gave up my plan to digest my lunch and focused my eyes on the property descriptions.

"What are they? I can't locate them without seeing the plat."

"Three hotels in Bur Dubai. The Malyakov villa," he answered. "A high-rise office building."

I riffled through the stack. "SerNa Corporation. Sergei and Natalie?"

"Exactly. There are bound to be more. Natalie's hangar, for one. These are just the ones I could pull up quickly. It looks like they have a small real estate empire."

"They have to put the profits somewhere besides diamonds."

Back at the hotel, I found Fred leaning against the wall by the door to my room, waiting for me. He needs a key, I thought. Inside, he popped a beer and sat by the window.

"There's a big black SUV parked across from Malyakov's gate," he said. "Yesterday there was one guard at the gate. Today there are three, all armed with Mac-10s."

"So something's happened."

"Yeah, something. Or the threat of something. Natalie's travel agency office at the Luxe is closed. The front window's boarded up. There's a bunch of broken glass still on the floor, and there are 'Warning: Wet Floor' signs posted around it. A uniformed security guard is posted by the front door."

"I guess the Luxe doesn't appreciate vandalism. Did you ask the guard when it happened?"

"Yes. He declined to answer. The offices at the Gold and Diamond Mart are also closed. Those movie theater barrier things—the posts with velvet-covered chains? There are three of them blocking the doors. No sign of vandalism there."

"The glass is probably too heavy to shatter. Did you ever check out the hotels Natalie books her tours into?" I asked.

"I went into one of them on the way home from the Gold and Diamond Mart. It is still open for business. It was hard to get to the registration desk for the mobs of whores."

"Central European?"

"Yup. Good-sized armful, every one, and blonde to the roots."

"I wonder if they're volunteers," I said.

"None of the ones I looked at seemed particularly unhappy, but I didn't make eye contact with any of them for fear I'd be dragged away for fifteen minutes worth of bliss."

I reached into my pack and pulled out some of the property deeds Willy had copied for me. Two of them were hotels. "It wasn't called the Ruskayia or the Sevastopol, was it?" I asked.

"The Ruskayia," he said.

"She owns it, or at least the SerNa Corporation does. Along with a lot of other real estate." I looked at my watch. "Dinnertime. Do we go somewhere together, or do I order from room service again?"

"There's a Pakistani place down by the spice bazaar that has good food. We could go there, and then drive over to Sharjah and look at Malyakov's place."

So that's what we did. The Pakistani place was packed, and service was slow, but the food was good. I like Mogul food. My stomach is getting middle-aged, and it's not as hot as some of the Indian food. It wasn't far to Malyakov's compound. There was still a large black SUV parked across the street, and the gates and walls of the compound were brightly lighted. No guards were visible, but they were probably behind the lights. We went back to the hotel, and I got Fred a key card to my room.

"This looks better than you standing out in the hall leaning up against the wall," I said.

"Aren't you afraid I'll come in and ravage you?" he asked.

"Not if you value your life, you won't. Get some sleep and then go over to Sharjah around three o'clock and see if anything's going on," I said. I looked at the notes I'd made. "And we need to find out what's happening at Jebel Ali. If the mafiya's playing games, they may play them there."

"It's not as if longshoremen were loading the ships. Big cranes do everything now," he said.

"Well," I said, "somebody operates the cranes. Somebody drives the containers to the docks. Somebody loads the containers. The whole operation is just asking for protection."

I put a yellow Post-it on the door and went to bed. There must be some way I can get in touch with the feet. Maybe I could ask for a phone number to call?

Chapter 35

LIVERWURST FOR BREAKFAST was beginning to bore me, so I returned to my usual baguette, butter, and cheese with coffee and some fresh fruit. Fred acquired his usual and poured ketchup all over it.

"I've decided how to handle the port," I said. "I'm going to be a freelance journalist putting together a series about ports. You're my cameraman."

"You're not a freelance journalist," Fred objected.

"I've got a card that says I am."

"And I'm not a cameraman."

"I have a camera. You point it and shoot."

"So who do we talk to?"

"There's bound to be a PR office."

Marty Worth's warehouse was on the fringe of the port area. Going there had given me no idea of what the whole port was like. By the time I got to Elliott Brewster's office, I was stunned by the complexity of it all. Brewster was a forty-year-old Wilbur with brains, tall and thin with straw-colored hair and pale blue eyes. He shook our hands and gave us chairs. I ran through my story.

"I'm putting together a series on ports of the world for Ryanback Advertising. It's to be a four-color, glossy brochure, a two-page spread for each port, text and photos, to give the clients an idea of what Ryanback can do. They're just getting into the field and want to hit it with a big bang."

"Well, Jebel Ali is a big bang of a port," Brewster said, laughing.

"I've done some reading, but I had no idea. It's huge! I'm just getting started too, so maybe I shouldn't be so surprised."

Brewster laughed. "If you're used to the dhow docks on the creek then you're right to be surprised. Dubai not only imports every single thing it uses, but is also a major transshipping point." He walked over to a chart on the wall. "There are over four hundred companies represented here, warehousing, hauling, forwarders. If it has to do with import or export, it's here."

"Do you mind?" I asked. "Fred, get a shot of Mister Brewster and the chart. If you don't mind?" I asked.

"Not at all. It is a good place to start."

With that, he took us to a truck, and we drove around the port area, stopping so I could take notes and Fred could take pictures. A US Navy destroyer was in port, and sailors were swarming on the dock.

"Which reminds me, do they give you any trouble? I know Dubai is a tolerant place, but sailors in port?"

Brewster laughed. "This is a special area reserved for the US Navy. Everything they'd ever want! They don't even have to go to town."

"Are they allowed to go to town?" I asked.

"Well—"

I grinned at him. "Never mind. Speaking of trouble, this is a huge place. You must employ thousands of people. Any trouble there?"

"We don't have any trouble. These are good jobs. If a man doesn't want to work here, he doesn't have to."

"He can always go home," said Fred.

Brewster nodded.

"To Pakistan?" I asked.

Brewster shrugged.

At least a dozen container ships were tied up along the dock, and the heavy cranes whined loudly as they hoisted heavy containers on or off the huge ships. I looked at Fred. He nodded.

"I think that's about all I can absorb right now, Mister Brewster," I said.

Brewster laughed and drove around the end of the dock to go back to the office. Docked in the far corner was a ship that looked tiny beside the container ships, an old, slightly rusty freighter. The containers stacked on its deck were wooden crates.

"What's that?" I asked.

Brewster looked embarrassed. "Just about the last of an old contract with a Pakistani outfit. A couple of their ships go back and forth between here and Karachi. I don't know why they're not down at the other dock. It looks a little shabby here."

We went back to his office.

"Thanks for the tour," I said.

"Where else are you going?" Brewster asked.

Fred looked at me. "I don't know," I said. "Ryanback is still trying to sort it out. They got Fred and me here yesterday with no advance notice. It is very kind of you to take us on without previous arrangements."

Brewster shook our hands. "Not at all," he said. "There's something in being the first. We got a chance to wow you."

I laughed. "You certainly did. I'll never forget it."

"Neither will I," Fred said as we drove away. "This assignment is not big enough for a professional."

"Don't be snobbish, Fred," I said. "I'm hungry. Let's go by the Luxe and have a look at Natalie's office and get some lunch."

The café on the first floor of the Luxe charged a king's ransom for a hamburger and fries.

"It's a good thing you're getting paid in diamonds," Fred said.

After lunch we strolled in the mall. Natalie's travel agency was still closed, but workmen were putting in a new window. We decided we might as well walk on their beach while we could use it for free. We strolled to the waterline, past the tourists rubbing sunscreen on each other, past the lovers walking hand-in-hand, past the children building castles in the sand, the afternoon sun casting small shadows in front of us.

I looked up at the sound of a small plane, a private jet climbing west into the sun. It was a pretty little thing with a nose like an insect. I stopped to look at it, and as I watched, the little insect exploded into a ball of flame, and debris twinkled down into the Gulf like fragments of a spent firework.

Fred and I looked at each other, and instinctively I moved closer to him. He put his arm around me, and I put my face into his shoulder, shuddering. Sunbathers rushed to the water's edge, the women screaming and picking up their children.

"I've seen a plane like that before, Lee," he said. "It's a Gulfstream. Natalie Malyakov owns a Gulfstream."

Before all the debris had finished hitting the water, the beach was filled with people who had come from everywhere to stand and gawk. Disgusted, I turned away.

"Come on, Fred, let's go," I said.

By the next morning, everybody in the Emirates knew that Natalie Malyakov had been killed in the explosion of her Gulfstream 150. Natalie was the third wife of a merchant of death to die within the last month after having had contact with me. I was beginning to feel like Typhoid Mary.

I sent Fred to the Sharjah airport to see what he could find out while I worked the computer to see what the press knew. It wasn't much—just the time the plane took off from Sharjah and its destination—Moscow. Either the police were keeping the lid on, or there wasn't much to know yet, but it's hard to hide a plane exploding over the Arabian Gulf off Dubai. Television news was running all-out coverage. Reporters and cameras were standing outside the fence at Natalie's hangar at the Sharjah airport. All you could see was a number of police cars and vans, but the reporter was talking anyway. Occasionally they switched to the Malyakov villa in hopes that somebody they could persecute would come out. Nobody came out. The reporter went on talking anyway. I didn't much like Sergei Malyakov, but I didn't want to see anybody stick a microphone up his nose and ask, "How does it feel to have your wife blown up in an airplane?"

Chapter 36

"WHO KILLED NATALIE Malyakov?" I asked Fred the next morning.

"The mafiya because of the Dumpy Lady's money?" Fred replied. "I've been telling you it's the mafiya."

"So why not kill Sergei?"

We went through what we knew, this time putting the mafiya in the center.

"Malyakov's manager, Evgeni Rostov, looked tight with the Nickolai woman," Fred said. "Look at the other guys. Willoughby says some of them worked for Malyakov after Gringikov disappeared, but he didn't know a lot of the others. Say they're mafiya. And the odd jobs boys will work for anybody who will pay them. Or Willoughby's wrong, and they all are mafiya."

"I don't see the mafiya using local talent," I said. "I think they probably have their own stable of odd jobs boys."

"Say this *is* their stable of odd jobs boys. Maybe that's why they were in the address book."

"But it was Gringikov's address book," I protested.

"Maybe you'd find the same names and phone numbers in Malyakov's address book."

"But that would mean that both of them are mafiya," I protested.

"Why not?" he asked.

I thought about that. Did it make any sense?

"All right. How about this?" Fred said. "That's the reason Gringikov split with Malyakov. Malyakov's organization was taken over by the mafiya."

"But it was Malyakov who split with Gringikov."

"We don't know that," he said.

"Okay. Say Malyakov shoved Gringikov out. Maybe made him disappear." I chewed on that. "But that would mean Roger Findley is mafiya."

"Why not? There may be a lot more money working for the Russian mafiya than there is in working for the CIA. Maybe it's time to send his kids to college."

"I can believe anything of Roger. The thing is, I don't see any of them being active in Dubai. That's why George Branson's death is so puzzling. Dubai is neutral territory. Everybody's okay so long as there's peace. Anything else will get them thrown out quick quick."

"Somebody took down that bank," Fred pointed out.

"And that doesn't make much sense either. Even if the shell company that owns the second half of the bank belongs to the mafiya, why would the mafiya take down their own bank? Piss off the Revolutionary Guard? If it's the Russian mafiya out to take down Malyakov, why move Malyakov's money and not Madame Nickolai's?"

"Maybe it's not the mafiya that owns that shell company," Fred said. "Maybe it's Malyakov. You said he owns a lot of real estate."

I shook my head. "Fred, maybe none of this matters. I'm here to find out who killed George Branson. Or was it Gil Brady who was killed?" There was one identity Fred didn't know about: Karl Spiegel. Was it Karl Spiegel who died?

Nothing at all happened for the next two days, and Fred wandered the town restlessly looking for clues to the plane bombing. As for me, I didn't do anything. When a case goes cold, it won't heat back up until something new happens. My Visa bill came in, and I knew I was going to have to sell a diamond soon.

On the third day, Malyakov held a memorial service for Natalie in the Russian Orthodox church in Sharjah, and then all hell broke loose.

The church with its blue onion domes and Romanesque arches stood in a plot of land donated by the emir. The domed interior was nearly full when Fred and I arrived. A large picture of Natalie adorned with black ribbons stood on an easel in front of the glittering golden iconostasis. As we entered, Sergei mounted the steps and stood beside the portrait, Evgeni Rostov at his elbow. A robed and bearded priest emerged from the sanctuary followed by altar boys swinging censers from which clouds of incense rose. The priest took one of the censers and blessed Natalie's portrait. Then he stepped in front of it and began to speak in Russian. People in the congregation crossed themselves in the Orthodox manner, so strange to a Westerner. After the priest spoke, it was Sergei's turn. He spoke in a broken voice, wiping tears from his cheeks. One by one, members of the congregation came up and stood beside Natalie's portrait and spoke. Off to the side stood Abdullah in full regimentals, his white costume standing out sharply against the gold background. I nudged Fred and pointed to the door. We worked our way as quietly as possible through the congregation, drawing glances as we passed. Outside I took deep breaths of air and apologized profoundly to my sinuses.

"I should have known that the service would be in Russian," I said.

"A lot of people are here," Fred said.

"Yes, and they don't look like Beautiful People. They don't look like mafiya either," I said. "Whatever mafiya look like."

"No, they just look like ordinary Russians. Maybe expats stick together in times like this?"

We sat in the car waiting for the service to end. It was more than an hour before Malyakov, accompanied by Rostov, Abdullah, and the rest of his entourage, left the church for their black limousines. We waited to see what would happen next. After all, there was no body to bury. The Malyakov limousines pulled away, and the rest of the people scattered to their own cars. Fred put the car in gear and pulled in behind the Malyakov limousines. It wasn't much of a trip from the church to the Malyakov villa. As the gates opened, a long black SUV whipped around us and raked the Malyakov limousines with rifle fire in passing. Fred slammed on the brakes, and we watched as the guards stepped out from the gates and fired at the SUV, missing it but putting plenty of pockmarks in the wall across the street. The guards took up positions around the car, and Malyakov and Abdullah were rushed inside, and the gates closed behind them.

"What was that?" Fred asked.

"I don't know," I said. "Your mafiya maybe. Who else?"

I heard sirens in the distance. "Let's get out of here, before we spend the night in jail."

Fred turned right at the next corner and then left.

"The number of people attending the service must mean something. I never thought of Malyakov as part of a community before, except the merchant of death fraternity. Funny, Gringikov and his wife did a lot of charity work in Istanbul. Maybe some of Malyakov's blood diamonds went to helping widows and orphans in Dubai."

"Ya think?" Fred said sarcastically.

"Stranger things have happened," I said.

Fred turned the corner and drove toward the hotel; I turned my phone back on and found urgent messages from both Willy and Ralph.

I called Willy and put it on speakerphone.

"There's a fire in Bur Dubai," he said. "One of Natalie's hotels is burning. They're trying to keep the fire from spreading."

We could see smoke billowing above the old quarter. Fred drove across the creek and headed for the fire. We left the car and made our way through the crowd to the fire lines. A dozen girls in various stages of dress stood weeping and hugging each other. Embarrassed men, barefoot and dressed only in their trousers, were trying to pretend they weren't there. I turned to the man standing next to me.

"Did everybody get out?" I asked. He shrugged and turned back to the fire, eyes glittering.

As we watched, a woman appeared screaming in a third-story window, her hair ablaze. She fell back into the room as the roof collapsed. The crowd sighed. I turned away, sickened, and Fred pointed me to the car. We sat there staring at the shops.

"Do you believe that?" Fred asked.

"No, I do not," I answered.

It was a while before we moved.

"Let's just go to Ralph's to see what he wants. He has quality gin. Although, after seeing that, I'd drink homemade raki."

When we walked into the South Seas, the bartender looked up from the paper he was reading and jerked his head toward Ralph's office.

"Gin," I said as I walked past.

"And Budweiser," Fred added.

Ralph was sitting behind his desk when we walked in. Walter W. Willoughby was leaning against the filing cabinet.

"Bring some chairs!" Ralph yelled through the door.

The bartender had his priorities straight. He handed gin to me and Budweiser to Fred before going back to get chairs.

"Don't you ever answer your phone?" he asked.

"Don't be peevish, Ralph. I turned it off when we went into Natalie's memorial service and forgot to turn it back on. What's so urgent?" I asked.

It was Willoughby who answered. "Three bodies have been picked up in the last two days. All of them are men in those pictures you showed me. Let me see them again."

I brought up the pictures from Karl Spiegel's lockbox. He flipped through them, pointing to first one and then another. All three were there.

"Tell me," I said.

He pointed to a picture. "This one was picked up on Russian Beach near where Gil Brady was found. Found above the waterline line, though. He hadn't been in the water. Shot three times in the back. Worked for Malyakov, I think." I had an ID for that one. I nodded. "This one was found this morning bound and gagged and shot in the back on Jumeirah Beach. He's one I don't know."

I did. He was one Marina Gringikov identified. He either worked for her husband or knew her husband. "He's Gringikov's," I said.

"How do you know?" Fred asked.

"I just know. Go on," I said to Willoughby.

"And this guy, he's one of the freelancers. Do anything for a buck. He was found in a dumpster in Deira."

"One of Malyakov's, one of Gringikov's, one maybe mafiya?" "What's going on here?" asked Fred. "None of this has been in the news."

"Think anybody's going to publicize a private war going on?" asked Ralph. "They'll keep the lid on, if only for the tourist trade, but the cops will be all over it."

"Somebody's broken the rules," I said.

"Somebody broke the rules when they blew up Natalie Malyakov's airplane," Willoughby said.

"Somebody shot up Malyakov's limousine as he was being driven home from Natalie's memorial service," I said.

"And somebody just set fire to one of her hotels in Bur Dubai," said Fred. "Not everybody got out alive."

Ralph and Willoughby looked shocked.

"Up to this point the conflict has been between the Gringikov and Malyakov organizations, and the violence was outside Dubai. This ratchets the war up by several degrees," I said.

"There must be a new element involved," Ralph said.

"And it's the Russian mafiya," Fred said.

We all looked at him.

"You don't know that," Willoughby said.

"Yes, I do."

Chapter 37

"LISTEN, IT'S THE only thing that makes any sense," he said. "Look at the timing. There's a meeting here, and the Nickolai woman moves a lot of money into the Dubai–Persian Bank. Why?" he asked.

"Who knows?" Ralph said. "What's this got to do with Gil Brady?"

"Hear me out," Fred said. "She and the money move here, it's like moving a headquarters here. She moves here to run things. She sees something wrong with Malyakov's outfit—"

"Fred, the only thing happening to Malyakov—" I protested.

He tanked over me. "Any of the stuff that happened to Malyakov could have been done by the mafiya. In fact, screwing up that Congo shipment would be easier for them to do than anybody else. That required a lot of work."

"Why would they try to bring him down if he's their man? If they've been doing all this stuff that's been going wrong, why? Why don't they just shoot him?" Ralph asked.

"Because they don't want to make a mess in Dubai," Fred said.

"Somebody's made a pretty good mess in Dubai in the last week," I said, "and the mess started when somebody took down the Dubai–Persian Bank. If you can think of any rational reason why they should take their own bank down, I'll be glad to listen."

"And how do you know that shell company belongs to them?" Fred asked.

"It's been a while since I've been in the business," Ralph said, "but when I was, they never did anything at my end. They got their cut from the suppliers. Easy enough to do. They've got organizations everywhere in the former Soviet Union. Why bother using muscle anywhere else where it would attract attention?"

"They're still doing it that way," said Willoughby.

"Anything else would cost too much," I said. "Come on, Fred. I've had enough mafiya for one day."

"So who do you think machine-gunned Malyakov's limousine?" he demanded.

"Shut up, Fred. Let's go," I said.

In the car Fred showed signs of wanting to continue the discussion. "I said shut up, Fred."

You could have played the banjo on my nerves they were so tight. I didn't want to think Fred was right. The Russian mafiya's too big. "It's another spaghetti Bolognese night," I said as Fred got off the elevator on five. "I'll see you in the morning."

Where could I get information about the Russian mafiya and arms dealers? Do I know anybody at the station in Minsk? I dialed a well-known number.

"Who do you know in Minsk?" I asked Sidney.

"I don't know anybody in Minsk. Why?"

"Who do you know that knows something about the Russian mafiya?" I asked.

"Carruthers, you're not big enough to mess with the Russian mafiya," Sidney said.

"I know. I'm trying to find out if I *am* messing with the Russian mafiya. So give me somebody who knows or somebody in Minsk."

"Nobody wants to know why George Branson is dead that badly. Get off that damned case before somebody kills you!"

I must know somebody in Minsk. I pulled up the embassy website. Too bad they never listed the chief of station. Kent Robertson was the political officer, though. I actually knew him. Knowing him and getting to him were two different matters. It's amazing how many people a simple political officer can hide behind. I think he finally answered out of curiosity.

"Hey, Lee. It's been a while. What do you want?" he asked.

"Hi, Kent. I'm just fine. How are you? I know you're a busy man. Four layers of secretaries told me so. Just give me the name of somebody in the station and transfer me."

He transferred me to Morris Ingram.

"Lee Carruthers. One of Sidney Worthington's."

"That's right," I said. "I need some information about the local mafiya and arms dealers."

"The local guy was Felix Gringikov. Missing two years ago and presumed dead."

"Yeah, I heard. So what's his connection with the mafiya?" I asked.

"No closer than anybody else. They take their half off the top before the merchant even gets hold of the stuff. Like old-fashioned robber barons. Nothing moves until they get theirs."

"Do you know anything about an Anya Markova Nickolai, age seventy-five, Moscow, Sevastopol?"

"Squat old dame with a baleful eye?"

"That's her."

"I saw her once. All I know is wherever she goes, trouble follows."

We parted the best of friends, and I promised to give his regards to Sidney. So the Dumpy Lady was trouble. Maybe Fred was right. I was chewing on that when the phone rang.

"Hi, Jerry. What do you have for me?"

"I'm just fine. How are you?"

"I'm just fine. What do you have for me?"

"That Russian stuff? Some of it's all messed up."

"I told you it might be. I had to jerk the drive out before the stuff was finished downloading. Can you read any of it?" I asked.

"So far it's just e-mails that seem to be personal to and from a man who might be her son. You remember she has one."

"I remember. She got him out of some kind of trouble. A firebombing?"

"That's it. She seems almost loving. Some of it's another e-mail account. None of that makes much sense. No context. I'll send you the translation. It might make some sense to you. The rest of it's financial records, spreadsheets. Seem to be credits from a variety of obscure places, big sums in euros. How are things?"

"Things have hotted up. It appears to be open season on Sergei Malyakov," I said.

"Do I want to know?" he asked.

"No," I said and then changed my mind. "Things have been going wrong for him for some time, but now it's ratcheted up. His wife's plane blew up, somebody machine-gunned him on his way home from her memorial service, one of their hotels burned, looks like arson. Recently, somebody's soldiers have been turning up dead. Fred thinks it's the Russian mafiya. Maybe it is, but the action in Dubai started with the crash of the Dubai–Persian Bank. Half of it's owned by people fronting for the Iranian Revolutionary Guard, and the other half is owned by a shell company chartered in London. My money man can't find out anything about the nominees. See what you can find."

Jerry said, "I'll get back to you."

I checked my e-mail and downloaded what Jerry had sent me. I'm supposed to do money but I hate spreadsheets. I'm glad I didn't have to see them in Cyrillic. He was right. The places were obscure. I copied the names and searched them. Some of them remained obscure, but some of them had military installations and thus arsenals. The sums were large. The mafiya did take its half off of the top. I could find no information about what they did with the money. The spreadsheets I had were for less than a year, and with that much money they could buy all of Dubai and half of Abu Dhabi. The big problem for the Bad Guys is always trying to figure out what to do with all that money.

The e-mails in her personal account could have been written by any mother. They were frequent, concerned, and loving. Hard to believe. Her son's responses were few, short, and sullen. Nice to know that mafiya leaders have family dynamics just like everybody else's.

I couldn't make much sense of the messages in the other account either. I think you had to be there. One thing I found was a list of twelve names with Sergei Malyakov's at the end. Right above that was Felix Gringikov. I knew about him. He was missing. I searched the other ten and found obituaries for eight. It was a list of arms merchants, and all were dead or missing except for Sergei Malyakov.

Chapter 38

"YOU LOOK MOROSE," Fred said the next morning.

"I feel morose." I told him about the list in the Nickolai files.

"It sounds like a list of arms dealers they've killed," he said, "and now they're after Malyakov. I told you so."

"Saying I told you so is not an attractive quality, Fred," I said. "Why would the mafiya want to kill arms dealers? They get their money up front. It doesn't matter who distributes the weapons," I said.

"Maybe they want to give the franchise to somebody else. Maybe that's the reason Felix Gringikov disappeared. Maybe they did him in too."

"Then why was a CIA officer closing up Gringikov's office in Istanbul?"

"You said Findley might be bent. Maybe it's the Russian mafiya that bent him," Fred replied.

I continued morose as the day went on. It looked very much as if Fred was right. Never mind the bank. There must be some convoluted reason for taking it down. I set out to find out why George Branson was dead and wound up entangled with the Russian mafiya. That was a fight I could never win. They could swat me like a fly and walk on by. Wasn't that the reason I left the Agency? Forever fighting battles I couldn't win? Why was I doing this? Not for God and country, that's for sure. Sidney was right. I hate it when he's right. Cynthia Branson was not my responsibility. Why did I even care? Did I? I'm tired of people shooting at me, I thought. One of these days somebody's going to hit me. I had baggies of diamonds. I began to think of places I'd rather be. Back to Paris? Cold and wet. Istanbul? Cold. Hong Kong was appealing and warmer. I hadn't been there a while. I didn't have any Chinese, but at least I could escape Arabic. I kicked the desk. I didn't need a place to go. I needed a *home*. I needed a *job*. I needed a life in which people didn't shoot at me. The thought made me even more morose.

I quit the Agency to get away from this stuff, I thought. Why did I take Cynthia Branson's job? Curiosity? My curiosity only got me more of the same, and one day was good to kill me. So what was I going to *do*? Maybe Jerry was right. Working with him would get me way away from this stuff, but did I want to go to Boston in the winter? Nobody in Boston wanted to shoot me. That was a plus. I checked the flights to Logan. There was one at noon the next day. So what if I didn't like Boston. I could always leave. Oh, the hell with it. I booked a seat.

I threw my suitcase on the rack. I was folding clothes when the phone rang.

"Leticia Habib is back in town," said Willy. "Do you want to meet her tonight?"

"Leticia Habib?"

"You sound tired, lady."

"I am tired. I'm tired of this damned case. I'm tired of this damned place. I'm going somewhere else."

"Sounds like somebody needs a nap. Leticia Habib is the diamond expert I was telling you about. Come to dinner and meet her."

I finished packing except for the last-minute things. Fred. I needed to do something about Fred. I called his cell phone, and my call went to voice mail. Why did he always have his phone turned off? I put a baggie of diamonds into the box from Sally's. I could give it to him tomorrow.

I arrived at Willy's just before eight with my tails in a taxi right behind me. Why shouldn't they know where I was going? Besides, it gave them something to do for their pay. Willy's gentleman's gentleman received me and escorted me to the lounge, where Willy and an elegant woman with classical features and a nose like the prow of a ship were waiting. Her face was unlined but showed no signs of surgical attention. The hair swept back into a chignon had not the faintest strand of silver. It was the hand—age spotted and wrinkled—that she gave me to shake that betrayed her age. Leticia Habib's little black dress had come from a Paris designer, and the rope of pearls hanging from her neck was worth at least a minor prince's ransom. I felt grubby in a pants suit of heavy black silk. Kemal's pearl would have looked good with it, but Kemal's pearl was gone. As gone as Kemal was.

The last time I was at Willy's we had gone straight to the kitchen, and I missed the wonders of the lounge. It was decorated in Art. The furniture, rugs, and wall colors were all neutral. What glowed were the paintings and the *objets d'art*. A Tang Dynasty camel lifting its head up in a bellow was displayed on a stand in the middle of the room. The celadon bowl in a lighted glass case looked old enough to be the ancestor of all the others. A Guan Yin that might be Song shed her radiance in another glass case. They lived happily with a Monet and a small Degas, but pride of place was an antique silk prayer rug of great beauty and tremendous value on the wall behind the sofa. At that point I stopped cataloging treasures. Willy grinned at me like a cheeky barrow boy and handed me a martini. Madame Habib had what looked like the driest of sherries. We chatted of this and that while I tried to beat down my art lust. I didn't have any place to put anything anyway, but I couldn't keep my eyes off that Guan Yin, and I heard the celadon bowl clamoring for attention. I grimaced at Willy and focused on Madame Habib. We found we had a mutual friend in Paris and descended into the delightful realm of gossip. We talked a bit about the couturiers, but I had to admit that I got my models from the consignment shop in the Fourteenth Arrondissement, and she told me about the Chanel suit in perfect condition that she had picked up there the previous year. We dined much more simply than Willy and I had the other night, on perfect lamb chops and roast potatoes followed by a tossed salad. More simply and better. I might leave the art behind and take Willy's manservant with me. We returned to the lounge for coffee and brandy, she and I seated on the beige nubby silk-covered sofa, while Willy took a matching chair across the carved lacquer coffee table.

I put my brandy snifter down and took a baggie of diamonds from my purse. "I have come into the possession of a number of uncut diamonds. I think this contains a representative sample," I said and handed her the bag.

Madame Habib looked at the baggie and over at Willy, who handed her a bit of black velvet. She placed it on the table in front of us and shook some of the diamonds from the baggie onto her hand, rubbing them back and forth and looking at them. Then she put them on the velvet and fixed a jeweler's loupe in her eye. She examined one stone after another while Willy and I sipped our brandy. She frowned.

"Where did you get these?" she asked.

"That would not help you answer my question," I replied.

She continued to look at me. I returned her gaze. She drew a deep breath.

"I do not buy blood diamonds," she said firmly.

"I don't wish to sell them," I replied.

"Then what do you want?"

"To know if anyone has offered you any similar stones recently."

She looked at Willy.

"She's a good guy," he said.

She turned her gaze back to me. "I have blood diamonds offered to me from time to time."

I brought up the pictures on my iPhone and handed it to her. "By any of these men?"

She scrolled through the pictures. "This one and this one." She continued to scroll. "All of them. This last one offered me a large quantity." She returned the phone to me. All of the men whose pictures were in Spiegel's flash drive had brought diamonds to her. Somebody had paid them in diamonds. I looked down at the picture of the man who had offered her a large number of stones. It was the picture of George Branson.

"When did this man try to sell you diamonds?" I handed the phone back to her.

She glanced at George's picture again and unfocused her eyes to think. "Ten or fifteen days ago," she said.

I looked at her in shock. "Ten or fifteen days ago," I repeated stupidly. "Ten or fifteen days ago he was dead."

But he wasn't, was he? George Branson was still alive.

Chapter 39

MADAME HABIB FINISHED her coffee and departed. Willy returned from seeing her out and poured me some more brandy. I drank it in a gulp.

"You see a ghost, doll?" he asked.

"My dead man? The guy I came to Dubai to look for?"

He nodded.

"He was alive ten days ago when he offered Madame Habib a large number of blood diamonds."

He sat thoughtfully. "You never said, but I assumed that he worked for your former employer."

I nodded.

"Doll, this is getting to be a very nasty situation."

"You have no idea, Willy, love. More than nasty." Some of the puzzle pieces clicked into place. One wouldn't fit. "Why did Langley want me to find out why he was dead if he wasn't?"

"Maybe they didn't know he wasn't?"

"Roger Findley told them he was dead," I said.

"Would he lie to Langley?" Willy asked.

"Maybe. If he was bent he would. What do I do now?"

I ran through a bunch of ideas and found all wanting except one. Roger Findley had told them George was dead and he wasn't.

"Ever since I got here, I've been working on the theory that George's death had something to do with the conflict between Felix Gringikov and Sergei Malyakov. That was before Malyakov's wife's airplane blew up. Since then it's been looking like the Russian mafiya is involved in the attacks on Malyakov."

"I don't see the Russian mafiya taking down the Dubai–Persian Bank, not when they probably own half of it," Willy said.

"But Malyakov's money was wafted off to safety in Zürich. If he's connected to the mob and his money is safe, then the mob doesn't own the other half of the bank. So who does?" I rubbed my eyes. "I've got to get some sleep," I said. "Let my subconscious work on it for a while."

"You're going back to the hotel?" Willy asked.

"Might as well."

I stood waiting for the elevator. When I got back to the hotel, I needed to call Fred. One thing I did know. Roger Findley lied. He knew that wasn't George's body.

The elevator doors opened. It was not empty. Roger Findley was in it, and he grabbed me, twisting my arm up behind my back.

"I told you to leave it alone."

He had company. George Branson was in the far corner. "Kill her," George said. So much for the old-school tie.

Felix Gringikov was by the call buttons. "We can't have her body turning up around here," Gringikov said. "Too many bodies been found lately, and everybody knows she's been asking questions." He pushed the up button.

"We can dump her where her body will never be found," George said.

"Which one of them killed Cynthia?" I asked George. He smacked me across the face. "Why did you send her the key? Why did you have that stuff in that lockbox in the first place? A little conflict among the troops?" This time Roger smacked me. The elevator doors opened. He clapped his hand over my mouth and frog marched me to Gil Brady's apartment. I bit his hand, and he hit me again.

Gringikov picked up my purse and followed, with George trailing behind. Inside the flat, Gringikov opened the purse. He raised his eyebrows when he saw the gun, which he tucked into the small of his back. Reaching into the back of the clutch, he pulled out the baggie of diamonds.

"Where'd you get this?" Gringikov asked, menace in his voice.

It's hard to be insouciant when somebody's trying to break your arm and your agent has just canceled your life insurance policy, but I gave it a try. Smiling sweetly, I said, "From Karl Spiegel's lockbox."

He looked sharply at George. "What!"

"Along with your address book and a flash drive with dossiers on your employees."

He moved toward George, who backed away.

"Stop it!" said Roger.

"Why did you send the key to Cynthia, George?" I asked. "Was it an insurance policy?" I turned to Roger. "Was that why you had Cynthia killed, Roger? To get the key back? Or was it because she saw George alive in Dubai?"

He jerked my arm farther up my back, and I yelped. I couldn't help it. It hurt.

"Shut up," Roger repeated.

"Why did you order them to kill Marina?" I pressed. "She didn't know anything."

"Marina is dead?" Gringikov grated. "She is not dead!"

He grabbed my shirt and twisted. That helped a lot. Front and back. Oh, well. Sidney always said my mouth would get me killed one day. This might be the day.

"Oh, but she is. Who do you know who can cause a heart attack, Roger?"

Felix reached for Roger.

"She's just playing with your head, Felix," Roger said. He pulled my arm higher and threw me on the couch.

"I told you to shut up!" he said as he stuffed a handkerchief in my mouth. I struggled against him. He held me down, and yelled, "Somebody get the drapery cord."

George and Felix looked at each other. Felix jerked his head in the direction of the balcony doors, and George ripped the cord from the draperies. He cut a length, and Roger turned me over for him to tie my arms behind me. I don't think I had much insouciance left.

"Call Worth—" Gringikov began.

"Call Worth," Roger said, "and tell him we've got another package for him."

So Worth did packages. Maybe Jason Hildebrand insured them? Right.

They both turned to George, who seemed to be the only Indian in the room. George flipped open his phone and made the call. Gringikov turned to George.

"What were you doing with that bag of diamonds? And what were you doing with a lockbox with that stuff in it?" he demanded.

"Things weren't looking good in Belarus," George replied.

"There was nothing wrong in Belarus that I couldn't handle," Gringikov retorted.

"Yeah, that's what you say now, but you went on the run for two years and left me in charge of the outfit. Who knew when I was going to have to run too? " George snapped. "The Agency had our backs? Right!" He sneered.

So the Agency was behind Gringikov.

"I said shut up!" Roger ordered.

Who was causing trouble in Belarus? And who is behind Malyakov?

"Malyakov—" Gringikov began.

"I said SHUT UP!"

No wonder George wanted some insurance. The three sat bickering until Martin Worth arrived. I watched as he opened a bottle and soaked a gauze pad with liquid, and I realized then how they got them. I started to struggle, but Roger flipped me over and pressed me down on the sofa, holding my head tight. Worth clapped the pad over my nose, and I tried desperately not to breathe, but I finally had to gasp for air. The last thing I remember is the taste of chloroform and a picture of Russian Beach.

I woke up in the dark lying on a hard surface. As I tried to make sense of where I was, I suddenly began to slide from side to side. Wherever I was it was swinging. I felt around, trying to find something to hold on to. Up. A ceiling. Close. Either hand touched something when I put my arms out. Something. I was in a box, and it was swinging from side to side. Then my stomach lurched, and I heard the whine. I was in a box. A box that had been dumped somewhere. I began to breathe rapidly. A small space. A really small space. I couldn't catch my breath. Where? I began to sweat. Control. Something bad. Only control. I kicked, which only showed me how small the box was. I heard the whine again and something bumped next to me. Another box? If they put a box on top of me—I wiped the sweat from my face. My lungs threatened to burst out of my chest, and I rocked from side to side. I hate small spaces. I *hate* small spaces. Dangerously near hysteria, I fought for control. Control was the only thing that would save me. Control. I breathed deeply once. Twice. Three times. I was trembling. Did I want to die there? More deep breaths. I became sane enough to think. My gun was gone, of course. I could feel the knife sheath on my ankle. Had they found the knife? I tried to sit up and banged my head. I tried to get to my ankle and bumped my knee on the top of the box. My breathing increased again. Stop it! Stop! I breathed deeply again and turned over on my left side. I pulled my ankle up and found the sheath empty. They got the knife too.

I lay on my side staring at the dark.

One day you will go too far.

Sidney was right.

One day I'll go too far.

This time I had gone too far.

I heard the whine again and knew another box was coming. I ran my fingers over what I could touch. Rough wood. Up to the seam at the top. Space between the two boards. With another strip of wood nailed into it? I ran my fingers along the seam. If only they hadn't found the knife. I rolled onto my back again. Getting restless in the small space again, panic not far behind, I rolled to my right and felt a lump in my pocket. My Swiss Army knife. Why had I taken it with me to Willy's? Who cared? The gods look after fools, even fools who have gone too far. I pulled it out of my pocket and felt it until I could pull out the biggest blade. It was so small. I reached up and inserted it in the crack at the top and wiggled it back and forth, pushed it along until I met resistance and wiggled it back and forth again. The seam gave a little, so I slipped the knifepoint further in and along the seam until it met resistance, and prayed the knife blade wouldn't break. I stopped to wipe the sweat out of my eyes. I returned to rocking the knife the back and forth as far as I could reach. I reached up and pushed the top. Did I feel it give a little? I brought the knife back and rocked it toward my head as far as I could reach that way. I turned to the other side and slipped the knife into the crack, rocked the blade back and forth, and felt it snap. Damn it! I lay back sweating. Now what? I began to shake. I heard the whine of the machine again. Frantically, I raised my knees and pushed. I felt it give. I dropped the useless knife and shoved again. More give. I shoved with all my might. The nails gave, and the top loosened. I could see bright light now, and I would be visible as soon I moved. I didn't care. I shoved the top of the box and looked up. I saw a crate coming toward me and pushed myself up and looked around. I was in a crate loaded on a ship, and the next crate was coming down toward me. I had to get out before they dropped the next crate on top of me.

I rolled the crate over on its side and looked down. There was one crate under me. What god to pray to in this situation? Why, the god in the machine, of course, I thought hysterically. I tried to miss the nails as I rolled the crate over and landed on my rear with the crate on top of me. I kicked it away and lay panting. Blessed flat deck! The light from the dock was fiercely bright, but there were dark shadows near the stack of crates. I could see only about fifty meters ahead to another stack. They might close the space between the stacks anytime now. I ran to the side and saw one of the mooring ropes where I could reach it. I ran to it and took my shirt off. I clambered over the side, wrapped the shirt and then my hands around the line and slid down until I reached the rat guard. I dropped my legs and hung by my hands, swinging my feet, but I couldn't reach around the rat guard. I put all of my weight on one hand and reached around the guard until I could pull my second arm around, losing my shirt in the process, but I could swing my feet to the cement dock. I threw myself flat in the shadows, heart pounding, arm and leg muscles quivering. It took my brain a while to thaw.

Jebel Ali is a huge place, but the ship I had been on was that rusted old Pakistani tramp docked near the east end. There were lights everywhere and probably security cameras. I sprinted into the first row of buildings and zigzagged my way toward the fence. I could see trucks waiting for clearance at a gate. I scampered to the fence and took advantage of a truck going out. While the guard and the driver complained about the price of gas I slipped through the gate. Where was I going in a bra and slacks in the middle of the night? Willy's place was three towers past the Palm Jumeirah. Two miles away? I was slowed by fatigue and having to fall on my face every time a car went by, but I eventually made it to the tower. I bent over and scooted across the driveway, and then lay flat, panting, my strength nearly gone. Eventually, the guard was going to have to go to pee. Maybe he wasn't allowed to pee while he was on duty? Every minute I waited restored my strength just a little. When he finally left the desk, I dashed in and ran for the fire stairs. If I get out of this alive, I vowed, I am going to improve the decoration of fire stairs. Murals, maybe, of fields of flowers or seascapes. Slowly, I climbed to the seventh floor. The hall was empty. I slid to Willy's door, rang the bell, and sank down against the door in exhaustion.

Chapter 40

WILLY'S MAN WAS shocked to find me at the door at three thirty in the morning, looking as if I had been pulled through a hedge backward. Fred was just shocked.

"Where the hell have you been?" he demanded and scooped me up in his arms.

"You?"

"You didn't come back. Your car is in the parking lot. Where the hell you been?"

"Nailed in a crate," I mumbled and rested my head on his shoulder.

He took me into the lounge and sat down with me in his lap. Willy joined the crew. They looked at me in my bra and slacks, dirty and scratched. I kept nodding off.

"Bathtub," Willy said.

Fred sat me gently in a tub of warm water and sponged me lightly.

"Have you had a tetanus shot recently?" he asked.

"Mmmm," I said and nodded off again.

He stood me up and dried me. "Can you stand up?"

"No," I mumbled.

He sat me down on the toilet seat and searched in the medicine cabinet until he found something. He started dabbing something on my scratches.

"Sssss," I hissed.

"Be quiet. It's iodine."

By the time he was finished, Willy was there with a terrycloth bathrobe. Fred wrapped me in it and followed Willy down the hall to a bedroom. He sat on a chair with me in his lap.

"Where have you been?" he demanded again. "What happened after you left here?"

I nodded off again.

He raised his voice. "Where have you been?!"

I nestled my head against his shoulder. "I'm going to stay here safe and warm for a while." I looked at him with an evil smile. "And then I'm going to do something really rotten to them," I said and went to sleep in his arms.

Sometime later, he sat me up in the bed and fed me chicken soup. Willy's man makes good chicken soup. I ate it, turned over, and went back to sleep.

When I woke, stiff and aching, I did a few stretches and wished I hadn't, but I moved better afterward. Fred had brought me fresh clothes. I put them on and looked in the mirror. My face was bruised. It and my hands and arms were scratched, painted iodine brown. The rest of me had brown spots too. I ran my hands vaguely through my hair and wandered down the hall to the kitchen. Willy's man was sitting reading a newspaper. He folded it and got up.

"Would you like something to eat?"

"Like what?"

"A small steak and some salad?"

"Perfect. Rare," I said and picked up the newspaper.

By the time I was half-finished with the steak Willy and Fred had returned.

"Before you ask, I was at Jebel Ali nailed in a crate on a ship bound for Karachi," I said through a mouthful of steak.

"I just know you're going to explain that," Fred said.

"George Branson and Felix Gringikov are alive. They and Roger Findley had me nailed in a crate and loaded on a freighter bound for Karachi. You remember that old rusty bucket we saw when we were there?" Fred nodded. "That one."

"George Branson and Gringikov are alive? And working with Roger Findley?" Willy said. "Why didn't they just shoot you? It sounds like the old 'put the heroine in the basement with water rushing in routine.'"

"A question I considered while I was walking here. They said too many bodies have been showing up. Fred, it's not the Russian mafiya."

"I don't see how you figure that," Fred said. "Branson and Gringikov being alive doesn't change things."

"Stubborn as hell, aren't you? It does change things. Willy, may I stay here for a while?"

"Of course," he said.

That afternoon I started thinking, and it was nearly midnight when I came up with a plan. The fact that I would not tell either Willy or Fred what I was going to do did not go down well, but I went to sleep with a smile on my face. The next day I drove to Sergei Malyakov's compound, where I stayed an hour. I drove back to Willy's tower and settled down in the car to wait. It was five o'clock when somebody opened the offside door. I jumped and went for my gun, but it was only Fred.

"What are you up to?" he asked.

"Shut up, Fred," I replied.

Not long after Fred got in the car, a black SUV with Roger Findley driving drove in and parked in the first row. I pulled out, stopped, and got out of the car. Bracing my arms on the roof, I fired a shot at the SUV, made sure that Roger saw me, then got back in the car and streaked out of the parking lot.

"What the hell?" Fred asked.

I turned left on Jumeirah Road and made sure the SUV was behind me.

"What are you doing?" Fred exclaimed.

"Shut up, Fred," I said and punched speed dial on my phone. "Now," I said.

I turned right into the parking lot of the Dubai Gold and Diamond Park and leaned on the horn. The SUV circled me, and Roger, Felix Gringikov, and George Branson got out. As they raised their guns at us, Sergei Malyakov and four men came out of the building, firing their guns. I revved my engine and started toward them. Fred jerked the steering wheel and pulled on the emergency brake. The engine juddered to a stop.

"What the hell do you think you're doing!" exclaimed Fred.

"They nailed me in a crate," I said and started the engine. I turned the steering wheel toward them again.

The men were hiding behind cars now and jumping up to take shots. I heard sirens in the distance.

"We've got to get out of here before the cops come," Fred urged.

He was right. I hate it when he's right. I drove around to the other side of the building and breathed deeply. My hands were still shaking a bit when I pulled out and turned left, crossing Jumeirah and driving to Sheikh Sayed Road. Turning left back to town I heard more sirens in the distance. I resisted the urge to go over and see how much damage I had done.

When we parked in the hotel garage and got out of the car, Fred put his arms around me and said, "You are out of your mind."

I pulled away. "Shut up, Fred," I said. "They nailed me in a crate."

I had missed my flight to Boston, but there was another one in three hours. I was putting my cosmetic bag in the suitcase when somebody knocked on the door. I picked up my gun, the third one. I've never had a three-gun adventure before. Sinbad should give me a discount. I looked out the peephole. It was Roger Findley. I opened the door and stepped aside, my gun firmly in my hand. He glared as he walked past me.

"Well, hello, Roger. The last man standing?" His left arm was in a sling. "Serious, I hope. Sit down over there or I'll shoot you in the other arm and shove you off the balcony like you did Cynthia."

He sat in stony silence.

"Why have you come, Roger? To thank me for completing your operation?"

"You finished it, all right," he said bitterly.

"Malyakov's dead."

"Gringikov and Branson are dead too."

"You've got your people in all the important positions in Malyakov's organization, Roger. You've got what's left of Gringikov's outfit. You and the Agency will be back in business supplying arms to terrorists under another name in six months' time."

"They are not terrorists."

"If they're not terrorists then what are they? And don't tell me they're freedom fighters."

"They are simply groups which the US finds impolitic to support openly."

"Pompous ass. Impolitic. You mean all hell would break loose if the press found out about it. Which side are we on in Congo? The one with the ten-year-old soldiers hopped up on amphetamines? Or is it the former government? Or the former government but one? Or is it both sides? You and Gringikov and George—or Gil Brady or Karl Spiegel, whoever—were getting along just fine doing the Agency's secret bidding, weren't you? Until Sergei Malyakov decided to set up for himself—"

"He didn't set up for himself. He had help."

"Whatever. He got so big he was taking some of your legitimate—you should pardon the expression—business with the dictators and rebel groups no other self-respecting merchant of death would arm. How much market was he taking from you?"

"Enough. Enough that we had to take him out."

"You mean you couldn't pay for your under-the-table trade anymore? So you infiltrated his organization, and strange things began to happen—like that screw-up in Kampala. I must say that was artfully done," I said.

For a moment he looked pleased that I had recognized how clever his plan had been. Then he remembered that he had come to threaten me.

"If any of this gets out, there's nowhere you can hide." He looked as menacing as a man can with his arm in a sling. "Nowhere!"

"And are your masters pleased with you, Roger? I'd worry about that if I were you. If it does get out, it won't be the Agency that carries the can."

"It was sanctioned."

"Tell that to Senator Feinstein. I'm glad you dropped by. Saved me from going to the consulate. It won't be just your arm that's in a sling, Roger. If I'm not living happily ever after, this will all come out, and, even if it was sanctioned, which I doubt, you'll never be able to prove it was. If I'm not safe, Roger, you're not safe." I gestured with the gun. "You said what you came to say. You threatened me. I've threatened you. Checkmate." I stood up. "Now get out."

I heard the door open and whirled round. It was Fred. He closed the door and leaned against it, his crooked little smile on his face, and a gun in his hand.

"I told you threatening her wouldn't work, Findley. Now I'm going to have to kill her."

Tears came to my eyes but they didn't spoil my aim. I shot him four times.

I've always had such a lamentable taste in men.

Chapter 41

SIDNEY EVENTUALLY GOT me out of jail, but I had to pay a price.

Sidney and I had dined with Willy and Madame Habib and were taking our coffee and brandy in the lounge. Madame Habib knew only that I had a bunch of blood diamonds to turn into dollars or Swiss francs.

"I do not myself ordinarily deal in such merchandise, you understand," she said, "but Willy asked it as a favor."

I nodded. "I'm grateful."

She handed me a slip of paper with the amount that had been deposited to my Geneva account. It was a surprisingly large amount. She finished her brandy and rose, and we rose too. I thanked her again, and Willy walked with her to the door. He returned rubbing his hands.

"You need to put that money somewhere, doll," Willy said. "Brandy?"

"I think I'll keep it in cash for a while, Willy, love, unless you need to make a payment on your boat. More coffee, I think," I said. "This is going to take a while."

Sidney looked as if he had just escaped from Yale in his blue blazer, flannel slacks, and bow tie. The bow tie was well known in Langley as a barometer of his mood. It got more and more crooked as he got more and more disturbed.

"The only way to understand this is to assume that there are two groups involved," I said. "We know Roger Findley and George Branson worked for the Agency. Let us assume that Gringikov did too, because of the link with Roger and George. If this is true, it makes the Gringikov operation an Agency operation."

He moved restlessly in his chair and opened his mouth to interrupt.

"Sidney, hear me out. Until you hear how I understand the whole case, any observations you make are just interruptions."

He did not look happy. He crossed his arms over his chest as if to protect himself from what I was going to say. His bow tie was nearly vertical.

"According to Gringikov, everything was going smoothly until something went wrong in Belarus. Then he found it necessary to pull in his horns. His relationship with Sergei Malyakov broke down, and eventually he found it necessary to disappear. It seems to me this suggests the entry of a new player into the game."

Sidney crossed his legs but made no comment.

"If it's true that Gringikov's business was an Agency operation, the new player would have to be large and powerful to compete. Here I think Fred was correct. The new player was the Russian mafiya. It's true that the mafiya took a percentage of the profits at the seller's end, but what if they decided to take all the profit by cutting Gringikov and others out of the market?

"The only way that all of what came down after I came to Dubai makes any sense is for there to be two players. When I got here, the first thing I heard was about the battle between Felix Gringikov and Sergei Malyakov. The second thing I heard was that strange things were happening to Malyakov's operation. Some of the things I discovered would profit Felix Gringikov and others would profit

Sergei Malyakov, but neither man would profit from everything.

"The lockbox key is a perfect example. George Branson sent the key to a lockbox in an Istanbul bank to his wife, Cynthia, the first of this year. Cynthia gave it to me when she hired me to find George. Cynthia called me for help, and I discovered that the man who killed her was looking for the key. I figured if they killed her for the key, they would soon understand that I had the key, so I took the key to Istanbul and opened the box."

Sidney stirred and ran his hands through his gray crew cut hair.

"In the box I discovered a bag full of uncut diamonds, an address book belonging to Felix Gringikov, and a flash drive which contained the dossiers of men who worked either for Gringikov or for Malyakov. Why did George send the key to his wife? He said it was for insurance, that he didn't know when he was going to have to disappear. Now he might have wanted the diamonds to fund a quick escape, but neither the address book nor the dossiers had anything to do with flight. They might, however, have something to do with the possibility of George turning on Gringikov and joining the other side. We know that, as Gil Brady, George worked for Malyakov. I assumed he was working as a penetration agent for Gringikov, but that need not be so. When he sent Cynthia the key, he might have decided to throw in with Malyakov for real."

Willy's man brought a tray with a small pot of coffee and a cup for me. I stopped talking to drink some. Talking, especially trying to convince Sidney of anything, is thirsty business.

"As a matter of fact, George had stashed diamonds in several places: in the Istanbul lockbox, in 'Gil Brady's' Dubai flat, and with a girlfriend in Dubai. Even if Gringikov or Malyakov were paying him in diamonds, it made more sense to sell them and put the money in the bank somewhere, unless he expected somebody to be able

to find his bank account. That would be the Agency, probably, although I suppose the mafiya could hack into bank
accounts as fast as anyone else.

"Or take the murder of Marina Gringikov. In Istanbul,
I rescued her from a fire at the Gringikov villa and discovered that she had been being held prisoner there after Felix
disappeared. I sent her to Paris with a bag of diamonds to
start a new life, but she died of a suspicious heart attack in
a taxi on the way from the airport to a friend of mine who
was going to buy the diamonds. It seems unlikely that
Gringikov would imprison or murder his own wife. These
are attacks on Felix by an outside source, possibly the
Russian mafiya.

"Or take the attacks on me. I was shot at while skiing
in Switzerland. I attributed that to Moroccan terrorists, but
that night I realized I was under surveillance. Both a ski
instructor and another man were very interested in my
movements. The ski instructor was determined to see me
get on the plane for Vienna and the other man was determined to discover where I was going from Vienna. Neither
of these men was an Arab terrorist. In Dubai somebody
stood outside my door every night as I went to bed, presumably making sure I was going to bed. I still don't know
why. I was also tailed around town by two Slavic-looking
men, men who had been identified as 'odds and ends men'
by arms dealer Walter W. Willoughby." I looked at Sidney.
"Those two were your men," I said, "because in at least
two cases they saved me from an attack."

Sidney nodded.

"You had to hire local thugs?"

Sidney cleared his throat. "I thought it best."

"Why were you having me followed?"

"Because you wouldn't get off the case," he said in
exasperation.

"There were at least two other attacks on me. When I
came back from Istanbul, there were two men waiting
for me in my hotel room. They wanted the key. Another

attack occurred after Fred and I had interviewed Martin Worth, who owns a bonded warehouse in Jebel Ali. Worth, incidentally, was the man who chloroformed me before I was nailed into a crate and loaded on a ship bound for Karachi. At any rate, after we had interviewed him, a black SUV ran us off the road, making us crash in a culvert and triggering a gas tank explosion. We got out of the car before the explosion, but we might not have. Worth worked for Roger Findley, so we'll chalk that up to the Agency. I'm not sure we can chalk the other attack up to the Agency, though. Neither Roger Findley nor Felix Gringikov seemed to know of the existence of George's Istanbul lockbox, and the Russians could only know if George had told them. We'll have to count that one as unclaimed, although the thugs looked Slavic.

"After the attack, when I got back from Istanbul, I hired a bodyguard. Fred Atkins, a Marine with a Bad Conduct Discharge, had been recommended to me by Ralph Prince, an old friend and retired gunrunner. I'm inclined to believe that Fred was clean when Ralph recommended him, but either just before or just after I hired him, Roger must've got to him. His BCD might have resulted from something more serious than the story he told me, and he was racked up on the beach with no visible means of support, so he was susceptible to being bought. It was his job, I think, to get me to trust him, and to blame all of the activity on the Russian mafiya. It didn't help that some of it actually was carried out by the Russian mafiya."

I looked at Willy. "What's the latest on the bank?"

"What bank?" asked Sidney.

"The Dubai–Persian Bank," replied Willy. "I'm virtually certain that half of it is owned by the Iranian Revolutionary Guard. The quarterly visitors from Tehran make that clear. I still have not been able to get behind the nominees of the shell corporation chartered in the UK that owns the other half. The law is designed, of course, to prevent that kind of knowledge from getting out. But still,

I can't understand why I can't get into it." He looked cross. He was used to being able to get that kind of information. "If it's the Russian mafiya, what do they care what I know? If it's the CIA, why should they care?"

"For one thing, the bank is probably busting sanctions all over the place. Have you traced any transactions?"

"No. I'll do that tomorrow. I spent my time trying to get into the shell company and worrying about you."

"I am truly sorry about that, Willy," I said. "I was worried about me too. I thought for a while I was going to Karachi in a box."

"I didn't worry so much about that, because I didn't know it was happening. What worried me was what you did next."

"I always preferred to read her reports rather than talk to her. She left out the most terrifying parts," Sidney said, "as well as the most illegal. Tell me about the bank."

"I think the bank is the key to all the rest," I said. "The last act began with a run on the Dubai–Persian Bank. A run on the bank is not hard to produce. All you have to do is start some rumors and draw your money out. The two groups I've charged with causing all the trouble—the CIA and the Russian mafiya—are fighting each other for control of the Russian arms smuggling trade. If they are the contenders, then who caused a run on the bank? It was probably not the Russian mafiya, because Sergei Malyakov's money was transferred to Switzerland just before the run started. But another mafiya creature, Madame Anya Markova Nickolai, had a lot more money in the bank, and hers wasn't moved."

"That's true," said Willy, "but what if the CIA started the run on the bank, as they might have if they had no connection with the bank or Malyakov? The result of the run on the bank was that Iran probably lost its investment, and if the mafiya owns the second half of the bank, it lost its investment and a high-ranking mafiya functionary lost a great deal of money."

"But why would they move Malyakov's money?" Sidney asked.

"To make bad blood between Malyakov and the mafiya," I said.

"So you think all the rest of it was caused by the mafiya? Natalie's assassination, the attack on Malyakov, the burning of Natalie's hotel?" Sidney asked.

"And the murder of a number of Malyakov's thugs. No, I think the rest of it was carried out by Roger Findley, Felix Gringikov, and George Branson under Agency orders and with Agency assets."

"Lee!" Sidney protested. "You have no proof that any of this was an Agency operation."

I laughed. "Sidney, how often does one get proof of a black Agency operation? What should I have? Memos? Orders? E-mails, perhaps? If it looks like a duck, walks like a duck, and quacks like a duck, it's a duck."

"Try seeing the run on the bank as a mafiya operation," Willy suggested. "The Nickolai woman didn't necessarily lose her money. When the bank is wound up, the largest depositors usually get most of their money. It's only the small depositors who lose. If the CIA owned the other half of the bank, then it lost a substantial sum of money. The transfer of Malyakov's funds may be a red herring."

"So why would they kill Malyakov's wife?" I asked.

"Maybe they didn't. Maybe the CIA did in revenge for the run on the bank or the killing of Marina Gringikov. Blowing up Natalie's plane, the attack on Malyakov, the burning of Natalie's hotel—they're all attacks on Malyakov, yes, but they're also attacks on a major Russian mafiya player," Willy suggested.

"A player that Gringikov had been trying to take down since Malyakov split and set up on his own. For Gringikov read CIA. I think that will do it, Willy," I said. "Working the bank into my theory has been the most difficult part of it."

"So you're telling me that the Agency has been running a major part of the illegal arms trade since at least the fall of the Soviet Union? That it's now locked in a gigantic struggle with the Russian mafiya for control of that trade?" Sidney asked. "I know we sometimes—"

"Sidney, you *know* we sometimes. You cut your teeth on selling counterfeit Vietnamese piastres on the Hong Kong black market."

"Somehow that's not the same as selling weapons to Congo. I'm not a part of that. I don't want to be a part of that."

I finished my coffee. "I don't want to be a part of it either. That's one of the reasons I quit."

Sidney joined me at breakfast the next morning. I could tell he wanted something, because he kept fiddling with his coffee cup.

"Spit it out, Sidney," I said.

"I need you to go to Hong Kong to find—"

"I'm not a missing person's bureau, Sidney," I said.

"That's not it. I need you to find—"

"I don't work for you anymore, Sidney."

"Consultant rates. And you can use Mike."

"And you want it untraceable to the Agency?"

"You're ultimately traceable to the Agency. I want it done right."

I sighed and poured myself some more coffee. "Tell me."

And so I missed the third flight to Boston.

About the Author

MARILYNN LAREW is a historian who has published in such disparate fields as American colonial and architectural history, Vietnamese military history, and terrorism, and has taught courses in each of them in the University of Maryland System.

Before settling on the Mason-Dixon line in southern Pennsylvania, she lived in Nebraska, Iowa, Missouri, Georgia, Wisconsin, Ohio, South Carolina, Maryland, in Manila, and on Okinawa. It's no surprise that she likes to travel. When she's climbing the first hill in Istanbul to Topkapi Palace, strolling around Hoan Kiem Lake in Hanoi, or exploring the back streets of Kowloon, she is not just having fun, she's looking for locations for her next novel.

When she's not traveling, she is writing or reading. She writes thrillers and likes to read them. She also likes to read Vietnamese history and Asian history in general, as well as military history. She lives with her husband in a 200-year-old farmhouse in southern Pennsylvania.

She belongs to Sisters in Crime, the Guppies, and the Chinese Military History Society.

She's busy on Lee Carruthers #3, *Hong Kong Central*.

She can be reached at larew_2000@yahoo.com.

Her website is www.mailynnlarew.com.

www.ingramcontent.com/pod-product-compliance
Lightning Source LLC
Chambersburg PA
CBHW031259170626
46807CB00001B/215